The COURTSHIP

Other Books by Gilbert Morris

Charade
Jacob's Way
Edge of Honor
Jordan's Star
God's Handmaiden
The Spider Catcher

The Singing River Series

The Homeplace
The Dream
The Miracle
The Courtship

GILBERT MORRIS

The COURTSHIP

⇥ THE SINGING RIVER SERIES ⇤

Book IV

ZONDERVAN®

ZONDERVAN.com/
AUTHORTRACKER
follow your favorite authors

The Courtship
Copyright © 2007 by Gilbert Morris

Requests for information should be addressed to:
Zondervan, *Grand Rapids, Michigan 49530*

Library of Congress Cataloging-in-Publication Data

Morris, Gilbert.
The courtship / Gilbert Morris.
p. cm. — (Singing River series ; bk. 4)
ISBN-10: 0-310-25235-0
ISBN-13: 978-0-310-25235-1
1. Domestic fiction. I. Title.
PS3563.O8742C59 2007
813'.54 — dc22

2007016776

Published in association with the literary agency of Alive Communications, Inc., 7680 Goddard Street, Suite 200, Colorado Springs, CO 80920.

Note: In this book, the author has taken deliberate liberties with some of the biographical details of early country musicians, the dates of their recordings and performances, and the publication dates of popular songs. This has been done strictly for dramatic purposes, and the author acknowledges that many of these details are not historically accurate.

The poems in this book were originally published in *Those Who Knew Him: Profiles of Christ in Verse* by Gilbert Morris, published by Fleming H. Revell, copyright © 1997 by Gilbert Morris. Used by permission.

Interior design by Michelle Espinoza

Printed in the United States of America

07 08 09 10 11 12 • 20 19 18 17 16 15 14 13 12 11 10 9 8 7 6 5 4 3 2 1

To Bobby and Helen Funderburk

I have had no better friends on this earth than you two!
Thanks for all the wonderful years
you have stood by me and brought joy into my life.
In my gallery of memories,
none is brighter or more comforting
than the ones which you two have given me.
Thanks for the memories.

The COURTSHIP

PART ONE

The Evangelist

❈ CHAPTER 1 ❈

I don't like the wicked witch, Lanie."

Corliss Freeman was sitting beside her older sister Lanie on the couch. They had been reading for some time, and as always, Lanie was amazed at how quickly the four-year-old was picking up the ability to recognize words.

"Nobody likes the wicked witch, Corliss."

"Then why is she in the book?"

"I suppose books have to have bad people as well as good people." She looked down at the book, *The Wizard of Oz*, and ran her hand over her sister's blonde hair. "Don't you worry about it. There's no such thing as witches anyway."

"I like the cowardly lion."

"Why do you like him?"

"Because he wanted to be brave but he couldn't. But he will soon, won't he? Let's skip ahead to the part where the wizard gives everybody what they want." Corliss's blue eyes lit up. "The straw man got his brain, the tin man got a heart, and the lion got courage. I like stories where everyone gets what they want."

The old grandfather clock sent its message across the room that time was passing. As Corliss picked out the words she knew— sometimes whole sentences—and read them aloud, Lanie thought how Mama would have loved her. Sadness filled her heart as she recognized this could never be.

Booger, the bloodhound, and Beau, just a pure hound, had been watching. Beau had been peaceful as long as he could. He got up, came across the floor, and rearing up, put his front paws in Lanie's lap, his eyes soulful as he sought her gaze.

"No, Beau, you can't get up in my lap! You're too big. Now go over there and be good."

Beau stared at her for a moment, then walked across the room and threw himself down, staring at the wall.

"You hurt his feelings again, Lanie."

"He gets his feelings hurt too easy. I think he's the only dog in the world that pouts."

"I pout too, sometimes."

"No, you don't, honey. You're always a good girl. Now, let's go on with the story, but you ought to know it by heart by now. We've read it so many times."

Indeed, the two had read the *Wizard of Oz* ever since Corliss had been able to talk, which was at a very early age. She loved books, and the *Wizard of Oz* was her favorite. If Lanie, Davis, or Cody tried to skip sections, she called them on it immediately. "You're skipping the good part," she always said.

Booger, the bloodhound, got up and stretched. The sunlight streaming through the window caught the gold medal around his neck, which spelled out HERO in capital letters. The town of Fairhope, Arkansas, had given it to him when he used his talents as a bloodhound to find Roger Langley who had been hurt and unable to move in the deep woods. Booger's picture had been in the paper and now was tacked up on the wall with other snapshots of the Freeman family. Booger had been one of the bloodhounds at Cummins Prison where their father, Forrest, was incarcerated for a crime he had not committed.

"Booger wants to go out." Corliss put the book down and ran to the screen door, Booger at her heels. On her way back to Lanie, she glanced toward the stairs, looking worried. "Aunt Kezia doesn't feel so good, Lanie."

"I know she doesn't, honey. She's pretty sick."

"She got a new bottle of medicine in the mail, but it didn't help her any."

Lanie frowned. "I wish she would stop taking that patent medicine. It doesn't do any good at all." She stirred restlessly, and then said, "You sit here and read your book, honey. I'll go up and see how Aunt Kezia is doing."

"All right."

Lanie, a well-formed young woman of eighteen with a wealth of auburn hair and striking green eyes, moved from the living room and quickly ascended the stairs. As she entered the bedroom at the end of the second story hallway, she found Aunt Kezia Pettigrew sitting in a rocking chair, staring out the window. Lanie was in awe of this ninety-two-year-old woman's adventurous life. When the state was going to separate the Freeman children after the death of their mother and the incarceration of Forrest Freeman, it had been God's miracle when Aunt Kezia was located and agreed to fulfill the state requirement of an adult in the house full of young people. She was a small woman, and age was beginning to tell its tale, but her eyes were still bright and clear.

"How are you feeling, Aunt Kezia?"

Ignoring Lanie's question, Kezia stared through the window. "I always liked fall the best of all. Back when we lived in Louisiana, there was no such thing as seasons. Look at the colors. The fall brings them out, don't it, now?"

"They'll be more colorful in October." Lanie moved closer and put her hand on the old woman's forehead. Aunt Kezia immediately struck it away and glared at her. "I will not be pawed at, thank you very much!"

But she did not fool Lanie. "I'm going to get Owen."

"You'll do no such thing. I'll be right fine. I've got me a new medicine." She picked up a brown bottle and held it high. "Doctor Oscar Bennett's Liver Rejuvenator. It's got four secret ingredients."

Lanie took the bottle, unscrewed the top, and smelled it. "Why, this is just plain alcohol, Aunt Kezia, with something put in it to make it taste bad."

"It is not! Doctor Bennett was brought up by the Cherokee Indians. An old medicine man gave him this recipe his own self."

"No, this won't do you any good. Don't you remember Estelle Tatum who started taking that patent medicine? It wasn't anything but alcohol. She became a regular addict."

"Well, she stopped aching, didn't she?"

"I guess so, but she was drunk all the time. I'm going to get Owen."

Kezia cackled and humor lit her dark eyes. "You likely won't find him."

"What are you talking about?"

"He's probably doctoring the widow Hankins. She's been after him ever since she lost her husband. She sees Owen Merritt as a likely prospect for number two."

Lanie bit her lip, for there was some truth to this. A small town like Fairhope had no secrets, and she was well aware that all the widows and single women in town suddenly enjoyed ill health. Doctor Owen Merritt was called regularly to treat women who had nothing wrong except loneliness.

"Now, you take that Ella Hankins. She wants a man. She's got her cap set for Merritt. Come to think of it, maybe you better go get him. I need to give him some advice on how to take care of these man-hungry females that are out to get him to the altar."

Lanie could not help smiling. She reached over, hugged Kezia, and nodded. "You just wait right here. I'll be back as soon as I can."

"Take your time, honey. I ain't going nowhere."

Lanie hurried downstairs and into the kitchen where a large black woman was ironing. Delilah Jones was the mother of the Reverend Madison Jones, the pastor of the Methodist Episcopal Church. She looked up from the cast smoothing iron she had just picked up from the stove, spit on it, and watched it sizzle. "This is the way to iron clothes. Them newfangled electric irons ain't worth spit."

"I'd like to have one all the same, Delilah."

"Them inventions ain't gonna do nobody no good. If these solid irons was good enough for my mammy, they're good enough for them women today. They's jist too lazy to work, that's what their problem is."

Lanie had learned long ago that it was useless to argue with Delilah Jones. She had a will as solid as the Rock of Gibraltar, and as far as anyone could figure out, the last time she had changed her mind it had been another century. "I've got to go get Doctor Merritt, Delilah. Aunt Kezia isn't any better. You take care of her and Corliss."

Delilah put the iron down on one of Davis's shirts and smoothed out the wrinkles. She quickly lifted the iron before it could scorch the material. "I reckon we could pray her through, Miss Lanie. I could get the deacons of our church to come, and that preacher of mine. We could anoint her with ile."

"Well, we maybe could do that, Delilah"—Lanie smiled—"but first of all, we've got to get rid of that awful medicine she orders by mail. I'm hoping she'll listen to Doctor Merritt."

"She ain't gonna listen to nobody," Delilah said. "She's stubborn as a blue-nosed mule."

And so are you, Lanie wanted to reply but did not. Delilah Jones had been the Freemans' strong anchor since the death of their mother. Lanie had been only fourteen when she was forced to take over raising her younger brothers and sisters. With the Depression at its worst, they could not afford much, and Delilah Jones had come day after day, and year after year, to throw herself into the lives of the Freeman children. Lanie loved her dearly. Going over, she hugged the big woman's shoulders. "You're a treasure, Delilah. I don't know what we would have done without you."

"I don't know neither. Now you go on and git that doctor. We'll let him try his thing, and then when that don't work, we'll let the good Lord have His way. I knows *that'll* work!"

Lanie left the house and turned toward town. The old Freeman home place was composed of five acres, all that was left of a large plantation that had belonged to Forrest's great-grandparents. It was all gone now. Sold off to make city lots, most of it, and as she hurried along, Lanie wondered what it had been like back in the days when this was all open fields with no town at all except a general store.

Turning left on Stonewall Jackson Boulevard, she made her way through the town. She passed the library where Cassandra Sue Pruitt, the librarian, waved to her, then turning right on Robert E. Lee Street, she passed the Rialto Theater and Planter's Bank directly across the street.

She arrived at the office of Doctor Oscar Givens and entered at once. A short stocky woman with her hair done up in a Pentecostal bun looked up. "Hello, Lanie."

"Hello, Nurse Pickens. I'd like to see Doctor Merritt, please."

"He's not here. He's gone down to get lunch, at least so he said. What he really likes to do is go down and listen to the gossip at the Dew Drop Inn. Who's sick?"

Lanie knew that she could get a full diagnosis from Nurse Pickens but did not want to get into that. The woman had served old Doctor Givens for at least thirty years and knew the ailment of every citizen of the county. "Aunt Kezia's not feeling well, but I'll go find Doctor Merritt."

"You tell him to bring me back Sister Myrtle's special. It's greens and fried pork chops—and bring me a piece of pie. Whatever she made today."

"I'll tell him, Nurse Pickens."

⚬══╾⚬

The Dew Drop Inn, being the only café in Fairhope, did a brisk business. It was pinched in between the barbershop run by Deoin Jinks and Gerald Pink's pharmacy. The parking spaces were all taken, as usual, around the Dew Drop Inn, for it was the social center of the town, almost as popular as Bud Thompson's Pool Hall.

Sister Myrtle Poindexter exited from the kitchen carrying two plates burdened down with food. Sister Myrtle was pastor of the Fire Baptized Pentecostal Church. She was a tall, angular woman with sharp brown eyes and her hair done up in a huge bun. She always wore dark clothing, sleeves down to her wrists and no jewelry except for a simple wedding band.

Charlie Poindexter, Sister Myrtle's husband, was a short chunky man of few words. This was just as well since Sister Myrtle had enough words for both of them. They had, however, a sound marriage, having raised six children with all of them turning out well.

The Ministerial Alliance of Fairhope was meeting at the Dew Drop Inn for lunch as they did every Monday at noon. Sister Myrtle did not even bother to take orders. They took the special or there was an argument. None of the preachers ever dared to order anything except the special. The plates were piled high with pork chops, collard greens, squash, and corn on the cob; in the middle of the table was a huge platter of corn bread.

Sister Myrtle slammed the plate down in front of Roy Jefferson, the Episcopal priest, and glared down at him. She had a running feud going with the priest about his collar. "I've told you before, Preacher, Jesus didn't wear no collar like that."

Jefferson looked up. "I don't expect he wore any kind of collar at all."

"Then why do you have to wear one?"

"It's just tradition among our church folks, Sister Myrtle. Now please don't start on me."

But Sister Myrtle plunked down a plate heaping with food in front of Ellis Burke, the Methodist preacher, and turned her guns on Reverend Jefferson. "You've got to make Carl Spivey go to work, Preacher."

It was difficult to have a ministerial alliance meeting at the Dew Drop Inn, for Sister Myrtle knew every member of every man's congregation (including all their shortcomings) and did not hesitate to bring them up in an open forum.

"I don't know how I could do that, Sister."

"He lets that poor wife of his do all the work. He's a lazy bum."

"He claims he's got a bad back," Jefferson protested.

"You bring him by our church, and we'll anoint him and get him healed. But it ain't his back. He's just lazy. All them Spivey men are lazy."

Jefferson caved in and nodded in surrender. "I'll have a word with him, Sister."

Ellison Burke, the Methodist pastor, was a small man with sharp, intellectual features. He was grinning at Roy Jefferson when Sister Myrtle turned to face him. "What are you going to do about that Bowden girl?"

"You mean Alice?"

"How many Bowden girls you got?"

"Well, I guess she's the only one, Sister Myrtle. What's she done now?"

"You need to keep up with your sheep, Preacher. She went over to Fort Smith with Aaron Dutton. He's no good, and he's going to get that girl in trouble. I think you got to jerk a knot in her and get her straightened out."

"I don't see I could do that."

"Well, the Apostle Paul would have did it! That girl's trying to be one of them flappers."

"I don't expect she means any harm."

"She wears ear screws. That's flat against the Bible, and you know it!"

"Where is that in the Bible?"

"I ain't got time for no theology lesson. You come by when this meeting's over, and I'll show you. But you've got to stop that girl before she goes plum down the wrong road."

"I'll see what I can do."

Sister Myrtle whirled and disappeared back in the kitchen. She came back almost instantly with two more platters. She put one of them down in front of the Presbyterian pastor Alex Digby. She opened her mouth but before she could speak Reverend Digby said, "Now don't you start on me, Sister Myrtle. I know some of my flock needs to be chastised, and I'll send them over for some of your sermon."

"Good! I'll give them a sizzling, red-hot dose of Gospel."

"I'm sure they'll profit by it."

Myrtle stared down at the plate of food and then at the rotund figure of Reverend Digby who was not pleasingly plump but downright overweight. "I've got a word for you from the Lord."

Laughter went around the table, and all the ministers kept their eyes on Sister Myrtle. She always had a word of the Lord for all of them, and Alex Digby flushed. "I don't think I want to hear it."

"Well, you're going to. You need to fast, my brother. You're digging your grave with that fork."

Colin Ryan, the interim pastor of the Baptist Church, was the youngest of the preachers at the meeting. He was twenty-six years old with black hair, dark blue eyes, a widow's peak, and a cleft chin. "Do you suppose we could just have the blessing and eat without the theology? These meetings always make me hungry."

Sister Myrtle suddenly laughed. She had a fondness in her heart for the young preacher who was anything but a typical Baptist. He often visited Sister Myrtle's church and was as loud with his amens and praise the Lords as any of her own flock. "You fly right at it, Brother Colin. You Baptists eat better than you do anything else anyhow."

Father Horatio Bates, the Catholic priest, always dreaded these meetings at the Dew Drop Inn. It humiliated him, somehow, that Sister Myrtle Poindexter knew at least as much of the doings of his flock as he himself knew. He bowed his head and said quickly, "Let's have the blessing."

"I'll ask it myself. I ain't sure any of you preachers are in fit spiritual condition to be thanking the Lord anyways," Sister Myrtle said. She prayed in a loud, strident voice as if she wanted the people across the street to hear. She put in not just a thanks for the preachers and their churches but for every item of food on the table.

Finally, as it went on and on, Colin Ryan broke in and said, "While Sister Myrtle finishes her prayer why don't we go ahead and eat."

Laughter went around the table, and Doctor Merritt, who was sitting at a separate table with the Sheriff Pardue Jessup, whispered, "I like this place, Pardue. You can get your stomach filled and your spiritual needs met."

Sister Myrtle whirled for she had excellent hearing. "I heard that. You missed the last two services at church, Doctor Owen Merritt. You're downright backslid."

"Well, I guess I may be, Sister Myrtle."

Sister Myrtle came over and stared down at the two men, both of them fine looking and in their late twenties. Owen Merritt was six feet tall, lean with crisp brown hair and warm brown eyes. Pardue Jessup, one year short of thirty, was even taller. He had hair black as a raven's wing, dark eyes, and rough good looks. He was the target of many of the single women. He and Owen Merritt were the prime bachelors of Fairhope. Sister Myrtle looked down at them and said nothing, and finally Jessup grew nervous. "What's wrong now? You want to preach at me about my sins?"

"Well, you need it, Pardue."

"What have I done now?"

"It ain't what you've done. It's what you *ain't* done. It's agin Scripture for a man not to take a wife, and you two need to be thinking on that seriously. As a matter of fact, I've got me a list. I've been thinking about the widows in our church who need husbands."

"We've got two or three of those in our congregation," Alex Digby said, "and I think Sister Myrtle is right. You two need to get yourselves married."

"That's right. You ought to be just as miserable as the rest of us," Aaron Burke said, a spark of humor in his eyes.

The meal continued with Sister Myrtle dispensing food and theology liberally. She looked up when Lanie came in. "Well, Sister Lanie, you come to get a bite to eat?"

"No, not this time, Sister Myrtle." She headed straight for Owen's table. "Owen, Aunt Kezia's not well. Could you come and see her?"

"Why, we'll take this whole bunch of preachers over there," Sister Myrtle said. "We'll pray her well."

"Well, who'll feed the people of Fairhope?" Alex Digby grinned. "Let them fast. They need it."

"Let's try Doctor Merritt first, Sister, and Doctor Merritt, Miss Bertha says for you to bring her one of the specials and a piece of pie."

Sister Myrtle scurried around, got the pie, and brought it covered with a clean cloth. She gave it to Lanie and said, "I'll be praying for Kezia. That's one fine woman."

Lanie smiled. "Thank you," she said and left with Owen Merritt.

As soon as they were out the door, the gossip started. "That young woman's got three men on the string," Sister Myrtle said. "She's a sweet thing, but she don't know much about men."

"Which three is that?" Father Horatio Bates asked curiously.

"You don't keep up with this town much, do you, preacher?" She refused to call him Father for the Bible said, *Call no man on this earth your Father.* "She's got Roger Langley downright silly over her."

"That's right. Owen Merritt's struck on her, too," Reverend Jefferson said. "That'd be a good marriage even though he's older than she is."

"Well, she ain't doing herself no good running around with that Brent Hayden, that writer fellow."

"I'm sure it's all innocent. She doesn't have anybody to talk to about her writing," Colin Ryan said.

Charlie Poindexter came out wiping his hands on his apron. Normally he kept his thoughts to himself, but now he jumped in, his voice its usual high-pitched tenor. "You watch what I tell you. That girl won't marry nobody until she gets her pa out of prison."

A silence fell on the group, and finally Sister Myrtle said, "I reckon you're right about that, husband. She's a fine girl with a strong sense of duty. I wish there was more like her in this town." Sister Myrtle turned and said, "Now, I got a list of Scriptures for your preachers to work into your sermons. Some of them women in your congregations are wearing their skirts all the way up to their knees. I want you to hit that hard, do you hear me?"

⚓

After Owen had examined Aunt Kezia, and talked her out of her liver rejuvenator, he left the house, accompanied by Lanie. As they walked toward his office, Owen was grinning. "You can always get any kind of words you need from Sister Myrtle."

"I like her."

"Well, I have one bit of good news. I got a letter from my brother in L.A."

"He's the policeman there?"

"He's a detective. He says he's got everybody looking for Thelma Mays." Thelma Mays was a witness who did not testify during Lanie's father's trial.

Owen looked down at the young woman with admiration. She had pride, which he appreciated. He was also aware of the supple lines of her body and remembered the young girl she had been when they first met. No matter the troubles that beset her family, she had handled life with a serenity he admired and seemed to grow prettier even as he watched. Now, he noticed afresh how her features were quick to express her thoughts, and how laughter and love of life seemed to lie behind her eyes and lips, waiting for some kind of release.

"I'm glad I've been able to help," he said. "I'll send the medicine out."

"Thank you, Owen."

⚓

The autumn air was cold in the hills of the Ozarks, and Lanie shivered as she pulled on the flannel nightgown that fell all the way to her feet. She put on a pair of wool-lined shoes, sat down, and began to work on a poem. She had been writing poems about the life of Jesus and the people who met Him while He was on earth, and today she had been thinking about the rich young ruler. Ideas, phrases, words filled her heart, and she wrote them in wonder, her fingers moving almost as quickly as the ideas came. Ten minutes later, she put her pen down and then read the poem aloud:

> *Seeing you, my son, standing all alone*
> *In growing dusk, is more than I can bear.*
> *Your heart is heavy — yet you must prepare*
> *To live life as a man, without a moan;*
> *Every day for weeks you've gone to where*
> *The Nazarene with his glowing eyes*
> *Entrances you — why, even now you stare*
> *As if you'd caught a glimpse of paradise.*
>
> *Paradise? No, Mother, be content;*
> *This very day I chose to live, not die.*
> *The Rabbi's price for heaven is too high.*
> *This solid earth must be my element.*
> *Sell all, he said — but when I passed him by*
> *A tear of purest rain shone in his eye.*

The poem did not please her completely, but her poetry rarely did. She put the notebook aside, then took up the journal and dated it August 3, 1932, and began writing quickly. Cap'n Brown, her cat, had leaped up on the bed and snuggled up close to her. Lanie rubbed Cap'n Brown's head then wrote:

> *I was mean to Owen tonight. He tried to talk to me about*
> *how people are gossiping about how I go to see Brent Hayden, and*
> *I lost my temper. I was sorry as soon as I snapped at him. I know*
> *I hurt his feelings, and I feel just awful about it.*
> *It seems strange that here I am, eighteen years old, and a*
> *lot of my girlfriends I grew up with are married — and I'm not.*
> *Roger's asked me to marry him, but I can't do it. About Owen, I*

guess I've been in love with him for years. I thought at first it was just a little girl admiration of a man that had done so much for our family, but I think it's more than that now. I don't know how to say it. And, of course, Brent. He's helped me with my writing, helped me to win the national contest, and he's the only one I can really talk to about writing.

She paused and shook her head fiercely then wrote:

I can't think about a home and a husband and children — not until Daddy's out of that awful place!

CHAPTER 2

The interior of the Blackjack Club was fully as grim and uninviting as the exterior. The club, built of concrete blocks, was set in the middle of an asphalt parking lot with grass springing up through the breaks in the surface. Its sickly green door was flanked by high windows on each side to let in light or air, and the roof was flat since there was no snow in California.

Every night the parking lot was filled with vehicles, mostly old trucks and rusted jalopies. The Blackjack Club was an island of concrete set in the midst of the lower edge of California society. Hockshops, tattoo parlors, ratty motels mostly covered with leprous pale gray stucco sat next to small frame houses, many of them with cluttered yards and a multitude of children. This dreary part of California had been so depressing to Maeva Freeman that she was ready to flee back to the green hills of Arkansas.

She had been prepared to see Gary Cooper strolling down the street followed by Paulette Goddard and other stars. She had seen pictures of the stars' palatial mansions and of the glorious city of Los Angeles with its palm trees, blue skies, and warm sun. The shock of the sordid world that she and Logan Satterfield had entered still lingered with her at times. The population was composed primarily of poor people who had fled other worlds looking for the magic of Disney and Hollywood. On the first day while they passed mile after mile of flat country, ugly and sparse, she had said, "This is a desert, Logan."

"Reckon that's what it is. There's another Hollywood, but we probably won't see much of that."

Indeed, they had not seen the beautiful side of Los Angeles, but had floated around the edges of the huge city and the small towns that seemed to have sprung up out of the sparse desert soil. True enough, the mountains were beautiful, but they were not the green mountains that Maeva was accustomed to. They were covered with scraggly trees and had little beauty, at least, in her sight.

Maeva had been accustomed to poverty, for Arkansas had plenty of that, and she had even been, despite her family's objection, to more than one social club, or saloon, as it might have been more properly called. They had been rough, noisy, and loud and filled with the twang of thick Arkansas voices, but there was something different about the clubs like the Blackjack on the fringe of Los Angeles.

Even now, as Maeva stood in front of the microphone singing a song called "Delta Dawn," disgust with the whole scene seemed to sweep over her. It was like being inside of a grotto of some sort. No sunlight ever touched the inside of the Blackjack Club, and only the few naked bulbs hanging from wires shed their feeble corona of light over those who filled the club. The air was thick with cigarette smoke and the pungent odor of alcohol.

The noise was deafening, the band almost drowned out by the shouts and raucous laughter and babble of voices that filled the interior of the club. More than once, men sailed by, dancing with women wearing too much makeup and clothes that were too tight. Often they called up rude, obscene things to Maeva. Mostly, she had learned to ignore them.

She turned and glanced at Logan who was in the middle of the small band composed of three guitars, a set of drums, a saxophone, and a piano. She knew her face was drawn with fatigue for it was late and the evening had been long indeed. Logan was studying her intently, his fingers flying over the frets of the guitar. She could barely hear the music he made, but she knew he was far better than anyone they had encountered on the travels throughout the bars, saloons, and clubs in southern California. In the pale light, his dark features were steady, his eyes intent. She thought how he had tried to discourage her from coming on this trip but finally relented after she had begged him.

The song ended, and Maeva moved away from the microphone. Several men grabbed for her arm, but she shook them off impatiently. She hurried through a door that led down a hallway to her dressing room. She stepped inside, shut the door, and leaned back against it, her head touching the wood, her eyes closed. For a long moment she stood still, the beat of the drums vibrating through the structure, muted wild laughter echoing. Wearily, she went over to the sink and stared into it. It was filthy. Taking out a handkerchief, she managed to wash her face with the tepid water, and then she straightened up and caught her reflection in the cloudy mirror above the sink.

"You look terrible, Maeva." The words were bitter, but indeed, she did look tired and washed out.

She turned away from her reflection, wet the handkerchief, and put it on the back of her neck. For a long time she stood there, memories of home flooding her mind. She thought of the house where she had been born and where her family still lived—except for her father who was incarcerated in Cummins prison. It was a big, rambling old house, and she had not known how much she loved it until she left.

The thought came almost unbidden like a burglar breaking into a house: *You're never going to find Thelma Mays, and if you did, it wouldn't do any good.*

As if to avoid the gloomy thought, Maeva turned and moved across the room. She kept her purse in a drawer of a painted pine dresser. Pulling it out, she extracted a comb and brush and began brushing her hair. It was impossible to get the smell of the cigarettes out without washing, and even that didn't seem to help. As she brushed her hair, she thought about how she had left home with one idea in mind—to find Thelma Mays.

Thelma had been a witness to the shooting that had sent her father to the penitentiary. No one had known she was there, and all the other witnesses had declared her father had murdered Duke Biggins in cold blood. Everyone in her family knew their father was innocent, but more than just believing in her father's innocence, Maeva had a fierce and angry hunger to find Thelma Mays and make her tell the truth—even if she had to shake it out of her.

She pondered her dilemma for a moment. What would she do if she did find her? *I'd make her go back to Arkansas and tell the truth.* And how would she make her go? Put a gun on her?

The rebellious thoughts coursed through Maeva Freeman. She had been through this almost daily since she had left Fairhope with Logan Satterfield, and now hope was a dim, vague light almost obliterated by the doubts that surrounded her.

With a sigh, she put the comb and brush back in her purse, concealed it in a drawer, and moved toward the door. She stepped outside and turned to go down the hall back toward where the raucous music seemed to be shaking the building, but a tall man wearing a white Stetson and a cowboy outfit with high-heeled boots blocked her path. She stopped abruptly, and her eyes went to his face. Cash Millard. The star of the show.

Millard had made one record that had sold fairly well and had an ego as big as the Stetson that he wore. He was a tall, lanky Texan who sang in a twangy voice, and the first time she had heard him and seen him Maeva knew he would never be another Jimmie Rodgers or A. P. Carter. He just didn't have the talent.

"Hey, sweetheart, I've been looking for you." Cash moved forward and put his hand on her shoulder. He was tall and lanky but had a strong grip.

"I've got to go sing, Cash."

"Aw, there's plenty of time. How about you and me cut away after we get through with this gig?"

"I'm tired, Cash."

"Don't be like that, honey."

Maeva had met men like Cash before. They didn't seem to know the meaning of the word *no*. She jerked her shoulder away and started around him, but he caught her and, throwing his arms around her, planted a kiss right on her lips. His arms were strong, but Maeva shoved him away, then swung her arm and caught him right in the mouth with her fist.

Cash blinked and put his hand to his mouth, stared at his fingers and saw that his lip was bleeding. He cursed her, but Maeva ran down the hall and stepped inside the maelstrom of the dance floor. She went at once to the stand and the manager, a short muscular man named Tommy Hart, grabbed the microphone and said, "And here she is again, folks, the Arkansas songbird. Let's hear it for Maeva Freeman!"

Maeva caught one glimpse of Logan, who was watching her, and then refused to look at him again. At once, the band swung into "A New San Antonio Rose," the theme song of Bob Wills, but Maeva did well with it. She finished that to a round of wild applause and then sang "I'm Thinking Tonight of My Blue Eyes" followed by "When My Blue Moon Turns to Gold Again."

After she had finished the third number Cash was suddenly there, and Tommy Hart introduced him once again. "Here's the star of our show, folks. Let's hear it for Cash Millard."

Cash's lip was swollen, and he gave Maeva a furious look. She ignored him, went over, and sat down on a chair close to the band.

"You all right?" Logan shouted over the din.

"Yes," she said, her lips barely framing the word. She sat there while Millard sang three songs, all of them loud and slightly off-key, and finally he stepped down and made his way to her. Without preamble, he pulled her to her feet. "Come on, we're going to dance."

"Let me go, Cash."

Cash laughed and simply dragged her out on the floor. He did not get far, however, for suddenly his grip was torn loose. He turned to face Logan.

"Wrong girl, Cash. Find yourself another one."

Cash Millard drew his arm back and threw a wild punch at Logan Satterfield. Logan almost laughed at the futility of it. He blocked the blow with his left arm and knocked Cash to the floor with a hard blow to the mouth. Cash got up, dazed, with blood running down the front of his shirt. Two of his admirers suddenly appeared, and one of them said, "We'll get him for you, Cash!"

Logan found himself embroiled in a wild assault by Cash Millard's admirers. He was a tough, hard, wicked fighter, but there were too many of them. Maeva threw herself at one who was lifting a beer bottle to hit Logan in the back of the head. She jumped on his back, bit him in the shoulder, and he let loose a wild scream.

And that's when the real brawl began.

⊂══✦⊷

"You got a lady to see you, Dave."

Sal Donatello, a lean Mexican-American detective, stepped inside the squad room. Dave Merritt was sitting at his desk pecking out a report on an old typewriter. "Who is it, Sal?"

"The same woman who's been here before. Says her name is Maeva Freeman. Just like always, she says she won't talk to anybody but you. I tried to turn on the charm, but it didn't work. Do you want to see her?"

Merritt grinned. He was a well-built man in his midthirties with a scar on his right cheek and crisp brown hair.

"Sure, Sal. Bring her in."

It was the late shift, and the dawn was just now breaking over Los Angeles. Dave Merritt got up, went to the window, and looked out. A pale wash of sunlight touched the earth and crept across the lawn. When he heard the door open and close behind him, he turned and saw the young woman standing there.

"My name is Maeva Freeman—"

"I remember you," he said. She had been here once before and told him she knew his brother, Owen, back in Fairhope. He had also received mail from Maeva's sister, Lanie.

"Sit down. How about some coffee?"

Maeva sat down but shook her head. "No, thank you."

Merritt poured himself a cup and sat down. The woman had red hair, startling blue eyes, and a figure that would turn men's eyes anywhere. "I guess you're here again about Thelma Mays."

"Yes. I've got to find that woman, detective."

"As I told you before, it's like looking for a needle in a haystack" Merritt studied Maeva carefully. There was a steadfastness in her that impressed him. She was good looking but was already beginning to show signs of a hard life. The first time they met, she had told him how she ran away from home with a friend named Logan Satterfield. He remembered they were both working in some dive called the Blackjack Club. It was a rough place for a young woman from Arkansas.

"I wish I had better news for you, but so far I haven't been able to find the woman. Got flyers out on her. A few leads, but nothing certain."

Maeva sat forward. "Anything will help, anything at all." Then she sat back again and added, "Your brother is a fine man, and I can tell you are too."

"Well, he's the good guy. I'm the black sheep."

"I don't believe that, but detective, before you tell me about those leads, I do have a more pressing problem."

"What's that, Miss Freeman?"

"Just call me Maeva. There was a fight at the club last night, and my friend Logan got arrested. He was the only one that they took."

"Why would they pick on him?"

"Well, there's a singer there called Cash Millard, and Logan beat him up."

"Yeah, I've heard Millard's record. Not much of a singer."

"Not much of a man," Maeva said bitterly. "They arrested Logan and took him to jail. I don't know what else to do. Could you see what it will take to get him out? We don't have much money," she added quickly.

"They probably took him to the Sixth Precinct. Let me call and see if they've got him." He picked up a phone, spoke briefly, and then nodded. "They're holding him there. Come on, we'll go see what we can do."

The detective picked the brown shapeless hat off the desk, crammed it on his head, and said, "The car's right outside." He stepped aside to let Maeva leave the room. He caught Sal Donatello's eye and knew that he was in for trouble. "I've got a hot lead on the case, Sal. Crime of the century."

"Sure, Dave. I'll call the papers and tell them to keep their front page open."

When they stepped outside, Dave opened the door to a black squad car. Maeva got inside, and Merritt went around and got in. He started the engine and pulled away from the curb. "You've had a pretty rough time since you got here, I'd bet."

"I'm not complaining."

"Tell me about my brother."

"Oh, everybody loves him in Fairhope. My sister especially."

"That's the one called Lanie?"

"That's the one. She's eighteen now, but we've known your brother since he first came to town. You see, my mama died, and my dad got sent to prison. You know about that."

"Yes, your sister's told me. So has Owen. They both say it was a frame-up job."

"It was, Mr. Merritt."

"Just call me Dave. So, Lanie likes my brother. He's a little bit old for her."

"Oh, I think it's just kind of a girlhood crush. She's so smart, Dave. She won a national writing award last year, and she's taken care of me and my sister and my two brothers. She had to quit school to do it, but she's done it. But she's so unhappy and so are all of us."

Dave Merritt was good at eliciting facts, and by the time he pulled up in front of the precinct house, he pretty much had the life history of the Freeman family—and even more of an inclination to help her.

"Come on. Don't pay any attention to what happens. We've got a sergeant here that thinks he's tough, but he's not as tough as I am." He shot her a mischievous, almost wicked, grin.

She followed him into a dingy room with benches occupied by three men and two women and a sergeant sitting behind a tall desk. He was overweight with piggish eyes.

"What do you want, Merritt?" he grunted, displeasure on his face.

"You got a prisoner in there, Simmons. Come to get him."

"What are you talking about?"

"I'm talking about Logan Satterfield. Trot him out."

Sergeant Simmons laughed harshly, but the laughter did not reach his eyes. "That'll be the day."

Dave Merritt was a big man, broad-shouldered, and there was something dangerous about him. He leaned over the desk and said, "Now listen, Artie, I'm not going to argue this. If you want to make something out of it, we'll go to the chief, and I'll tell him about that kickback you've been getting from the chippies over on the south side. I got three of them that'll be a witness against you."

"You wouldn't do that."

"Oh yes, I would. I'd love to do that. Now, what'll it be?"

"There's a fine. You can't have him until he pays his fine."

"You pay it. He's a witness in a case of mine. Now get him out here. Why was he the only one arrested? There must have been a dozen guys in that brawl."

Simmons could not answer. He knew Dave Merritt's reputation and knew that he had little choice. "I don't care," he said. He raised his voice. "I'll get him, but you owe me one for this."

"Yeah, come around anytime. We never close."

"Will you get in trouble for this?" Maeva asked.

"No, not likely. He's a sorry excuse for an officer anyway."

A few minutes later Simmons came back followed by Logan, who looked a bit worse for wear. His ear was red, but his expression was cheerful.

"Are you all right, Logan?" Maeva asked quickly.

"Right as rain. How'd you pull this off?"

"This is Doctor Merritt's brother, Dave. I've told you about him. He's a policeman, a sergeant."

The two men shook hands, and Simmons said, "Take him out of here, Merritt. You're cluttering up my precinct."

"And a princely domain it is. Thanks for the cooperation, Simmons."

The three moved outside the precinct house, and as soon as they were clear, Dave said, "It looks like you two aren't finding California very receptive."

"I guess not, but there's some good folks here—especially one detective."

"I'm doing it for Owen. He helped me out a lot when I was growing up. As a matter of fact, I think I'd be on the wrong side if it hadn't been for him."

"You were going to tell me something earlier about Thelma Mays. You said you might have a lead."

"I'm not one hundred percent sure, but it looks like the woman might be in Bakersfield. I got a tip that she was there. Come on back to the office. I'll make a few calls."

As they drove back toward the station, Dave Merritt studied Logan Satterfield and decided by the time they got there he was a straight arrow. "So you just upped and left home for California, brought this young lady along with you? You come here to be a star?"

"I came because my family pretty well kicked me out."

"They kicked him out because two of his brothers were beating Owen up. Logan stepped in and made them quit. His daddy didn't like it. They're real clannish, the Satterfields."

"Put me out kit and caboodle so I had to do something. I won't ever be a star though. I found that out already."

When they reached the station, Dave nodded toward a café that had just opened up across the street. "Come on, I'll buy you breakfast."

"You don't have to do that, Dave," Maeva said.

"I always have breakfast. Come on." He took them inside the Elite Café, and a pretty waitress came up, her eyes dancing. "Hello, handsome."

"Hello, beautiful. You give these folks whatever they want for breakfast. Fix me up the usual. I'll be right back. What time do you get off?"

"The same time as always."

"I'll see you then."

The waitress watched him go. "Isn't he fine looking?"

"You ought to see his brother. He's even better looking." Maeva smiled.

"Really? I didn't even know he had a brother. What can I get you?"

"Well, since it's on the policeman I guess we'll have whatever's the best."

"How about eggs and bacon and pancakes and biscuits?"

"That'll have to do, I guess." Logan nodded. "Bring two orders of that."

The two sat there, and Logan touched his ear. "I got bobbed in the ear, but I think I gave as good as I got. Good thing you found Owen's brother. It saved my bacon."

The two talked until the food came, and they plunged into it. They were halfway through when Dave Merritt came back. "Okay, Betty, bring on the feed."

"I'll be right here, good looking."

She disappeared, and Dave leaned forward, his eyes bright. "I think we've got something. She's in Bakersfield. I'm ninety percent sure it's her." He wrote out an address on a piece of paper. "I can give you the name, but I don't know what you'll do with it."

"What do you know about her, Dave?" Logan asked.

"Well, she's living with a thug named Bobby Dean Loy. We know him pretty well," he said. "He's done two stretches in the pen. A real rough one. If you bump into him, don't give him any trouble. He's a shooter."

Maeva said, "I've got to go there."

"I'll go along," Logan said. "Haven't had any excitement in a while."

Dave Merritt leaned back. "Well, watch out for Loy. We think he's killed two men, but there was no evidence, so he walked." The waitress brought his breakfast. He winked at her and something passed between them. "Real sweet kid," he said. "Going to college. Works here to pay her tuition. Wants to be a teacher."

"She seems like a fine young woman," Maeva said.

Dave looked at the food and shook his head. "It'll be hard to get the Mays woman to testify. That kind doesn't talk."

They finished breakfast, and he took them back to the rooming house. Maeva said, "Thanks so much, Dave. I'll tell Owen what a help you were."

"I hate to let you two go. Loy's a pretty tough cookie."

"We'll be okay," Logan said. "I'll see to it."

"Okay. Write me and tell me how it comes out, will you? Or give me a call."

"Yes, we'll do that."

They watched as the police car moved away, and Maeva said, "How are we going to get to Bakersfield?"

"How much money have you got?"

"About twenty-three dollars."

"Well, I got twenty-nine. Tell you what. You go pack your stuff."

"What about our jobs?"

"Oh, didn't I tell you? We got fired. Don't have any jobs to lose."

"That's not enough money to get to Bakersfield."

"I have a master plan. You go get packed up. Stay there until you hear from me."

Maeva was sitting outside the apartment house, and she looked up to see an old dilapidated automobile with Logan at the wheel. He brought it to a squealing halt and got out. "Some car, huh?"

"Where did you get this thing?"

"I saw it last week in front of a garage with a for-sale sign on it. I hope it'll get us to Bakersfield. I've got nineteen dollars left."

"How'd you buy that car for that little money?"

"Ah, I made a deal."

Maeva did not find out what "the deal" was until they were packed and ready to go. "Where's your guitar?"

"I had to throw it in to get this car."

"You shouldn't have done that." The flat top guitar was the one good thing that Logan Satterfield owned.

"We got to get to Bakersfield, don't we?"

"I feel terrible letting your guitar go like that."

"Well, I'll find some way you can pay me back. Now, we're on our way."

They found the address that Dave Merritt had given them, and it was every bit as run down as the rooming house where they had rented rooms.

"They're not living very high on the hog are they, Maeva?"

"I'm a little bit scared. You know what Dave said about Bobby Dean Loy."

"I'll charm him with my wit and sophistication."

"You're crazy," she said, but she could not help but smile. "Well, let's find her."

Finding Thelma Mays was not difficult. The landlord grunted, "She's upstairs in room 203. Don't give me no trouble."

"No trouble," Logan said. The two ascended the stairs and knocked on the door. A woman dressed in a housecoat opened it. She had bleached blonde hair, green eyes, and bruises on her face. She stared at them suspiciously. "What do you want? Who are you?"

"My name is Maeva Freeman. You're Thelma Mays?"

"That's right. I don't know you, do I?"

"No, we're from Fairhope. Could we talk to you?"

"About what?"

"Could we come in, do you think? It's kind of public out here."

"I guess so." The woman moved inside the filthy wreck of a room then turned to face them defiantly. "What do you want with me?"

Maeva took a deep breath. "My daddy's in prison for killing Duke Biggins."

Thelma Mays stared at her. "What's that got to do with me?"

"You were there when the shooting took place, weren't you, Thelma?" Maeva said, her eyes fixed on the woman.

"No, I wasn't there."

"Yes, you were. We know you were, and you know my daddy didn't kill Duke Biggins like the witnesses said he did."

"You get out of here. I don't want nothin' to do with you."

"Doesn't it mean anything to you, Thelma, that an innocent man's in prison? He's got a family."

"It ain't my fault. Now you get out of here."

The door suddenly opened, and a big hulking man stepped inside. He had the face of an unsuccessful prizefighter, and there was a sullenness in him. "Who are you?" he demanded.

"My name's Logan Satterfield. This is Maeva Freeman. We're from Arkansas."

"Are you Mr. Loy?" Maeva asked.

"Who told you that?"

"A friend of mine, a police detective in Los Angeles," Logan said. He stepped closer to put Maeva farther away from Loy. "We need to talk to Miss Mays here about going back to Arkansas to get Miss Maeva's father a new trial."

Loy stared at him and then his eyes went to Thelma. "What they talking about, Thelma?"

"Oh, some story they made up. There ain't nothin' to it, Duke. Now you folks get out of here."

Loy said, "You heard her. Now git!"

Maeva started to argue, but Logan said, "Let's go, Maeva."

Loy grinned. "That's pretty smart." He stuck his hand inside his coat. "I got the difference here."

"We're leaving," Logan said. He took Maeva's arm and led her outside. They got in the car, and he started it up. "We'll have to go at this some other way. She's not going to talk until she has to. Wouldn't do any good to get into a brawl with Loy."

"No, he might hurt you."

"Or I might hurt him."

He looked around and said, "Well, Bakersfield's bound to have some kind of a dive where we can get a job playing at least for enough money to get a room." He moved the car away from the curb, and they began cruising the streets, looking for a sign.

Maeva said, "I wish I was a praying woman, but I'm not."

It was the first time Logan had ever heard Maeva say anything like this. "You think you ever will be?" he asked curiously.

"I don't think so. I was born bad."

"Yeah, me too. I've been told that all my life that I was no good."

"You got some good in you. You're helping me get my daddy out of jail."

He reached over and tugged a lock of her hair. When she turned to face him, he grinned crookedly. "Maybe I'm just trying to get on the good side of you. You know, make up to you like men do."

Maeva laughed. "No, I know when a man's after me. You're not that kind, and you dragged me all the way out here to California when I asked you to. You never once tried to get at me." She was quiet for a while and then said, "I guess you want a good woman, Logan, and I'm not like that."

"Don't talk like that. Maybe both of us will turn the corner. Become good instead of bad."

"Well, what do we do now?"

"Get a job, hang around, go back, and see Thelma. Sooner or later, that sorry man of hers will beat her up again or kick her out. We'll wait until she hits bottom, and then we'll make our move."

⭳ CHAPTER 3 ⭳

"I got me a new plan, Booger, and it's a lollapalooza."

Cody Freeman often talked his plans over with the big blood-hound. When he tried talking to human beings, they usually argued with him, trying to talk him out of what he wanted to do, but Booger was far more understanding. The big dog moved closer, leaned forward, and licked Cody's face. The creases in Booger's own face were deep and furrowed, and his eyes were sad, but this was an illusion, for actually Booger was a very happy dog indeed. He was wearing his medal. It caught the sunlight, and Cody took it between his fingers and admired it.

"They're going to give me a gold medal, too. It's going to say GENIUS just like yours says HERO." He stroked the big dog's head and said, "It'll take me a while, but I'm going to do 'er. Here's what it is, Booger. I've been reading in the Bible, and it says 'Go ye into all the world and preach the gospel to every creature.' Well, Booger, I ain't been doing that, but I intend to start."

Booger edged closer and leaned up against Cody, who was sitting on the ground. The big dog's head was on the level with Cody's, and he whined softly as if he were trying to say something.

"What I'm going to do is witness to everybody in this whole dadgummed town! It'll take a while just to get this town seen to, but I'm going to do it. Let's go. You can go with me."

Booger got on his feet instantly, and Cody picked up the cotton bag that he had carried his Bible in. He had also composed a tract that made him very proud. The title of it was *Turn or Burn!* It set the tormenting flames of hell forth in dramatic terms, and at the last offered the Gospel to anyone who wanted to be saved. It was liberally larded with Scriptures, not all of them seeming to fit the tract, but Cody was proud of it and revised it from time to time.

When he left the house and started down Jefferson Davis Boulevard, the first person he saw was Mrs. Agnes Jinks, who lived right across the street. She was the wife of the barber Deoin Jinks, and Cody had known her all his life.

"Hello, Cody, where are you off to, you and that beautiful dog of yours?"

"I'm out to be a witness. Have you ever been saved by the blood of the Lamb, Mrs. Jinks?"

Agnes Jinks stared at him. "Why, Cody, we belong to the same church. You know I'm a Christian."

"Well, people make mistakes. Here, you better take this." He handed her one of his tracts.

Agnes scanned it and frowned. "Why, I've been saved since I was sixteen years old."

"I'm going to talk to everybody in this town. I think there's hypocrites among us. Not everybody that says they're saved is really saved."

"That's — that's crazy, Cody."

"Oh no, it's scriptural. Well, you're my first witness. I'll see you later, Mrs. Jinks."

Agnes Jinks watched him and despite herself felt almost something like despair. "That boy! What will he think of next? I'll have to talk to Lanie about this. Maybe she can do something with him."

❧

Francis Butterworth, the owner of the Rialto Theater, was putting up new posters outside the theater. The one he was working on was a movie called *Red Dust* staring Clark Gable and Jean Harlow.

"Mr. Butterworth, you don't need to be showing that movie."

Francis Butterworth turned and blinked with surprise. "What'd you say, Cody?"

"I'm telling you that movie's not fit to be seen."

"Red Dust? Have you seen it?"

"No, but look at the picture. That woman's clothes is about to fall off, and while I'm here, I've got to tell you that *Tarzan* movie that has that woman Jane in there—I did see that, and she hasn't got enough clothes on to be respectable. I'm telling you, Mr. Butterworth, you've got to get rid of them sinful movies!"

Butterworth stood there staring at Cody who ran through a list of movies he thought unsuitable. Finally, Francis Butterworth, who was a fine Christian man, said, "Go on, Cody, leave me alone."

"All right, but I'll be back. And here—I'm leaving this for you." He reached in, pulled out a Bible that looked rather thin, and without even looking, he tore a page out of it and said, "There. Read that."

"What's this?"

"Why, it's the Bible, Mr. Butterworth. It'll tell you about them bad movies." Butterworth looked down at the page of the Bible. "This is a page from the book of Leviticus 11:2 and 3. 'These are the beasts which ye shall eat among all the beasts that are on the earth. Whatsoever parteth the hoof, and is cloven-footed, and cheweth the cud, among the beasts, that shall ye eat.'"

Francis threw up his hands. *What in the world is that boy thinking of now? This doesn't have anything to do with movies. It's all about the Jewish dietary laws. I'm going to have to talk to his family. He's going to shame them sure as the world!*

Elspeth Patton, editor of the local newspaper, stared at Cody as he announced, "Miss Patton, you've got to be more careful what you put in the newspaper."

"Well, good morning to you, Cody. What particular editorial do you object to?"

"It ain't the editorials," Cody said. He was standing there before her, a fine-looking boy, and one that Elspeth liked a great deal. She loved the whole family, in fact, and thought Cody was one of the wonders of the natural world.

Withholding a smile, she said, "Well, suppose you just show me. Here's the paper. What is it that's not Christian?"

"It's right there on page three." Cody took the paper and ruffled it. "Right there. There's a woman wearing her underwear."

"That's a corset ad paid for by Cole's Department Store."

"You call it anything you want to. She's wearing her underwear right there for everybody to look at."

"And that offends you, does it, Cody?"

"It sure does. We got to get these things cleaned up. Here, take this." Pulling out his Bible, he ripped a page out and handed it to her. "I'll be expecting to see some changes made."

Elspeth Patton waited until Cody was gone and then looked at the page. It was from the book of Ezekiel, a part of the Bible she found very difficult anyway. She shook her head, a smile touching her lips, then murmured, "Well, I'm glad Cody brought this by. It'll certainly make a better newspaper woman out of me—although I don't know how."

⌖

Effie Johnson, the president of the Planter's Bank, looked up as the door opened. "Hello, Cody," she said. "What can I do for you? You want to make a loan?"

"No, ma'am, I don't. I'm just out on my mission today."

"You have a mission?" Effie knew the Freeman family well and had been instrumental in saving their home place from the clutches of Otis Langley. It had been a close call, but she had a special interest in Forrest Freeman and in all of his family. She greatly admired Lanie for holding the family together single-handedly.

"Well, go ahead. What's your mission?"

"I'm going to preach the Gospel to every creature so I thought I might as well stop in. Bankers need the Gospel, too."

"And you don't think I'm a Christian?"

"Oh, I expect you are, but I'm passing the Gospel along to everybody. Here, Miss Effie, take this."

Effie took the page that Cody ripped out of the Bible. "You're tearing your Bible apart?"

"It'll help make you a better Christian."

"Did you pick this page especially for me?"

"Why, no," Cody said, a puzzled look on his face, "I didn't do that."

"Well, why do you think I need this particular page?" She looked down and saw that it was part of the book of Revelation. She had puzzled over that particular book for years, and now she said, "This is all about the four horsemen. Do you know what that's all about? What it means?"

"I'm working on that, Miss Effie, but you just hang onto it. It'll do you good. Well, I've got to go. Lots of folks to see."

"Well, God bless you, Cody." Effie waited until the door was closed and then began to giggle. "That boy! What will he think of next?"

In the church office, Colin Ryan leaned back and studied Louise Langley. She was a beautiful young woman, and one who had despised him utterly when he had first come to town. She had been filled with pride, and Colin's laid-back approach to practically everything had not pleased her. It had taken a miracle to break her pride, and another miracle had made her fall in love with the handsome young pastor. They were engaged now somewhat to Colin's surprise, but women had a way of doing things like that.

Louise was going over the possibilities for the things she wanted in their wedding, and Colin leaned forward, took her hand, and held it tightly. "Aren't you getting ahead of yourself, Louise?"

"What do you mean?"

"Well, I'm just interim pastor at this church. That means when the new pastor comes I'll be out of a job."

"I think you should be the pastor."

Colin laughed. "I know you think so, but I'm really not suited for this church, and I think the Lord has other things in mind."

"I know what you want to do. You want to start a mission work somewhere."

"That's right. I do. I think that's what God has called me to do."

"Daddy will fund it for you. He'll back you in any mission work you like."

He suddenly moved and pulled her into his lap. "I'll tell you what. Let's smooch a little bit. We can talk about business later."

"You let me go, Colin Ryan. We're not married yet."

At that moment, the door opened, and Pardue Jessup stepped in. He stopped abruptly, amused by the embarrassment of the two young people. "Sorry, didn't mean to intrude."

Pardue had no chance to say any more because Geraldine Delaughter, the mayor's wife, came bustling in. "You've got to do something about Cody Freeman, Pastor. It's your job."

"What's he done now?" Colin moved away, putting a safe distance between him and Louise.

"He's passing out literature that's not fit to read on the street. Here, he stopped me and asked me if I had ever been washed in the blood of the Lamb and then he gave me this."

"Why, this is a page from the book of Song of Solomon."

"I know what it is. I don't want him passing out things like this to me on the street. Look what it says." She grabbed the sheet. "It says,

'Thy breasts are like two young roes that are twins, which feed among the lilies ... Thou art all fair, my love: there is no spot in thee.'"

"It's part of the Bible, Sister."

"It's a part that ought to be read quietly and silently and not shouted in public and not handed out to church members." She turned and said, "Pardue, you ought to arrest Cody."

"On what charge? Being a religious fanatic? That ain't against the law."

Mrs. Delaughter had no chance to say more for others had begun to arrive. They all had encountered Cody, and all of them had either the *Turn or Burn!* tract or parts of the Scripture. The office filled up, and finally Colin said, "All right, let me talk to the young man. He's got a good heart."

"You've got to make him stop this foolishness," Mrs. Delaughter said. "You mind what I say. You're the pastor, and it's up to you."

⊶

Cody was working on one of his inventions, very few of which were ever successful. He looked up when Colin came into the yard. "Why, hello, Preacher," he said. "You're just in time. I want to show you my new invention."

Colin edged closer and said, "Well, actually I've got to talk to you about something else."

A large hen of a peculiar dark red color was clucking around Cody's feet. He shoved her away with his toe. "Get away, Priscilla. You're going to get stepped on. That's Lanie's favorite hen. She lays an egg a day just as regular as the sun comes up."

"Cody, I want to talk to you about your witnessing."

"Ain't it great?" Cody said proudly. "I got rid of a whole bunch of tracts and pages of the Bible."

"You've got to be a little bit more — tactful."

"What does that mean? The Bible says go preach the Gospel to every creature. Fairhope's full of creatures, ain't it, Pastor?"

"Well, yes, but I'm not sure that God intended for us to stop everybody on the street."

"Why not?"

"I just don't think it works too well for one thing."

"But you witness to people all the time."

"But not to everybody I meet." Colin cleared his throat. "What I do is I try to make myself available, and I might pass by five people and God wouldn't do anything to push me toward them. Then I'll see another one, and God will sort of say to me, 'There's the one. Share the gospel with him.'"

"Is that the way you do it? Well, I might miss some like that."

The conversation went on for some time, and finally Cody rather reluctantly agreed to pray about the matter. Colin said, "I admire your boldness, Cody. It's a rare quality. You have a good heart and a fiery heart for the lost. God's going to use you greatly."

"Well, shucks, I hope so." Cody shrugged his shoulders then his eyes lit up. "Now, can I tell you about my invention?"

"Why, sure. What is it?"

"Get away, Priscilla, you're going to get stepped on." He shoved the hen away and said, "Look at this." He reached into a paper sack and came out with a handful of what seemed to be broken up concrete. "That's my new invention."

"What is it?"

"It's power, that's what it is. That's what all inventions are about. You take the steam engine. That's power! A gasoline engine, that's more power. All inventions have something to do with power. Look, let me show you." He put the sack down, pulled out a small crumb of the material, and put in on a flat rock. He picked up a six-pound sledgehammer with a short handle. "Now, you just watch this." He lifted the hammer and struck the crumb of what looked like concrete. *Bang!* "You hear that?"

"I heard it. What was it?"

"Why, that's power. Now, look at this. I've been trying it out on little bitty pieces, and there's always a bang. I've been waiting to try it out in a big way." He pulled six or seven chunks of the mixture out and put it on the flat rock.

"You're not going to hit that with that sledge, are you?"

"That's what inventors do. They keep trying things until they work."

"You don't know what will happen, Cody. If a little piece of that makes a bang, there's no telling what it'll do if you hit a big chunk."

"You just step back. I got my mind made up."

Colin backed up, protesting all the time. "It's too dangerous, Cody. You could hurt your eyes or something."

"No, I'm going to turn my head away. See." He took the short, heavy hammer in his hand and measured the distance. "Now look. I'm turning away, and I'm raising the hammer. Now watch this!"

Colin had backed away fifteen feet. He saw the hammer fall, and the air was suddenly rent with a tremendous explosion.

"Cody, you all right?"

Cody stood there looking stunned. When he turned around Colin said, "Your eyebrows are gone." He looked down and said, "The hair's all gone off of your arm too."

"What? Why are you whispering, Preacher?"

Colin Ryan stared at him. "I'm not whispering."

"I can't hear you."

"Well, you're deaf then." He started to say something else, but at that moment, the sledgehammer descended. It had been blown high in the air, and what goes up must come down. It came down, unfortunately, on Priscilla and killed the big hen instantly.

Cody was staring at the dead hen and poking at his ear when Lanie came out of the house. "What was that?"

"I'm afraid there's been an accident," Colin said.

"Are you hurt, Cody? What did you do?" Lanie suddenly stopped, and her face turned pale. She bent over and said, "Priscilla! You killed Priscilla!"

Cody turned his good ear and tried to think of some excuse. "Well," he said finally, "it was — it was her time to go."

"You fool boy!" Lanie screamed. "You did that, not God!"

"It is appointed unto a chicken once to die. The Bible says that, don't it, Brother Colin?"

Colin cleared his throat. "I'm afraid it says it is appointed unto a *man* once to die."

"Well, that's all the same."

"Come inside. Are you hurt?" Lanie said, putting the death of her pet chicken aside. The family gathered and everyone was babbling.

Aunt Kezia had come downstairs and stared at Cody. "What happened to your eyebrows, boy?"

"They got blown off," Colin said.

She looked puzzled and worried at the same time. "What was that stuff you hit?"

At the age of seventeen, Davis was taller than most and had auburn hair and startling blue eyes. He narrowed his eyes at his brother. "I'll tell you what it was," he said, his face flushed. "He's been taking dynamite caps away from the brakeman, Tim Carter. You know they put those things on the railroad tracks and when a train hits them, they explode. That's a signal for the train to stop."

"You stole dynamite caps?"

"I think he meant to throw them away," Davis mumbled.

"Well, it looks like you could have killed yourself. If that hammer had come down on your head," Colin said, "you'd be dead instead of the chicken."

"Which chicken is dead?" Kezia said.

"Priscilla, my favorite," Lanie said mournfully.

"Well, boy, you done it this time. You're a fanatic, but God bless you." She thought a while and said, "There's a lot of dead folks in the church so it's a lot easier to restrain a fanatic than it is to resurrect a corpse."

Colin Ryan found this extremely amusing. "I'm glad you're all right, Cody, but you've got to watch yourself about this witnessing."

Lanie frowned. "What witnessing is that?"

"My office was filled up with people. He decided to witness to everybody and give them a page of the Bible and one of those tracts."

"He's made a public nuisance out of himself is what he's done," Davis said with disgust.

Cody sat there feeling miserable. He looked around and said, "Well, everybody makes mistakes. I made one with that dynamite, but it ain't wrong to witness."

Colin Ryan put his arm around Cody. "You're a good boy, Cody. You're going to be a fine, fine man. We just got to stop you from hurting anybody until we get you grown up."

⊸⊸ CHAPTER 4 ⊷⊷

The news of Cody Freeman's Dynamite Caps Escapade spread all over Fairhope within twenty-four hours. Dorsey Pender, the mailman, recounted the story at every house where he stopped to deliver mail and even at those that had no mail for the day he stopped anyway. Henrietta Green, the telephone operator, did her bit by informing everyone she spoke to, whether to give a long distance number or express her opinion of a boy who would kill a chicken with dynamite.

The story swelled with the telling, as gossip always does, and one overzealous citizen even called the FBI to inform them that a foreign agent had taken up residence in Fairhope, Arkansas. The FBI disregarded the message.

The inhabitants of the Freeman house were, more or less, accustomed to Cody's shenanigans and escapades, so they were not as shocked as other citizens were. Lanie was the most outspoken for she greatly mourned the loss of her favorite chicken Priscilla. It was while she was putting ointment on Cody's blistered arm that she delivered a stern message concerning his behavior.

"I think you should have had better sense, Cody," she said, smearing the ointment on his arm liberally and ignoring his flinching. "Dynamite is so dangerous. Didn't it ever once occur to you not to blow up something?"

"Aw, Sis, it was just an experiment. I was trying to find a new source of power."

"Well, you didn't find it. All you did was find a way to kill Priscilla."

Cody shut his eyes and winced as she slapped more ointment on. "Ouch, that hurts! Anyway, I told you it was Priscilla's time to go."

"It was *not* her 'time to go.' *You* made her go. If you hadn't pulled that silly stunt, she'd still be laying an egg every day just like she always did."

Cody opened his eyes to slits and saw that Lanie was angry. It was unusual for her, and he decided it would be the better part of valor to ignore the subject. He thought he could straighten her out about predestination when she was in a better mood.

"And another thing, this crazy witnessing program that you're on—"

"It's not crazy. The Bible says to share the Gospel with every creature."

"It doesn't say that any one of us has the responsibility for every other human being. Besides, you're hurting people's feelings."

"Well, Jesus hurt people's feelings. He called the Pharisees vipers, snakes. I haven't done that yet."

"You'd better not." Lanie dropped his arm and shook her head. "It's a wonder you didn't blow your ear off. Look, your hair is all blown off your eyebrows and the side of your head. You look lopsided."

Cody tried to look ashamed. "Well, inventors sometimes aren't recognized for genius in their own lifetime."

Lanie was not through talking about Cody's program of winning the world through witnessing. "You are absolutely wrong to call Mamie Dorr a scarlet woman." Mamie Dorr was the operator of a beauty salon, and she was indeed suspected of having rather loose morals. "You didn't have any business calling her a scarlet woman."

"Well, she is!" Cody protested.

"What's a scarlet woman?" Corliss had come in to watch the healing operation and now turned her big blue eyes on Lanie. "Is she really red? The kind of scarlet woman like a Christmas ornament?"

Lanie knew it would be hopeless to try to explain the situation to Corliss. "You go out and play, honey. This is grown-up talk."

"Well, shoot. How am I going to learn anything if I don't listen? I bet I'll find out though what a scarlet woman is." She ran off singing a little tune under her breath as she almost always did.

Lanie was wiping her hands off on an old towel worn thin. "Mamie isn't a Christian, Cody, but some of us have been praying for her for a long time."

"Well, I just made it plain to her. She needs to get right with God."

"No, you embarrassed her and humiliated her in front of her friends. It's going to be much harder now to win her to Jesus."

"Well, she needs to hear the Gospel," Cody protested.

"She needs compassion, Cody, and that's what you didn't give her."

"She's a loose woman, Lanie, everybody knows that."

"Listen to me, Cody. God is her judge, not you. Don't you know that judge-not-that-you-be-not-judged principle?" She shook her head and knew that he would have an answer.

Cody said adamantly, "By their fruit you shall know them. We've got a right to be fruit inspectors, Lanie."

"Oh, it's hopeless talking to you! You're going to have to apologize to Mamie and ask her to forgive you."

"Jesus never apologized!"

"You are *not* Jesus, Cody. Sometimes it occurs to me that you think you are. Only God can judge people, not you, and not me." She saw the hurt look on his face, reached out, hugged him, and managed a smile. "You are the most aggravating young man in this world, Cody Freeman—but I'll say this for you. You make life interesting, and when you learn to show a little common sense, you're going to be a wonder."

Cody said, "Can I have some gingerbread?"

"You don't deserve it but yes, you can. Leave some for Davis."

Lanie went into the kitchen and doled out a generous wedge of gingerbread for Cody. He went off, and Lanie wondered what impractical and foolish scheme was hatching in his head. "I wish I could read his mind. Then I could put a stop to some of these things."

Going over to the stove, she lifted the lid on a pot, dipped out a deep dish full of chicken soup. She put two pieces of homemade bread and butter on a plate and then got a glass of milk from the ice box. Putting it on a tray, she went upstairs and entered Kezia's room. "Here's your lunch, Aunt Kezia." She was relieved to see that the old woman looked much better. Color had returned to her face, and her eyes were clear.

"What is it?"

"Chicken soup."

Kezia suddenly cackled a high-pitched laugh. "I'll bet I know which chicken it was."

"You're right. It's Priscilla. She was tough, but I boiled it down. I can't eat any of it. It makes me feel like a cannibal."

"Well, I can eat it. Put it right down there, girl."

Kezia leaned forward and smelled the soup. "Well, I will say this. That chicken died in a good cause. You're a fine cook, Lanie."

"Thank you, Aunt Kezia. There's plenty more soup if you want it."

"No, this will do me fine." Kezia slurped the soup loudly, for her table manners were not the most delicate in the world. Finally, she looked up and said, "You written any more of them poems about people in the Bible?"

"I just finished one last night. Would you want to hear it?" Lanie took a strip of paper out of her pocket.

"What's it about?"

"You know the first song I can remember learning in Sunday school was about Zacchaeus. It went something like this:

"Zacchaeus was a wee little man
A wee little man was he
He climbed up in the sycamore tree
His Savior for to see."

"I reckon they're still singing that song. I heard Corliss singing it just the other day."

"Well, I've always been interested in Zacchaeus. It's all in the nineteenth chapter of Luke. It just says that he was a rich man, and he was very short so that he couldn't see over the heads of anybody. So he climbed up in a tree. Jesus looked up when He passed by and said, 'Zacchaeus, I'm going to have dinner with you today.' That was a good thing for the Lord to do, wasn't it? He was a publican, a tax collector, and all the Jews hated him."

Kezia pushed the dish away and leaned back in the chair. "Well, how did you come up with a poem about a fellow like Zacchaeus?"

"Oh, I try to think what was he like, how he heard about Jesus, where he got his money, if he had a family. So, then I try to see him as a human being just like all the rest of us. I imagine he had his hard times so I just thought I'd have him talking to one of his relatives, a nephew in this case, telling about how he met Jesus. You sure you want to hear it?"

"Read it, girl — read it."

"I always put a Scripture at the top of these poems about Jesus. This one is from Luke 19. 'And behold, there was a man named Zacchaeus, which was the chief among the publicans, and he was rich. And he sought to see Jesus ... and could not for the press, because he was little of stature.' I call this poem 'Sycamore Tree.'"

Who's that? Who calls Zacchaeus? — why, Nephew,
There you are, beneath this tree I've climbed;
Strange fruit on this old sycamore, eh, Micah?
A miserable old publican dangling
Like a withered time-burned grape.
Ha! I read your eyes: **The old man's cracked!**
I hope he made his will before he perched
Up there, blinking like a sun-struck owl!

Not mad, Micah — just a little desperate.
(Let us say I play the fool in age
Because in youth I never dared to dare.)
O Micah, you are a mirror! In you I see

Myself as I was forty years ago —
Face set for getting, grasping, keeping!
No time for dreams, or friends, or joy!
It was those barren years that put me here,
Risking my brittle bones up in this tree.

Would you believe I'm here because I'm lonely?
What's that? I'm too rich to be lonely? Fah!
I'm so rich my soul can taste the bite
Of poverty so deep it starves my soul!
My early hopes have twisted into nightmare
Shapes that mock me day and night, laughing
At my empty yesterdays and dark tomorrows.

Why am I here, Nephew? Laugh if you will
But by this tree must pass the prophet, Jesus.
By the synagogue I heard him preach;
My prisoned heart opened like a door,
Loneliness faded like a mist.

And so, I ran ahead, and now I wait.
Yet — it is a foolish hope; why should
God's prophet look at me, a publican?
When last did I see love in any face?

But see, he comes, Micah!
At least I'll see his face — but everything
I'd give if this man Jesus would simply stop,
Look up, and with a smile,
Fill up this empty, frightened heart!

Kezia had listened intently, and when Lanie had finished she nodded vigorously. "Well, isn't that fine! I never was one much for poetry, but I like that kind."

"Thank you, Aunt Kezia. I'm glad you liked it."

"What you going to do to Cody for nearly killing himself and the preacher and actually wiping out your favorite hen?"

"I don't have the heart to really fuss at him. I'm just glad he didn't hurt himself."

"I hear he's created a ruckus going around passing out that tract, *Turn or Burn!* and tearing pages out of the Bible."

"Well, I've had a talk with him about that too, and so has Brother Ryan. I made him promise to apologize to Mamie Dorr."

"What'd he say to make her mad?"

"Went right into her beauty shop and called her a scarlet woman."

"Well, that wasn't too smart."

"No, it wasn't. He's got all kinds of enthusiasm."

"Well, he goes about things full speed ahead. Still, he's got a heart for God. Wouldn't surprise me if he wound up being a preacher."

"Well, he'd better be an evangelist. He wouldn't last long as a pastor of a church! He has no tact whatsoever. I'm going over and see Nelson and Cass and their new baby."

"That fellow is plum foolish about that child. You'd think it was his own."

A young woman named Cass had been brought home by Davis, and it had developed that she was pregnant by some man she refused to identify. A neighbor, Nelson Prather (called Nellie by most) had fallen in love with Cass, and they had married. The baby had been born, and the new parents were foolish about him. They had named him Nelson Davis Prather and were the proudest parents in the world.

Lanie decided to ride Davis's bicycle into town. She put a bundle of paper in a cotton bag and tied it onto the handlebars, then pedaled through town smiling and waving at people. She passed by several empty buildings that had once been prosperous businesses, but the Depression had left its mark on Fairhope as it had on every town in America.

At the end of Confederate Boulevard, she turned onto Highway 16 and headed toward the Prathers' farm. As she pedaled along, she thought of the story that had been in the morning paper. There had been a bonus march by veterans of World War I. They had come by the thousands to Washington and camped out in a tent city there, asking the government to reward their services with a cash bonus.

It had not worked that way, however, for President Herbert Hoover had ordered the army to move them out. Led by General Douglas MacArthur and Major Dwight Eisenhower the soldiers struck the bonus marchers, injuring some of them and killing one. It had saddened Lanie, and she had said to Roger Langley, "I don't see why the government couldn't give them a bonus. They won the war for us."

She pulled into the driveway leading to the Prather house, a two-story white frame building as neat as any in the county. She saw Nellie coming out to meet her, and he grinned at her broadly. "I bet you come to see that pretty boy of mine, ain't you?"

"I sure have."

"Well, come on in. I'm trying not to get swollen up with pride, but it's mighty hard with a son like that."

Lanie moved inside, listening to Nellie brag on the new baby, and as soon as she got inside, Cass greeted her, holding the new arrival.

"Let me have that beautiful baby!" Lanie exclaimed. She took the boy from Cass and looked down into his face. She touched his cheek and said, "Look, he's going to have dimples, I think." He suddenly grinned at her toothlessly, and she shook her head. "You're going to be a charmer, you are."

"Come on in. You're just in time to get a bite to eat," Nellie said.

"No, I've got several stops to make. Thanks very much."

Nellie and Cass would hear nothing of her leaving. "Come on in," Nellie said. "You've got to taste some of my sweet potato pie. It's the best in the world, or anywhere else for that matter."

Indeed, it proved as excellent as all Nelson's cooking was known to be. His mother had been an invalid and left a widow at a young age, so Nelson had raised his brother and his sister working in the fields and in the house.

As Lanie ate the pie, Nelson remarked, "Well, we got bad times a-coming."

"I thought they were pretty bad already with this Depression."

"Going to be something extra bad. I heard a dog howl last night at midnight. You know what that means."

"I guess it means he's lonesome."

"It means bad luck is what it means." Nelson was one of the most superstitious men that had ever drawn breath. Everything was a sign to him, of good luck or bad, and now he shook his head gloomily. "We got to be careful and ward off bad luck."

"Oh, that's foolishness," Cass said. "God's been good to us."

Nelson grinned. "She's trying to get me to give up my superstitions, and I guess she's right about it." He changed the subject, as he often did. "What do you think about this coming election? Who's going to win?"

"Well, it won't be Hoover. Everybody blames him for all the troubles of the country," Lanie said. "I like this man Franklin Delano Roosevelt."

"Well, he's a Democrat and most folks around here are yellow-dog Democrats."

"Yellow-dog Democrats?" Lanie looked at him, puzzled. "What's that?"

"They'd vote for a yellow dog as long as he was a Democrat."

Nellie took Nelson Davis Prather in his arms and said, "I got to show this boy what's going on out in the big world. You two can gossip while I'm gone. Talk about what a good looking husband Cass got herself."

"He's such a mess," Cass grinned. Tears came into her eyes. "He's so good to me and the baby. You wouldn't believe it."

"I guess I would. I've always thought Nelson was one of the best men I've ever known."

"Do you ever think about getting married yourself and having children, Lanie?"

"Well, I've got too much to do right now taking care of my brothers and sisters, and trying to get my daddy out of jail."

Cass took Lanie's hand. "You've done so much for me, you, and your family. If Davis hadn't found me and brought me to your place, I think I'd have died. Now I've got everything. I just wish you had a husband." She hesitated and gave Lanie an odd look. "I thought you'd have married Roger by this time."

"No, I can't think about things like that," she said. "Well, I've got to go. I'm going over to Brent's to show him some of my new writing."

Cass followed Lanie outside. "Do you like him a lot?"

"Well, he's been kind to me, Cass. He encouraged me in my writing. He helped me get published." She saw that Cass was troubled and shook her head. "I see you've heard the gossip about us."

"I don't believe a word of it, Lanie. I just hate to hear people talking about you."

"People are going to talk as long as there's a Dorsey Pender and a Henrietta Green to keep the gossip going. They're good people, but they're gossips."

"Just be careful, Lanie," Cass said. She embraced Lanie and kissed her on the cheek. "I pray for you and your family, and especially your daddy, every day."

Lanie was touched. This girl had come into her life from nowhere with nothing, and God had touched her and given all she longed for. It made Lanie happy that some stories did have good endings. "I'll stop on my way back."

"All right. Be careful, Lanie."

Lanie pedaled quickly down the highway. The trees were not yet starting to turn, but they would be soon. The woods were full of maple trees and they turned the autumn into a flaming rainbow of colors—scarlet, yellow, and gold—all mixed in with the evergreens.

Lanie could not help but think about the talk about her and Brent. When she pulled up to his cabin, she almost changed her mind, but she wanted him to see her new work. Leaning the bicycle against the front of the cabin, she knocked on the door. It opened at once, and

Brent stood before her, smiling. "Well, come in. I was about to cut my throat because I'm so lonesome." He had left Fairhope to take an editor's job, but had returned after a few weeks to begin his writing again.

Lanie went inside and glanced around. She had found this house for Brent who had come from the north to find solitude and do some writing himself. She had helped him furnish it, and it was a cozy looking, though small, cabin. A fire burned over in the fireplace, its yellow flames leaping upward, and the wood crackling making a counterpoint to the ticking of a clock on the wall.

"This is such a nice place, Brent."

"Well, it ought to be. My best girl found it for me and helped me decorate it. I'm glad to see you. Come on. I've got coffee made and cake."

"Did you make it yourself?"

Brent laughed. "Not likely." He was medium height with chestnut hair and gray eyes, and he was twenty-eight years old and had gone to college. Lanie had never known a writer before, and Brent had shown her how to submit her poems for publication. He had also encouraged her to submit her work to a national contest, which she had won.

"No, I didn't make this cake. I bought it from Mrs. Swinder. I buy lots of meals from her. She's having a hard time with four children and her husband off somewhere looking for work."

"I'm glad you're helping them, Brent."

They sat down, and she ate the cake and drank the coffee while he looked over the last poem, the one about Zacchaeus.

"This is really fine. You know, when we get enough of these we'll put them all together in book form, and I'll start looking for a publisher."

The two sat there talking, and finally he said, "Come on, let's sit in front of the fire. It's not all that cold, but I love to sit in front of a fire, listening to the crackle and snap, watch the flames."

They sat on the couch, and for a time he talked about writing. He was the only one who could talk with her about such things, and she treasured the moment. Finally, she said, "Brent, I've got something new."

"More poetry?"

"No. This is different." She hesitated and shook her head. "I almost didn't bring it, but I wish you'd look at it."

"What is it? A short story?"

"I don't know what it is. I've kept a journal since I was ten, writing about everything I did and thought, but I never let anyone read it."

"By George, I wish I'd done that."

"I thought about writing a novel, but then I think I'm crazy. I can't do that."

"Why can't you?"

"Well, it just seems like such a big thing to do. I did write the first chapter. It's about when my mama died and how it just about destroyed all of us."

"Let me take a look."

Lanie reluctantly passed a sheaf of papers to him then sat quietly as he read. He did not speak, nor did he comment, until finally he looked up and shook his head. "Lanie, you don't have any idea how good this is."

"Oh, not really, Brent."

"Yes, really. I served as an editor for a publisher, and one of my jobs was reading new manuscripts that came in over the transom."

"Over the transom? What does that mean?"

"Writers just send manuscripts directly to the publisher. They don't have agents. Most of them are terrible, but this has real potential. It needs work, of course, but it's alive. Is this all you've written on it?"

"Yes, I feel so silly trying to think about writing a novel. I like to read them, but writing is different."

"Well, let me tell you about the publishing world." The two sat on the couch, enjoying the warmth from the fire, and after a few minutes he put his arm around her shoulders, laughed, and hugged her.

Lanie did not know what to make of this, but it bothered her somehow. He was an affectionate man, she knew that, but she did not want the gossip to become truth.

"I asked a publisher once, how do you know what to publish and what will sell? You know what he said?"

"What?"

"He said, 'Brent, if you want a sure thing, go to the racetrack and bet on horses. You'll have a lot better chance of picking a winner than you will publishing a book.' Wasn't that encouraging?"

"Did he really say that?"

"He really did, and it is a hard world." They sat there for nearly an hour, Brent speaking easily. From time to time, they got up and got another cup of coffee but always came back to the couch. Finally, Brent fell silent and said, "I'm boring you with all of this."

"No—no, you're not, Brent. I love to hear you talk about writing."

Brent was quiet, and suddenly he reached over and pulled her close. He kissed her, and for that one moment, Lanie could not tell whether she was frightened, excited, or pleased. It was a mixture of all. She stood up quickly and said, "Brent, I probably need to stop coming to your house alone. There's been talk."

"We've done nothing wrong."

"I know, but—" Lanie couldn't put into words the discomfort she felt but also the strange pleasure his kiss gave her. She admired him so much, and she felt completely different from when Roger had kissed her or even Doctor Owen Merritt. She said, "I'm afraid I'll have to stop coming here."

"Well, if it troubles you, you can bring somebody with you. Or we can meet at the library. They've got a little room there. You've got a great talent, Lanie. You just can't waste it."

"I'll think about it, Brent." She hesitated then put her hand on his chest. "You've done so much for me. I don't want anything to spoil it."

"Bring me some more of your novel when you get it done—or let me know and we'll meet at the library."

"All right."

Lanie left the room, got on her bicycle. She started down the road and encountered Dorsey Pender. He was driving his old Ford pickup, and he stopped and leaned out. "Hi, Lanie, you been visiting?"

It was an innocent enough question, but Lanie knew that she might as well have put the record of her visit in the front page of the newspaper. She said simply, "Yes, I have," and then pedaled away. The sun seemed to be less bright, and some of the pleasure had gone out of the day.

Why can't people just let other people alone? She did not speak the words, but a sadness came to her as she realized that with that kiss her relationship with Brent had become imperiled and that she had lost something important. She pedaled faster as if getting away from his house would put him out of her life.

⊸ CHAPTER 5 ⊷

Lanie took the dress that she had just washed and held it to the wringer. As the garment passed through, she was thinking, *How wonderful it is to have an invention like this! It's so much better than wringing it out by hand. Someday they'll invent a machine that will dry clothes just like they invented one to wash them.*

Corliss suddenly appeared beside her on the back porch. "Lanie, come and read my book to me."

Looking down, Lanie saw that Corliss had brought the *Wizard of Oz* and was holding it to her chest. Her blue eyes were bright and alert.

"I can't right now, Corliss. I have to finish washing the clothes."

"Can I help you?"

"Of course you can. Here. When the clothes come out over here you put them in this basket, then we'll take them outside and hang them on the line. The sunshine is out today, and it'll dry them, and they'll smell good."

Corliss suddenly turned and said, "Somebody's at the door."

"How can you tell?"

"Don't you hear Beau barking? He always barks when somebody's at the door."

"Well, let's go see who it is. Maybe it's the straw man looking for a brain."

"No, it couldn't be him. That book is just imaginary."

"Yes, it is, but it's fun. Come along."

The two of them moved off the back porch and made their way down the hallway. Opening the door, they found Roger standing there with a large bunch of flowers in his hand. "Hi, Lanie. Hello, Corliss."

"Hello, Roger. Did you bring those flowers to me?" Corliss smiled.

"I sure did, half of them anyway, and half for your lovely big sister."

"Oh, Roger, I'm such a mess. Every time you come I'm wearing my work clothes."

"Well, I think you look good." She held the door open, and he came inside and divided the flowers up. "Half for you, Corliss. Half for you, Lanie. I tried to write a poem, but it all ended with words like moon-June-spoon."

"It sounds wonderful. Where is it?"

"I couldn't stand it. I threw it away."

"Well, the flowers are lovely. They smell so good. Do you want some gingerbread? I just made a pan."

"I feel strongly led by divine providence to become a glutton."

"Does that mean you're going to eat the gingerbread, Roger?" Corliss demanded.

"It certainly does. Come along. You can listen to me eat."

The three of them went into the kitchen, and Roger sat down. Lanie went to the oven, took out the pan of gingerbread, and cut out a very small piece no more than an inch square. She put it on a plate and her eyes danced with mischief. "There, you think that will be enough?"

Roger stared at the small morsel of gingerbread. "Why, shucks, Lanie, I spill more than that. Here, you eat this, Beau."

Beau, who had followed them in, caught the morsel that Roger tossed to him, and Lanie laughed. "I guess you'll need a bigger piece at that." She cut a large slice, put it on another plate, and cut smaller portions for herself and Corliss.

Corliss pulled at Roger. "Hold me in your lap. You can read my book while we eat."

Roger laughed, reached down, pulled her up, and put her on his lap. He kept his arm around her and with his free hand began to attack the gingerbread.

"I can read some myself." She began to read, picking out the words, and Roger stared at Lanie. "How old is she? Four?"

"That's right."

"I don't think I could read until I was ten."

"Oh, of course you could, but she just picked it up. I don't know how. I put my finger on a word as I read, and somehow she was able to read them. You're a bright girl, aren't you, Corliss?"

"Yes, I am." Corliss crammed a bunch of gingerbread into her mouth and mumbled as she read another sentence. "This book isn't true, Roger."

"It's not?"

"No, it's a made-up story. It's all about Dorothy who doesn't like where she lives, and a tornado picks her up and puts her down in the Land of Oz, and she finds out that there's no place like home. That's what the story's all about, you see."

"You mean about there's no place like home?"

"That's right," Corliss nodded solemnly. "She meets the cowardly lion and the straw man and the tin man, and they all need something. And when they get to the Wizard of Oz, he gives them what they needed. He gave the tin man a medal, and he gave the straw man a heart, and he gave the cowardly lion courage, but he couldn't get Dorothy home for a while. But he finally did so it all ended when she got back home. That's what the story's all about, you see."

"Well, that is a wonderful story."

Roger sat there holding Corliss as she continued to read, and finally Lanie said, "You go outside and play. Find a doodlebug and bring it to me."

"All right, Lanie." She went off, holding the book, and Roger shook his head.

"She is one smart kid."

"We're very proud of her. She's musical, too. She can already pick out tunes on the piano."

"Maybe I better have another piece of gingerbread just to keep my strength up."

"You are a glutton." She gave him a piece of gingerbread, another glass of milk, and he plunged in at once but with his mouth full said, "I heard about Cody's invention. It's a wonder he didn't kill somebody."

"He did kill my best hen Priscilla. That hammer went up in the air, came right down, and killed her. I cried about it. She was such a faithful chicken. Laying an egg every day just like the sun coming up."

"Well, at least he didn't kill himself or brain the preacher. I heard it was pretty close."

Roger was one of the handsomest young men she had ever seen. When he was a high school senior she was a mere freshman, and she had beaten him out for the prize student of the year. Roger's whole family had hated her for that, but Roger had only laughed. He had been the most popular boy in school with all the girls falling madly in love with him, but he had never noticed Lanie—until she reached the age of seventeen. Then it was as if his eyes suddenly opened. He started talking to her and finally asked her out. Since then he had dated her regularly.

"Why are you looking at me like that, Lanie?"

"Just thinking of all the good times we've had."

"We have, haven't we?"

Lanie shook her head and said, "I don't know what we're going to do with Cody."

"What's he done now? Oh, you mean handing out his *Turn or Burn!* tracts. Boy, they are scorchers! Did you ever read it?"

"Oh yes, it's full of fire and brimstone. He's decided to scare everybody into getting saved, and he's handing out pages in the Bible. Doesn't make any difference what page it is. He thinks it's all good."

"I know. He gave my mother a page from the book of Ecclesiastes. She didn't know whether to hit him with her umbrella or laugh.

I think she finally decided he was incorrigible, so she just laughed at him."

As if on key, they heard a door slam and Cody came in, heading straight for the gingerbread. "Did you save me any of that or did you let this hog have it all?"

"The hog has saved you a few morsels," Roger said. "Sit down and eat. Tell me about your invention."

Cody stared at Roger. "It would have worked, but something went wrong."

"It killed Priscilla. That's what went wrong," Lanie said severely.

"Well, it didn't kill me or the pastor or any of the kids so stop griping about it." He turned and said, "Roger, are you sure you're saved?"

"Cody, don't start," Lanie, cried her eyes flashing. "You know Roger's a Christian."

"Well, I thought maybe he had backslid. He works with a bunch of heathens."

"They're not all heathens," Roger protested. "Ed Chandler's my boss. He's a deacon at Shiloh Baptist Church, a fine Christian man."

"Well, I'm going to come over and give tracts to all of the fellows you work with. Warn them I'm coming, will you?"

"Go away, Cody. Work on another invention that'll maim somebody."

Cody grabbed another piece of the gingerbread and walked off with a grin. "I'll see you tomorrow, Roger. I'll bring plenty of tracts, and we'll get them fellers saved."

"I'm sorry about that," Lanie said. "He's just lively. He'll be all right."

"He's lively all right. Too lively at times. What do you hear from Maeva?"

"I got a letter from her yesterday. She's still singing in those awful saloons, or whatever they are."

"You worried about her?"

"Of course I am. She doesn't have any business being in places like that."

"Well, Logan's there. He'll take care of her."

"Well, I hope so."

"How about we go to a movie tomorrow? There's a new one called *Dracula*. It's about a vampire, a man that goes around sucking young girls' blood."

"I'm not going to see an awful thing like that!"

"Well, you can take me." Kezia hobbled in, her eyes snapping. "Sounds like a movie I really would enjoy."

"All right, Aunt Kezia. You put on your best dress, and I'll put on my graduation suit. We'll be the best-looking couple there. What time could you two be ready?"

"I can't go," Lanie said quickly. "Davis and I are going to visit Daddy."

"So, how are you going to get there?"

"Owen is taking us." Lanie saw Roger's face change expression, and she said quickly, "He wants to examine Daddy to see if he's completely healthy."

"Well, I know you need to do that."

"We can go the next day if you can wait, Roger."

"That'll be good," Roger brightened up. "You be ready, Aunt Kezia."

Roger left and as soon as he was gone, Kezia said, "That young man's jealous of Merritt."

"Oh, I don't think so."

"Have you gone deaf and blind at your age? I tell you he's miserable. But it's good for young fellows to be miserable. Does them good to suffer. When you get to that prison you tell your daddy I'm praying for a miracle to get him out of that place."

"I will, Aunt Kezia. We're all praying for that."

◐══◇═◦

The weather had been cool, and Owen had driven with the windows down. Davis had gone to sleep in the backseat, after coon hunting with his friends all night. Lanie glanced back and said, "Davis is worn out, but they got two coons. Now I've got to cook the dratted things."

"I don't think I could eat a coon. They're too cute."

"I don't think I could either, but Davis says he likes it and so does Aunt Kezia." She turned and said, "How do you think Aunt Kezia's doing? She just never seems to get completely well."

"Well, she's ninety-two years old, Lanie. God has given her a long life, but you know she's nearer the end than the beginning."

Lanie looked out the window and was quiet for a while. When she looked back at Owen, he saw that her eyes were glimmering with tears. "I don't think I can bear the thought of losing her."

Owen shook his head. "She won't be lost. If you know where something is, it isn't lost."

Lanie was surprised, for Owen sometimes came up with statements like this. "That's right, isn't it?"

"Oh yes. The doctor's always right. I'm hoping we keep her for several years yet. How's your writing going?"

"Well, the poems are going fine, but I'm trying something new."

"What's that?"

"I'm going to try to write a novel."

"Is it going to be a romantic novel with lots of steamy love scenes?"

Lanie laughed. "Of course not, silly. It's going to be a novel about my family."

"Well, you've got enough material there. Your family's had lots of ups and downs. I think they call that conflict, don't they, in literature?"

"Yes, Brent says it's good. He thinks I can do it."

Owen frowned and shook his head. "I'm worried about all this talk about you and that writer."

"You know his name. Why don't you say it?"

Owen glanced at her. Her temper was up. He saw that at once and said, "I didn't mean anything by it, Lanie."

"Yes, you did. You're as bad as Cody! He's always judging people, and you're doing the same thing with me."

Lanie waited for Owen to respond, but he didn't say a word. She knew she had hurt his feelings, and when he pulled up in front of the prison she started to apologize, but Davis awoke and rubbed his eyes. "Are we here?" he demanded.

"Yes, we're here. Come along. We'll go find your dad."

"Your girl's here, Forrest, and that doctor. And your son too. That girl of yours has sure grown up." Warden Gladden had come to where Forrest was feeding the bloodhounds. They had a bad reputation for tearing prisoners to pieces, but actually, they were very gentle dogs.

"Yes, Lanie's growing up. So is Davis. They all are."

"Well, she was just a scrawny little fourteen-year-old when she first came here, but she sure is a fine young woman now. How's your other daughter, Maeva?"

"She's still in California looking for Thelma Mays."

"You think she could clear you, Forrest?"

"She was there that night, though I didn't know it. She saw the whole thing. The other two witnesses lied. Maeva's gone out to find her. She's stubborn enough to stay until she does."

"Well, you let that doctor look you over and make sure you invite them all to eat lunch."

Owen had listened to Forrest's chest, taken his pulse, and now he stepped back and nodded, "You seem fine to me. You're the old Forrest Freeman."

"Well, Doc, I feel real good."

"You should, Daddy," Davis said. "God did a miracle for you. Made that old tumor just disappear."

Forrest grinned at Davis. "The doctors never have believed that. They think something was wrong with the X-ray machine. They claim I never had the tumor to begin with."

"That's pretty stupid," Owen said. "I've got the original X-ray that shows that tumor as big as Mount Hood, but it's gone in the later ones. I'm going to visit some of the inmates." Without another word, he turned and walked away.

Forrest was surprised. He watched Owen leave and then turned and said, "What's wrong with Owen?"

"Well, I was sharp with him. I shouldn't have been but I was."

"Why'd you do that?"

"Oh, I just lost my temper."

"I wish you wouldn't do that, Muff." He used his old nickname for her. "Don't put him down ever. He's done so much for all of us."

"He sure has. Well, look. We've brought you some pictures. I know how you like them, Daddy."

For the next ten minutes, Forrest looked at the pictures including those of Booger, who had been his favorite bloodhound at the prison, Beau, and Cap'n Brown.

"I wanted to bring you a picture of Priscilla, but, of course, I can't."

"What happened to Priscilla?"

"Cody killed her," Davis said. "In one of his fool inventions." He went on to tell the story, and when he was through Forrest couldn't help grinning. "Well, that's Cody. He hasn't changed a bit."

"Aunt Kezia has been ailing, but Owen says she's going to be all right for a while."

Davis said, "Here. We brought you a bunch of goodies. Lanie cooked all day yesterday."

"Well, look at these!" Forrest exclaimed with delight. "Oatmeal cookies, fried apple pies, brownies, and fudge. Why, I can't eat all this."

"I thought you could share it with some of your friends here."

"I sure can, but I'm going to try some of this right now."

Davis watched his father eat, and finally he blurted out, "A scout for the Cardinals wants me to sign a contract to play baseball. Do you think I ought to do it, Daddy?"

Forrest stopped chewing and studied the tall, young man in front of him. He had changed a lot since Forrest had been in prison. He was seventeen now, and his lanky form had filled out. Forrest studied him for a while and said, "I had a chance to play pro ball when I was about your age or a little older maybe, but I didn't do it."

"Why not, Daddy?"

"Because I didn't want to leave you and the family." Forrest chewed slowly on an oatmeal cookie. "Minor league baseball can be a real hard life. You travel on buses and eat bad food in cheap restaurants, sleep in terrible places that sometimes have buggy beds. A few make it to the show, but most of them don't."

"The show? What's that?"

"The big league. Most minor league players spend a large part of their lives under miserable conditions with almost no money, and then they have to go find another job. They've missed out on college and getting training at other work so it's real hard."

"You don't think I should do it?"

"I'm telling you the bad part. It's a hard life, Davis. You might have the talent to make it, but everybody you see in the minor league was a star at their high school. If you have to do it, you know I'd support you. But I'd rather you didn't."

"I'll think about it, Daddy, and you pray that I do the right thing."

"I'll do that. You can be sure. Now, let me have one of those fried pies ..."

❦

As soon as they pulled up in front of the house, Davis yawned and got out of the car. "I'm going in. Good night."

"Good night, Davis," Owen said. He sat there and waited for Lanie to get out, but she turned to face him. She had been thinking all the way home how to apologize and tell him how sorry she was for losing her temper. Finally, she knew there was no other way to do it except to come right out with it. "Owen, I'm so sorry I snapped at you."

"It's all right."

"No, it's not all right." She reached out, took his hand, and held it with both of hers. It was a strong hand and a skillful one, and she stroked it while she tried to put the right words together. "You've done more for our family than anybody. We were just about falling to pieces when you came to town. And you doctored us and looked out for us, and you took us to see Daddy. We all think of you as a member of the family. The boys love you and respect you, and of course, Corliss hangs onto you like a leech." She suddenly put his hand against her cheek and held it there. "I'm so sorry I snapped at you. You're my best friend." She suddenly leaned forward, kissed him on the cheek, and then quickly stepped out of the car. "Good night, Owen." She ran into the house, and Owen sat there stunned.

As soon as she went upstairs, she found Kezia waiting for her. "I was watching you out my window. That wasn't much of a kiss."

"I was mean to him, Aunt Kezia."

"Well, sometimes women don't have much sense."

"I never thought I'd fall for a doctor, but I guess I've fallen for Merritt."

Kezia grinned. "Now, you sit down and tell me all about Forrest ..."

·⇒ CHAPTER 6 ⇐·

Thursday was the day that Lanie took the Freeman's Rolling Emporium on the route over to Pineview. She had been doing this now for what seemed like a long time, and she had learned the regular houses where she would stop. The sales were never large, but put together they did help to pay the bills.

As she drove along, she saw that the September weather was turning crisp, and one day the frost would come, and the leaves would change almost magically. Already the younger ones, because of the dry year, were putting out gold and scarlet leaves. As she drove along, she thought of the visit she had made the previous day with Owen and Davis to visit her daddy. She still felt guilty over snapping at Owen.

When she had kissed him on the cheek, he had sat there perfectly still. *I thought maybe he would put his arms around me like he did once before, but he didn't. I guess I hurt him worse than I knew.*

A strange feeling sliced through her, and she knew that it had to do with her feelings for Owen. He was older than she was, thirty to her eighteen, but such age differences didn't seem to matter in the mountains. It was not unusual for a much older man to marry a very young girl. Lanie was a girl with great vitality and imagination, but the hardness of her life had caused her to hold these things under careful restraint. She sometimes wished she could be more outgoing like Maeva, but that was not the kind of young woman she had become.

As she thought of Owen, her lips made a small change at the corners and her heart danced like a young girl's as she drove along. The cool breeze touched her face, rouging her cheeks and putting a sparkle in her eyes. She had a beautifully fashioned face, all of its features generous and capable of showing emotion.

She swerved to avoid a large pothole and managed to put the thought of Owen out of her mind, at least temporarily, when she saw Mrs. Ellen Taylor waiting for her. Mrs. Taylor always bought a few things but wanted company more than anything else. Lanie stopped the Emporium and got out. "Hello, Ellen."

"I'm glad to see you. I thought maybe you wouldn't come today."

"I'm a little bit late."

"Do you have time for a cup of tea?"

"Of course I do."

She followed Ellen into the house and sat there smiling and carrying on the conversation, passing the talk of what was happening through the county. Ellen followed her out and bought a few things, and when Lanie drove away, she saw in the rearview mirror the woman staring after her. *She's so lonely. I know she misses Thad.* Ellen had lost her husband two years ago, and the loss was still a keen, biting memory for her.

Suddenly Lanie put the brakes on the Emporium and brought it to a stop. She saw a man sitting with his back against a large walnut tree. He had made a small fire and was adding sticks to it. She didn't know why she stopped. Ordinarily she would not, but somehow the man drew her attention as he sat there huddled up, an ill-fitting ragged coat and a hat pulled down over his face.

She stepped down from the Emporium and went over to him. "Good afternoon."

"Hello, miss." The man stood up at once. He was thin with intelligent features. When he pulled his hat off she could see a thatch of salt and pepper hair. He was in his late forties, she guessed, and had the haunted look of so many men and women on the road. She had seen that look on a lot of faces since the Depression had displaced so many people.

"I've got some extra food here. Maybe we could have a picnic."

"Why, that would be prime, miss. My name's Dan Reilly."

"I'm Lanie Freeman. How about some hot dogs?"

"Sounds wonderful."

Lanie entered into the Rolling Emporium, got six weenies, buns, mustard, and relish. She came out and said, "We can use your fire. I like mine done pretty well."

"So do I. We'll have to cut some sticks. I'll do that." Reilly went to an oak tree, cut two of the lower branches and sharpened them. He threaded one of the weenies on for himself and another for her then he put some more twigs on the fire. "I'm surprised you stopped, Miss Freeman. It's a little bit dangerous, isn't it?"

"Oh, I trust the Lord to keep me safe. Where are you from, Mr. Reilly?"

"Just call me Dan. I'm from Cleveland."

"You live there long?" The two sat there, and the weenies began to swell and blacken in the flame.

Reilly said, as he critically turned the weenie over, "I worked in a factory there for twenty years, but it failed last year."

"Where are you headed for?"

"On my way to Florida. I have a brother there who says he can help me."

"Do you have a family?"

"A wife and a baby girl two years old. They're staying with her people—but they're not able to keep them long. I'm hoping I get work soon."

When the weenies were done, they both pulled them off. She split the buns and put them inside. "I like lots of mustard on mine, and this relish I made myself. It goes good with hot dogs."

Reilly fixed his hot dog and despite his obvious hunger, he was a dainty eater. "Nothing better than a good hot dog out like this. My wife and I used to go out camping. We always took some weenies along and made hot dogs."

The two sat there talking, and something was working inside of Lanie. She was thinking about how Cody had made up his mind to witness to everybody he met. Somehow, she knew this would not work, but something had made her stop for Dan Reilly, and she prayed a silent prayer. *Lord, if you want me to share the Gospel with this man, I'll do it.* She heard no voice, but somehow she knew that was why she stopped. She was in no hurry and let him talk about his family, and she told him a few facts about hers. She ate two of the hot dogs and gave him the extra ones. He took a handkerchief out and wiped the mustard off his mouth and said, "That was so good, miss. I appreciate it so much."

"Would you mind if I tell you something about myself?"

"Why, not a bit, Miss Freeman."

Lanie began to tell a little of her history, how her mother had died, and she'd had to take over as a surrogate mother. Then her father had gone to prison on a false charge, and she had been mother to her other brothers and sisters.

"That must have been real hard."

"It would have been impossible, but God always made a way. We nearly lost our place, but He did a miracle and showed us a way to pay off the loan." She hesitated and then said, "I was saved when I was very young."

"Is that right, miss? I don't know much about that. We've never been churchgoing folk."

"Well, it was a very simple thing. I heard a sermon about how Jesus died for sinners, and the evangelist said we were all sinners. I left the meeting, and the next day I went out in the woods. I hadn't slept much, and I was worried about myself. So, I began to pray, and something happened to me. I began to cry, and I didn't know why. But I was scared, and I felt I had to have God. So, right there in the middle of the woods, I just called on God."

"What did you say?" Reilly said, his eyes intent.

"I just told Him that I was a sinner, and that I had done wrong things and asked Him to forgive me."

"Was that all?"

"No. I knew Jesus was the answer, and so I asked God to forgive me in the name of Jesus, and then I asked Jesus to come into my heart." Her eyes filled with tears, and she wiped them away quickly with the back of her hand. "And He did, Dan, and He's been there ever since."

Dan Reilly was staring at her. His mouth began working, and he whispered, "That's a wonderful story. That's so beautiful."

"Well, I think God wants to do that to everybody." She took a deep breath and then said, "He'd come into your life if you'd ask Him."

Dan Reilly stared at her in disbelief. "I haven't been a good man."

"Jesus died for sinners. That's all of us. Let me show you something." She ran back to the wagon and brought her Bible out. It was an old one that she had marked in, and she turned to the tenth chapter of Romans. "You see, I've got this underlined. See what it says? 'If thou shalt confess with thy mouth the Lord Jesus, and shalt believe in thine heart that God hath raised him up from the dead, thou shalt be saved.'"

Reilly took the Bible, and his lips moved as he read the verse silently. "It sounds too easy."

"I think it has to be easy or none of us would ever find God. But look over here in Acts. There's a story of a man called Paul and his friend Silas." She repeated the story of Paul and Silas who were cast into prison. "There was an earthquake," she said, "and the keeper was going to kill himself because in those days if a prisoner escaped, the jailer paid with his life. But look what it says here. Paul cried out, 'Do thyself no harm ...' And the jailer came then and said, 'Sirs, what must I do to be saved?' Then look what Paul said."

Reilly took the Bible and read the words where she placed her finger. "Believe on the Lord Jesus Christ and thou shalt be saved, and thy house." He was absolutely still, but when he turned his face toward her, she saw tears in his eyes. "Do you think that would work for me and for my wife and baby?"

"Yes."

"I don't know how to do that."

"Let's just pray. You let me pray out loud, and you just tell God you're a sinner and that you want Jesus to save you and come into your life to take care of your wife and your little girl, and He'll do it. I know He will. Will you do that, Dan?"

He hesitated and then swallowed hard. "Yes," he whispered.

She bowed her head and prayed a simple prayer, but it was a prayer full of compassion. God had given her a great love for this man that she had never seen and probably would never see again this side of heaven, but she prayed fervently that God would take care of his wife and baby and would provide work, and most of all, that he would be saved. When she said amen, she looked up and saw tears running down Dan Reilly's face. "Did you ask God to come into your heart, Dan?"

Reilly nodded. He could hardly speak. "I did."

"Then you're a Christian now. Here, I want you to have this."

Reilly looked at the Bible and flipped the pages. "But this is your Bible. You've got it all marked up."

"I have another one at home. I want you to have this one, and I want us to write on the front page how you called on the name of the Lord. We'll put the date in here and my name and address, and you can write me. When you get a place I'll answer you, and I want you to know, Dan, that I'll have our church praying for you and for your family every day."

Dan Reilly took the Bible and ran his hands gently over the surface. He was silent for a time, and he looked up and said, "Why did you stop and talk to me? Do you talk to everybody like this?"

"No. God just put you on my heart."

"I can't thank you enough."

"Now you wait right here. I've got one more thing for you." Lanie turned and went back to the Rolling Emporium. She had a cotton sack there, and she filled it up with groceries, came out, and held it out to him. "This ought to get you to Florida."

He took the sack and said huskily, "I'll never forget you, Miss Freeman, not ever."

The two wrote in the Bible the date and what had happened. When they had finished, she put out her hand, and he took it. He could barely speak, but he said, "I guess this means I'm going to heaven now."

"Yes, it does."

"Well, if I don't see you on this earth, I'll see you there."

"That you will, but you're going to see God do miracles. You just drop me a postcard and let me know when you get your wife and baby there in Florida on your new job."

Lanie left and shut the car door, but she could see that Dan Reilly was watching her. He was holding the Bible in both hands, but when she waved he quickly held the Bible up and a beautiful smile touched his lips. He said, "God bless you, Miss Freeman," and she smiled, then drove away. A great feeling of joy came to her, and she knew she had done God's will and not hers.

⌐═◄►

Roger refused to take Lanie to see the movie called *Dracula*. They went instead to the next town where a Marx Brothers film was on. They laughed until they were practically helpless, and when they came out Lanie said, "I wish Aunt Kezia could have come. She just wasn't up to it tonight."

"She would have enjoyed *Dracula* better."

They got into Roger's car and headed back for town. When they were almost there, he pulled over by the Singing River, and she looked at him with apprehension. This is where courting couples came to do things that weren't always right. But Roger just sat there and looked out over the river. "Beautiful, isn't it?" The moonlight touched the river, and as usual, the river sang with its sibilant cry over the stones. Roger turned and said, "I want to tell you about what I want to do with my life."

"What, Roger? What is it?"

"I want to become an engineer. I want to build things — bridges, buildings, and roads. I've always wanted to do that. That's been my dream."

"We all should have a dream."

"Well, a dream doesn't mean much if you don't have someone to share it with." He reached out, took her hand gently and said, "I want to share it with you."

Lanie squeezed his hand and said, "I'll always share that dream with you."

"What about us? You know I want to marry you."

"I can't even talk about that until Daddy's out of jail."

"You're a loyal girl, Lanie, and I honor you for it." He started the car, and they moved along the river road, and Lanie thought, *So many young women would give anything to have a young man as good as this, but I can't even think about that now.*

September was winding down, and Maeva was exhausted. She had worked a long shift as a waitress and then gone to the Grotto, a combination beer hall and dance hall. When she went inside, she was struck by the raucous noise and the ever-present smell of sweat and booze and cigarette smoke. She had gotten sick of the life and looked over to where Logan was playing. He too had a day job, but they had to take everything they could get for the two rooms and meals.

"You're Maeva Freeman?"

Maeva looked up and saw a heavyset man with swarthy features. "I'm Pete Causin. You ever hear of me?"

"I don't think so."

"I handle singers and bands and make dates for them. I've been hearing you sing here at night. I want to make you an offer."

Maeva stared at the man. "What kind of an offer, Mr. Causin?"

"Well, you'd be starting at the bottom, pretty well, but I can get you something better than this place. I think I can get you on with some of the Grand Ole Opry stars from their own tour. You've got a great voice, and you look good."

"I don't know. I don't want to leave Bakersfield."

"It's a dead-end town, kid. You're not going anywhere here."

Maeva knew this was right, and he said quickly, "Come on. We'll sit down and talk about money."

⚬⚬⚬

Logan stared at Maeva. "You're going to leave with Pete Causin?"

"He's made me a good offer, Logan."

"You know what he is? He's a womanizer."

"No, I didn't know that."

"Everybody in the business knows it."

"Look, Logan, we're not getting anywhere here." She told him about the offer and said, "If I can do that for a month, we'll have enough money where we won't have to have two jobs."

The argument went on for some time and became rather sharp, but Logan did his best to talk Maeva out of it. But in the end she said, "I've got to do this thing, Logan. We're wearing ourselves down with this life."

"I think you'll regret it," Logan said heavily.

"It won't be the first thing I've regretted."

"When will you be leaving?"

"Tomorrow."

Logan shook his head but said no more. "Well, you know how to get in touch with me if you need me."

⚬⚬⚬

By the end of the first week in her new job, Maeva was convinced that she had made a bad decision. She was on her guard against Pete Causin from the first, but was confident she could handle him.

Olene, the drummer's wife, tried to warn her. She drew Maeva aside just before a performance and said, "You better watch out for Pete."

"I can take care of myself, Olene. I've had men after me since I was fourteen."

"Yeah, but not many guys are a bad as Pete." Olene was a short blonde-haired woman with hard green eyes. "Don't let yourself get alone with him. Keep your door locked. And you'd better get a black-jack or a knife."

"Oh, he can't be that tough."

She kept on her guard, but fending off Pete became more difficult than the travel or the performances. Every time he came close, he tried to put his hands on her, ignoring her protests.

More than once Maeva decided to leave, but she needed the money. *If I can get enough saved, I'll quit and go back to Logan.*

She kept Olene's warning in mind and kept her door locked. Almost every night Pete came tapping at the door, whispering to her, but she ignored him.

On Friday of her second week, the performance went on until long past midnight. Maeva was so exhausted that when she finally got to her room she forgot to lock the door. She undressed, put on her gown, and went to bed. She fell asleep almost instantly.

The touch of hands on her body woke Maeva, and when she cried out, a hand on her lips cut the cry short.

"Now I got you, girl!"

The hand that covered her mouth kept her from screaming, but as Maeva felt Pete's free hand tearing at her gown, she clawed at him. She felt her long nails dig into Pete's face. He shouted a curse and turned her loose.

Maeva was a strong woman, and she used all her strength to pull herself free and roll off the bed. She knew Pete would come at her, so she seized the heavy brass lamp on the table beside her bed. She lifted it high then brought it down with all her force on the man's head. The blow flattened Pate, but she hit him again and again, all the while calling for help.

The door opened, and Bert, the drummer, and his wife Olene came in along with Jimmy Dortch, the bass player. Bert flicked the switch, took one look at Pete's bloody head, and then grinned at Maeva. "Well, girl, I see you done the necessary."

"Good for you, Maeva!" Olene nodded with satisfaction. "I've wanted to see some woman put this scum out for a long time."

"Get him out of here, will you?" Maeva said. "I'm leaving."

"Don't blame you," Jimmy said, grinning. He went over to Pete, pulled his billfold free, and opening it, gave Maeva the bills inside. "Here's your severance pay."

"You won't get into trouble, will you?" Maeva asked.

"Naw, ol' Pete's gonna be plumb quiet about this little play party."

"I can take you to the bus station," Bert said, staring down with pleasure at his employer. "Looks like he's gonna need some stitches. His nose is broken."

"I hope it heals crooked." Maeva gathered her thoughts for a moment and then said, "I need to use a phone. I have someone who can come get me."

"Hope he's better than Pete," Jimmy said.

"He is!" Maeva smiled. "He's a lot better."

Logan was playing the cheap guitar he had bought after selling his to get the car, and the manager came up and said, "Phone call for you, Logan."

"For me?"

"Yeah. Take it over there."

"Thanks." Logan walked over and picked up the phone. "Hello."

"This is Maeva."

Instantly, Logan heard something in her voice. "What is it? You don't sound right."

A silence was punctuated by a sigh, and then Maeva said, "You were right. Can you come and get me? I'm in a little town called Fairbanks. I'll be at the bus station. I don't have the money to get home."

Logan said, "Stay right there."

He hung up the phone, walked in, and said to Larry Prescott, "I've got to leave, Larry. It's Maeva. She's in some kind of trouble."

"I hope it works out for you. Here, I'll pay you for the night."

He took the money, went out and got into the car, filled it with gas, and at once headed toward Fairbanks. When he got to the bus station, he saw Maeva sitting on her suitcase out in front. He stopped the car, got out, and said, "Why didn't you wait inside?"

"I didn't want to."

"Are you okay?"

"Yes, I'm okay. I could kill that man—and I'm afraid I almost did!"

"He come on to you, did he?"

"Of course he did, just like you said he would. You were right, Logan—I should have listened to you."

"Well, I'm right about once every two weeks." He grinned, pulled her to her feet, and then picked up her suitcase. "Come on."

He put her into the car and stopped at a restaurant. She had not eaten, he discovered, in a couple of days, and he was hungry. They had hamburgers with French fries, and then he drove on into Bakersfield. He didn't turn toward the rooming house though, and she said, "Where are we going?"

"We're going to see Thelma."

"Thelma Mays?"

"The only Thelma I know. She called the day before yesterday. She's in the hospital, Maeva. That sorry buzzard beat her up and left town. Good thing. If I'd have found him, I would have parted his skull. I've been to see her twice, and she's right at the bottom. I think maybe she might be willing to go back with us."

Maeva stared at Logan and whispered, "If God would get my daddy out of jail, I'd do anything for Him."

"I don't think it works that way."

"What do you mean, Logan?"

"Well, I'm no expert, but I think the way it works is you have to give yourself to God first—and then after you do that God can do some things with you. I don't think He makes bargains though."

Maeva Freeman stared at this man, one of the few that she trusted. She turned and faced out the front windshield. "Maybe you're right, Logan. I sure enough need God."

"Well, that makes two of us. Come on. Let's see what we can do with Thelma Mays."

PART TWO

The Glory Road

⫸ CHAPTER 7 ⫷

B y the time Logan and Maeva had arrived at Bakersfield, the sun
was almost hidden beyond the western mountains. Logan pulled
the old Ford to a stop. It groaned and gasped and backfired, and for
a moment he sat there, then shook his head with something close to
despair. "This old buggy's not going to go on forever," he muttered.

Maeva had been looking at the square brick building which con-
sisted of three stories that covered a square block. The sign outside
read Mercy Hospital, and when she turned to face Logan, doubt dark-
ened her expression. "How is Thelma, Logan?"

"She's in pretty poor shape, Maeva. She's scared about as bad as
a woman can be."

"What's she afraid of?"

"Well, she's afraid that Loy will come back and beat her up
again—or even worse. She's got no friends and no family, nobody to
take care of her. I don't want you to show what you feel when you see
her, but she's in terrible shape."

"You think we can get her to go back and testify?"

"It's going to take a miracle. It's hard to even get her to talk."

Maeva turned her eyes back to the hospital. It was a utilitarian
building without grace or charm, and she watched the front door open
and a man in a white uniform pushed a wheelchair out. Maeva's gaze
took in the man who was sitting in it. His face was as pale as wallpa-
per paste, and he was emaciated, with no light of hope in his eyes.

"I hate hospitals!" she murmured.

"Might be good for a body to come and sit in one for an hour every day. It'd make his own problems look mighty small. I know what you mean, though. Every time I come here, I go away feeling terrible."

Maeva watched as the attendant loaded the patient into an old Oldsmobile. A small plainly dressed woman stood and watched, then nodded her thanks to the attendant. She got in and drove away, and Maeva took a deep breath. "I never felt so helpless in all my life."

"Well, we've got to have hope, Maeva. From what you tell me, all your family is praying for your daddy to get out of prison—and they've got the church there praying too."

"But I can't pray, Logan," Maeva said in a tense voice. "I wish I could."

"I guess you and me are alike. We've left God out of our lives. Now that we need Him, it's kind of hard to call on Him. Come on, let's go inside." Getting out of the car, the two went to the front door and stepped inside. It had all the smells of a hospital that Maeva had always hated. A woman to their right sat at a desk with a sign marked Information. She looked at them as if they had come in to steal something, but Logan whispered, "Come on. I know her room number. We don't need any information from her."

They took the elevator up to the second floor, and when they stepped off, Logan nodded. "It's down the hall here. Room 223."

They started down the hallway and then turned down a long corridor. They passed women in white uniforms who were pushing dollies filled with trays of food. "Supper time," Logan said. "Maybe we can get a free meal out of it."

Maeva didn't answer. She was feeling more depressed all the time. The experience with Pete Causin had shaken her. She was used to men making advances, but he had been crude beyond belief, and she had been fortunate to escape a real tragedy. They passed by a nursing station, and one of the nurses, a tall angular woman with stiff gray hair, said, "Hello, Logan. Come to see Thelma?"

"Sure have. How is she doing?"

"Well ..." The nurse shook her head, and her mouth turned downward in a frown. "Physically not too bad, I guess—but she's in poor shape emotionally."

"Can she talk?"

"Doesn't say a word unless you force her to. She's real fragile, but I expect she'll be released pretty soon. Nothing much we can do for emotional problems here."

Logan muttered his thanks and the two walked down the hall. He stopped beside a closed door marked 223 and tapped on it, but there was no response. He pushed it open and stepped aside to let Maeva enter. When Maeva entered the room, she saw that there were two patients there. A stiff fabric curtain could be drawn between the two beds, but it was now pushed open. Thelma Mays had the bed over by the window. The other bed was occupied by a young woman who stared at them curiously. She had black hair and a California tan. "Wake up, Thelma," she said. "You got company."

"How you doing today, Ann?"

"Doing fine, Logan. I'm going home tomorrow."

"That's good to hear. You have to be careful and not fall off any more horses."

"I didn't fall off," the young woman said indignantly. "He threw me off. He won't do it again."

As Logan spoke to the young woman, Maeva moved over to the bed. Thelma Mays was lying flat on her back. Her complexion was washed out, and her eyes were closed. When Maeva leaned over and called her name, the eyelids fluttered and then opened wide. Her bleached blonde hair was in disarray, and her light green eyes were full of fear. She had been a pretty girl once, but a hard life had left its marks on her. She suddenly cried out in a meaningless phrase and put her hands out in front of her in a defensive gesture, crying, "Don't hurt me!"

Logan left Ann at once and came over. "It's just us, Thelma. You remember me—Logan."

Thelma Mays looked around the room wildly, then fastened her eyes on Logan. She watched Logan but seemed to be agitated.

"Who are you?" she said, directing her gaze at Maeva.

"I'm Maeva Freeman."

Thelma closed her eyes and began to cry. Maeva looked quickly at Logan, and he shrugged.

"She does that all the time," the patient next to her said. "All she does is cry and carry on."

Maeva stood there uncertainly, waiting for Thelma to stop crying, but she didn't. Finally, the nurse they had seen at the station stepped inside. She had a needle in her hand and came to stand beside Thelma. "She's worse today, I think." She turned Thelma over and gave her a shot then shrugged. "That'll quiet her down, but you won't be able to talk to her. Come back early in the morning. She's usually a little better then."

"You say she's going to be released pretty soon?"

"We'll have to let her go. She doesn't have any money to pay the bill, and there's nothing much we can do for her physically."

"I wish I had the money to pay for her bill, but I don't."

"You're not her kinfolk, are you, Logan?"

"No, we come from the same town." He nodded and looked at Thelma who was now absolutely still. "We'll do the best we can for her, Nurse. Let's go, Maeva." They left the room, and as they walked down the hall, Maeva was silent. They passed by a chair-lined room, filled to overflowing with families waiting to see patients.

"What are we going to do, Logan?"

"We don't have money for a room, but I'll go sweet-talk the nurses. You stay here, and I'll get us something to eat."

"How can you do that?"

Logan grinned. "I've fallen into mighty poor ways, Maeva. They put the trays in the rooms, and some of the patients don't even touch them. When I was here before, I lived off the food here. Hospital food isn't much, but it's better than starving. You go on out to the car."

Maeva agreed. She left the hospital and sat down in the car. Her mind seemed to be in a whirl, but in a very short time, it seemed, Logan came out with food on a tray. "I put it all on one tray so I could carry it and came out the emergency entrance. Looks like it's mostly some kind of meat. Hard to tell what it is, and the vegetables are over-cooked, but we get to eat."

He got into the car and balanced the tray on the seat beside him. He had brought flatware, and the two ate hungrily. The food wasn't the best, but Maeva ate it gratefully. "What if they arrest you for stealing food?"

"Nah, they don't care. They'll just throw it away anyhow."

"How are we going to sleep, Logan?"

"You sleep in the backseat. I'll sit up here. If you have to go to the bathroom, you can go in the hospital there." He sounded somewhat cheerful, even though she knew he had lost both his job and his room.

Maeva had little enough appetite, but she forced herself to eat. When she had finished Logan said, "You curl up back there. I'll bring us back some coffee. If you're asleep, I'll drink it for you."

"I just don't know what we're going to do, Logan."

"We're going to take Thelma Mays back to Arkansas, and she's going to testify about what happened at that shooting. You've got to keep the faith, Maeva."

Maeva watched him as he left. He had lost a little weight, but still he was a tall, strong man, and she realized how much she had come to depend on him. She was weary to the bone. She lay down in the backseat and never knew when Logan came back, for she fell at once into a deep, profound sleep.

❦

The sun touched Maeva's face, and she woke at once. She moved stiffly on the seat, then sat up. She saw Logan sideways in the front seat, with his back braced against the car door, watching her. "What time is it?" she said hoarsely.

"About daylight. Breakfast time, too. I'll go scrounge us something to eat. I'll bring some coffee this time."

Maeva watched him go and got out of the car. She put her suitcase on the seat, opened it, and rummaged around for her brush and comb. Standing beside the car, she felt the stiffness of her body but managed to brush her hair into some kind of order. By the time she had finished, Logan had come out whistling and bearing a tray.

"We got a fine breakfast here, Maeva. Scrambled eggs, toast, some bacon. Got a little bit of everything and hot coffee."

"I never thought we'd be reduced to stealing food from a hospital."

Logan grinned at her. He had not lost his tan, and his white teeth made a brilliant contrast. "They're just going to feed it to the hogs or throw it away. Come on, eat up."

When Maeva finished eating, they went inside. Logan took the tray back, and Maeva went to the restroom where she worked on her hair and washed her face. When she came out Logan was talking with a pretty blonde nurse. He turned to her at once. "Come on down to the waiting room. Thelma should be awake pretty soon." He led the way to the waiting room on the second floor then said, "You want to wait here while I go see if they're through fixing her up yet?"

"All right, Logan." Logan turned and left at once, and Maeva sat down. She felt the need for a bath so fiercely that it was almost like hunger for food. There were fewer people in the waiting room than there had been the night before. Her eyes met those of a poorly dressed woman who sat across from her. She was wearing a thin print dress and had taken off her coat and put it on the chair next to her. Her shoes were worn, Maeva saw, and the marks of the Depression showed plainly.

"You got family you're waiting on here, dear?" the woman asked in a kindly fashion.

"No, just a friend. You have family here?"

A sadness touched the worn woman's face. "It's my son. He's only sixteen."

"What's the matter with him?"

"He was in an accident." Her fingers plucked at a handkerchief, limp and damp. "Well, he's not doing good." Tears came to her eyes, and she mopped them with her handkerchief. "The doctors say they don't know if they can save him."

"I'm so sorry," Maeva said, and indeed, she felt compassion for the woman.

"He's my only child. I lost my husband two years ago."

Maeva struggled to find some word of comfort, but could find none. She had never known what to say in situations like these, and the grieving woman touched her in a way that moved her to a depth of sadness. A feeling of helplessness came over her, and she said finally, "I'm sure he'll be all right."

Logan came back and said, "She's awake. Come along."

Maeva stood to her feet, and when she got to the door, she turned back and saw that the woman was watching her as if she had some kind of answer. She had none and could only say, "I hope your boy gets well."

Quickly, she turned and left. Logan caught up with her. "Lots of sad people in there. I spent some time in that waiting room. I heard one of the doctors say that woman's son is not going to make it."

"I felt bad for her."

Logan studied her face. This was a new Maeva somehow. Before she had been self-centered and cared little for the feelings of others, but the rough times they had in California had worn her down, and Logan saw that she was not just saying words, but had a real concern. "You've changed, Maeva," he said quietly as they walked down the hall.

"What do you mean?"

"I mean you never cared all that much about people, but you do now. It looks like—hey, there's Doctor Jackson. I met him a couple of times."

Doctor Jackson turned as the two approached him. He was a middle-aged man with a shock of salt and pepper hair and a pair of snapping, black eyes.

"How is Miss Mays doing, Doc?"

"Physically she's going to make it, but she's in bad shape emotionally. Sometimes that's worse than the physical problem."

"Anything at all you can do for her?"

"Not here. I think it's going to take a lot of care to pull her out of it." He hesitated and then said, "We're going to have to release her. It's hospital policy. I know it sounds heartless, but when people can't pay their bills we have to give their bed to somebody who can."

"That doesn't sound exactly right."

"It's not right and it's got to be changed," Jackson said sharply. "I guess you'll have to sign her out."

Logan stared at him. "I'm not kin to her."

"Somebody needs to be responsible."

"All right, Doctor. We'll take her."

"You go down and stay with her. I'll get her release papers drawn up." He suddenly put his hand out and shook his head regretfully as Logan took it. "I'm sorry I couldn't do more for her. That woman's had a hard time. I wonder if they caught up with the bozo that beat her up."

"Not that I've heard."

"I'd like to work him over with a baseball bat."

"Well, maybe something bad will happen to him."

Jackson studied Logan's face, and the two men understood each other. "Yeah," he said, "maybe so."

Logan and Maeva went into the room and found Thelma awake. She was still wearing her hospital clothes, and Logan said, "Well, it looks like you'll be leaving, Thelma. This here is Maeva. You remember her?"

"No."

"She'll be going with us, I guess. Where are your clothes?"

Thelma's mind seemed clearer, and she nodded at a closet. "Just got the clothes I wore here when they brought me in."

"Maeva, why don't you help her get dressed. I'll wait outside."

As soon as Logan left, Maeva went over and opened the closet door. There was only a slip, a worn dress, and a thin cloth coat. She brought them over. "Thelma, you don't have any friends here in California, do you?"

"No."

"No family either?"

"No. I got nobody."

Maeva had been thinking how to approach Thelma Mays. She decided to be as straightforward about it as possible.

"Thelma, I want to tell you about my daddy. He's the most wonderful man I know. He didn't do what Alvin Biggins and Ethel Crawford and Willie Biggins said he did. You were there that night the shooting took place. You're the only one who can help my daddy, Thelma. It's your chance to do something good. Will you help us?"

Thelma's eyes suddenly filled with tears, and she began to tremble. Maeva sat down suddenly beside the thin woman and put her arm around her. "What really happened that night?"

"It wasn't like they said. I was at the trial. They said your daddy just came in and started shooting Duke, but that wasn't the way of it."

"What did happen?"

"Your daddy had a gun, but it was in his belt. Alvin began cursing him, pulled a knife, and came at him. Your daddy pulled the gun out and told him to stay away. Duke grabbed him from behind, and he reached down and got your daddy's wrist. They was wrestling all over the room, and the gun just went off. Your daddy didn't mean to shoot nobody."

"Where were you, Thelma?"

"I was in the bedroom, but the door was open. I could see everything."

"Why did they lie, do you think?"

"Ethel hated your dad. She wanted to be his woman, but he'd never have anything to do with her, and the Biggins brothers worked for him, but they were sorry trash. After the police took your daddy away, I heard them make it up, Alvin and Willie and Ethel. Alvin said, 'We're going to put him in the jail. We're going to tell the story that he come in here and just started shooting.' And that's what they done too."

Maeva tightened her grip. "Would you be willing to go back to Arkansas and testify to that, Thelma?"

"I'm too sick to go anywhere."

"We'll take care of you, Logan and me." At that moment, she had no idea how they could take care of a sick woman, but she knew she would get this woman back to Arkansas no matter what it took.

"If I go back there, the Biggins family will kill me. They've killed people before. I — I can't go. I'm afraid, and I'm too sick."

Logan came back shortly after that and leaned up against the wall. He said nothing, but Maeva kept talking softly to Thelma as persuasively as she could. Thelma kept saying that she couldn't do it, and finally, Maeva said, "Come on. We've got to get out of here."

They left the hospital and got to the car. "Do you have any things, clothes and things like that, Thelma?"

"At my rooming house. It's over on Paloma Avenue."

"Take us there, Logan," Maeva said.

Logan drove away from the hospital. He came to the Paloma, found the old rooming house, and said, "Maeva, you stay with Thelma today. I guess you may have to spend the night here until we can work out something better."

"Will that be all right, Thelma, if I stay with you tonight?"

"I guess so."

Maeva got out of the car. Thelma was so weak she could barely walk. "When will you be back, Logan?"

"I'll see you probably later this afternoon."

Maeva helped Thelma into the rooming house, and as she had expected, the room was in as poor condition as you could imagine.

She got Thelma into bed and then sat down on the chair, and there was nothing to do but wait.

⬥

The day had passed slowly, and Logan had come back once. "I'm still working on some things. You stay with Thelma tonight."

"Where will you be?"

"I'll sleep in the car. I'll see you in the morning." He stopped and looked in her face and said, "We'll get out of this somehow. We found her and that's the big thing."

"Thank you, Logan. I'll see you later."

Maeva watched as Logan left, then went inside and spent the rest of the day in Thelma's room. The doctor had given them some sample medicine that made Thelma sleep most of the day. Maeva dosed off and on in a chair, and that night she had a strange dream. It was very brief, but when she woke up with a jerk, she realized that it was different from any dream she had ever had.

When Logan came the next morning, she told him about it. "I had a dream last night, Logan. Usually I don't remember my dreams, but I remember this one."

"What was the dream?"

"It was just me and you and Thelma. We were in the car, and we were going through mountains, and I heard a voice. Couldn't see anybody, but it said, 'I will guide you and plant you in the mountains.'"

"Was that all there was to it?" Logan asked when she paused.

"That's all. You think it can mean anything?"

"Well, we sure need to be guided, and we need to get back to the Ozark Mountains, so maybe it's the Lord talking to you."

"God never talks to me."

"Me either, but maybe He is this time."

"How we going to get to Arkansas even if Thelma agrees to go?"

"Well, I don't know. That old car is not likely to make it, but if you want to try it, I'll go with you."

"How much money have we got?"

"Less than a hundred dollars, considerably less."

"We've got to do it, Logan."

He smiled at her. "You've got nerve, Maeva Freeman. Let's get Thelma, and we'll make a start at it."

Maeva got Thelma dressed and packed what few things she had in a worn suitcase. All the while, Thelma protested weakly. "I can't go back to Arkansas. The Biggins family will kill me."

"No, they won't. You're going to save my daddy, and my family is going to take care of you."

They got in the car, and Logan said, "Well, here we go."

"We won't ever make it in this old car, and we don't have enough money."

"We'll go until the money's gone, then we'll see if God will help us out."

Thelma stared at him. "Are you two Christians?"

"Nope, but we will be before this is over, I reckon."

Maeva smiled. "Take us to Arkansas, Logan."

~☞ CHAPTER 8 ☜~

Lanie entered the living room to find Cody playing Monopoly with Corliss. They were both sprawled on the floor, and Corliss was laughing.

"I win, Cody—I win!"

"No, you don't win. You don't know how to play this game."

"I like to play it my way." Actually, Corliss loved to play with the paraphernalia of the Monopoly game. She liked the red hotels and the tiny green houses. She liked to roll the dice and move the tiny metal figures of cars and boats around the board, but she cared little enough for the other aspects of the game.

Cody looked up and frowned at Lanie. "She doesn't play this game right."

"She plays it the way she likes it, Cody, but I don't have time for this. Aunt Kezia is feeling worse today. I won't be able to go off and leave her tomorrow."

Thursday was the day that Lanie took the Freeman's Rolling Emporium on the route. Davis had a driver's license and could go alone, but he had gone to Fort Smith for two days to play in a baseball tournament. Cody could drive, and he at once piped up saying, "I can take the Emporium."

"No, you can't. You don't have a driver's license, and I can't go away and leave Aunt Kezia and Corliss alone. We'll just have to wait until Davis gets back."

Cody shook his head, and a stubborn look appeared on his face. "I can drive as good as Davis can."

"Yes, but you don't have a license."

"That don't matter."

"Yes, it does. If you get arrested, we'd have to pay a fine. That wouldn't be very smart, would it?"

"I hear somebody coming." Corliss jumped up from the floor and ran to the window. "It's Nellie!"

"You're supposed to call him Nelson," Lanie said.

"We always called him Nellie before."

"Well, Cass doesn't like that name, so we'll call him Nelson, all right?"

"I'll let him in!" Corliss cried. She ran to the door and opened it, and Nelson Prather came in bearing two large buckets. "Hey, Lanie. Hi, Corliss. Hello, Cody."

"What you got in your buckets?" Corliss demanded.

"Fresh blackberries. I picked them myself." He looked over and grinned at Lanie. "I thought you might take them along the route. Some people would rather buy berries than get out and pick them."

"I would," Cody said. "Every time I go, I get chiggers all over me."

"Me too," Nelson nodded. "Nothing worse than a chigger bite. I'd just about as soon get snake bit."

"Why, thank you, Nelson, for the berries, but we won't be going out tomorrow."

"I thought that was your day on the Emporium."

"Well, it is, but Aunt Kezia's not feeling well, and I don't have anybody to stay with Corliss."

"I told her I could take the Emporium," Cody said.

"And I told you, you don't have a license. You might get arrested and go to jail."

"Hey, maybe I could get loose long enough to drive," Nelson said.

"No, you've got plenty to do."

"If I find out somebody that's got a license that's not doing anything, I'll send them by."

"I wouldn't trust just anybody with our Emporium," Cody said. "It'd have to be somebody responsible."

"I'll see what I can do. Lots of people have driver's licenses. Surely ought to be one that could get off long enough to drive you around, Cody."

"I'm pretty particular who I let drive our Emporium. Besides that, whoever it is I'd have to spend all day with them."

"Oh, I'll try to find somebody that you'll like. See you later."

Cody sat up abruptly, his eyes flying open. The banging somewhere had awakened him, and he looked out the window to see that it was still dark. He leaned forward and saw by the old clock beside his bed that it was only five thirty.

"Who could that be coming at this time of the night?" He came out of bed and pulled on an old bathrobe that had belonged to his father and left his room. By the time he got to the front door, Lanie was there. "Who could that be?" she said. She too was wearing a bathrobe and a pair of fleece-lined slippers.

"I don't know, but they ain't got no manners," Cody said. "Listen to them bang." He opened the door and peered into the darkness. He could see a figure there, but he couldn't make it out. "What do you want? Who are you?"

"Why, Cody, don't you know me?" Cody flipped on the porch light and stared at the speaker. "It's me—Lolean."

"Why, Lolean, what are you doing here this early?" Lanie said. Lolean Oz was the daughter of Harry and Maxine who owned the hardware store in town. She was seventeen now and had grown amazingly in the last year.

Lolean stepped inside at Lanie's invitation. "I've come to drive your vehicle for you."

Both Lanie and Cody stared at the girl. Lanie exclaimed, "How did you know about that!"

"Nelson Prather asked me if I had a license, and I told him I did. He told me you couldn't go tomorrow on your route, and you needed somebody to drive the truck."

"You can't drive the Emporium!" Cody exclaimed. "It ain't no job for a woman."

"Why, Lanie drives it all the time," Lolean said. She was a flaming redhead, as all the Oz children were, had light blue eyes and a peaches-and-cream complexion. She had been a lanky, skinny adolescent, but during the last year, she had entered into young womanhood in a manner that had been amazing. She had been in Lanie's Sunday school class, and Lanie had always liked Lolean for her cheerful spirit.

"Why, that's very thoughtful of you, Lolean," Lanie said quickly. "It would be a great help to us."

"Well, it won't do," Cody said. "It would be unseemly."

"What would be unseemly?"

"Well, a single man and woman ought to have some kind of supervision. They might get into trouble."

Lolean suddenly giggled. "Were you thinking to be forward with me, Cody?"

Cody flushed. "No, I wasn't!"

"Well, then you must think I'm going to make advances to you." Lolean winked at Lanie. "Tell you what, Lanie. I'll bring my daddy's .410 shotgun to fight your brother off when he tries to force his attention on me."

Cody sputtered and for once could find nothing to say, and then Lolean added innocently, "Everybody knows that Cody's a real lady's man."

Lanie knew that Lolean was adept at teasing, and it amused her that she was getting the best of Cody. He got so unbearable sometimes that he needed somebody to put him down. "Come on in, and I'll fix you a good breakfast. Driving the route is hungry work."

Cody glared at Lolean. "You just remember that you're the driver, but I'm the boss." He turned and stomped upstairs.

Lanie laughed. "Are you sure you can put up with him all day?"

"I've always liked Cody. I had a crush on him when we were in the fifth grade, I think. He's afraid of girls, but this will be my chance to get better acquainted with him."

Lanie fixed a huge breakfast: ham, eggs, biscuits and grits, and fresh blackberries covered with rich cream.

Cody watched Lolean eat and said grumpily, "You eat like a starved wolf. Don't they ever feed you at your house?"

"I'm a growing girl, Cody."

Corliss, as usual, was examining their visitor. She knew Lolean from church, but now she began to pepper her with questions. "How old are you?"

"I'm seventeen."

"Well, how much do you weigh?"

Lolean giggled. "A hundred and twenty-six pounds."

"Do you have any dolls?"

"Yes. I don't play with them anymore, but I'm keeping them for my little girl."

"How many little girls do you have?"

"None yet."

"Stop pestering Lolean," Lanie said.

"I'm going to get married, and I'm going to have three little girls and one boy," Corliss announced.

"Oh, who are you going to marry?" Lolean said, winking at Lanie.

"I'm going to marry Owen."

"Doctor Merritt? He'll be too old for you."

"No, he won't."

Lolean glanced slyly at Cody. "I've always known I was going to marry a younger man. That way I can raise him up the way I want him to be. Like if I married you, Cody—I'm older than you are."

"Just a year. That's all."

"Well, that's older, and girls are older than boys anyhow, for their age. So, I can get rid of all your bad habits."

"I don't have any bad habits," Cody said self-righteously.

Lolean Oz suddenly grinned broadly. "That's not what Mae Simpson says."

Cody blushed and got up from the table. "That's foolish talk. I wouldn't marry a woman older than me. I'm going out and get the stuff loaded."

Lolean helped Lanie clean up the breakfast dishes, and when they were through Cody came back in. He looked at Lolean and said, "You can change clothes before we leave."

"Change clothes? Why would I do that?"

"Why, you can't wear that dress on the Rolling Emporium."

Lolean looked confused. "What's wrong with this dress?"

"Well, it ain't fittin'."

"Not fittin'? Why not?"

"It's too tight."

"It fits me just fine," Lolean said. Lanie had been taking all this in with a smile. She was accustomed to Cody correcting young women for their taste in dressing. "You let Lolean alone. She looks fine. Here, here's some money to make change with, Cody."

Cody took the bag full of change and looked at Lolean. "If you've got to go, let's get started. I ain't got all day."

"Oh, it's going to be such fun, Cody!"

"No, it won't," Cody said and stomped out.

"He's grumpy, isn't he?"

"Yes, he is, Lolean. You'll just have to work on him."

Lanie watched as the two got into the Rolling Emporium, and it drove off. She went upstairs to talk to Kezia. "Who was that young woman? I seen her from the window."

"That's Lolean Oz. She's seventeen and has a driver's license. It really irked Cody that he couldn't drive."

"Right pretty young woman."

"Cody didn't think so. He's all embarrassed because he can't drive."

"That's what he needs, a young woman to take the starch out of him."

"Lolean told him she was going to marry a younger man so she could cure him of all his bad habits."

"All three of my husbands had bad habits," Aunt Kezia said. "I had to work on them. Even Mr. Butterworth."

Lanie said, "Did they work on your bad habits?"

"Law, they was so foolish about me they never even noticed my bad habits!"

"They were foolish about you even after they married you? Lots of men don't seem to have much romance."

"Well," Kezia said, "I knew how to handle them, honey. A woman can make a man love her if she knows a few tricks."

"I wish you'd tell me some of those tricks."

"Well, I'd be proud to," Kezia said. She settled back in her chair and nodded confidently. "The big secret is to be affectionate."

"Affectionate? What do you mean?"

"Why, I mean some women are cold. They don't show their love for their man, but I found out men like a woman who's always ready for loving."

Lanie hesitated. It was an area that she was curious about, and since Kezia had had three husbands, she should know.

"I thought a man was supposed to always be the one who, well, made up to a woman."

"Why, that's foolishness!" Kezia snapped. "A woman has needs just like a man. They need a man. Most women are scared to let that side out, but most men love for a woman to show that they've got a tiger inside. Just go to loving on them and make them feel like a big man. They'll come running every time you snap your fingers."

Kezia went on for some time giving her rules for making a man downright foolish about his wife. Lanie was stunned. "I never heard of such a thing."

"Well," Aunt Kezia smiled and reached over and patted Lanie's cheek, "if you'd listen to me more, you'd know more. I'll give you some more lessons after my nap about how to bring a man around ..."

⊂━⋖⊷

Lolean had enjoyed one of the best days of her life. Driving the Emporium was no problem, for she was a fine driver. She chattered constantly to Cody who had only short answers, for the most part, and she got out at every stop. She quickly learned that if a man was involved, she could charm him with a smile, and if it was a woman, she could talk about the things women talk about.

It was late afternoon when they were on their way back to the farm when Lolean noticed the engine had overheated. They were on the highway that ran beside the Singing River, and she pulled over at once. Cody looked up and said, "What are you stopping for?"

"I think the truck needs some water."

"Well, shucks, it does that. I've got to have a new radiator put in."

They got out of the truck and lifted the hood. Lolean said, "Be careful. Don't pull that radiator cap off until it cools off."

"I guess I know how to—" Cody pulled the cap off and steam blew everywhere. Cody let out a yell and jerked his hand backward.

"Did it burn you, Cody?"

Lolean came over and attempted to take Cody's hand, and he pulled it away rapidly. "Don't mess around with me. Don't paw me, Lolean. It didn't hurt."

"I'll tell you what. Let's go down to the river. You can soak your hand in it, and we'll bring some water back. But you're not supposed to pour cold water into a hot engine. It will bust the block."

Cody stared at Lolean Oz. "How'd you know that?"

"Because my daddy did it once, and I saw him. You always learn from watching people, Cody. Come on. Let's go down." She paused suddenly and said, "I know what. It's going to take a while for this truck to cool off. Let's have a picnic."

"You fool, girl, we can't have picnics! We're working."

"We're through with the route. We've got plenty of stuff in here to heat up."

Cody opened his mouth, but somehow he found himself down on the riverbank building a fire. Lolean chatted constantly, and they wound up with a fine picnic lunch of baked beans, hot dogs, and cookies.

When they had finished, Lolean said, "That's the prettiest river I've ever seen. You know, I'd like to go swimming."

"It's September. That water's cold."

"I like cold water."

"You can't go swimming. You don't have a bathing suit."

"Well, I can go wading." Lolean took off her shoes and moved out into the river. She lifted her skirt to keep it dry, and Cody was shocked at the sight of her bare legs. "That's unseemly," he said.

"What's unseemly?" Lolean asked with surprise.

"Pulling your skirt up like that and exposing your legs."

Lolean laughed. "You're so fussy, Cody." She came in, dried her feet off, and put her shoes back on. The two sat there, and she said, "Did you know I liked you all the time we were in school together?"

"You were always in a grade ahead of me."

"I know it. You never paid any attention to me, but that was when I was all skinny. You liked Mae Simpson and I hated her. Tell me about the other girls you like."

"I ain't talking about that."

"Irene Perkins likes you, but she wouldn't be any good for you, Cody."

"Why not?"

"She's spoiled. She wouldn't make a good preacher's wife. Hey, I've got something I want to show you." She jumped up and ran back to the truck, and Cody watched her go. When she came back, she held up something.

"Look at this."

"What is it?"

"It's a bottle of perfume called Evening in Paris. I got it for my birthday." She uncapped the perfume, put some behind her ear, and then put the cap back on. "Smell it."

Cody sniffed, but Lolean said, "You can't smell from there. Come here closer."

Cody moved closer and sniffed at her ear. "Do you like it?"

"Yeah, it smells good all right."

"How many girls have you kissed, Cody?"

"It's unseemly to talk about stuff like that!"

"You kissed Clara Mayhan at the State Fair. She told me."

"Well, it was her fault. She done the kissing, not me."

Lolean laughed, and her eyes were sparkling. She moved closer and said, "Do you really like my perfume?"

"It's all right." He turned suddenly and there was Lolean's face only inches away from his own. He was acutely aware that she was pressing against him and was watching him with an odd expression. He could not get over how she had grown up in the past year, and once again, even in the falling darkness, he admired the smoothness of her skin. She suddenly leaned forward and kissed him right on the lips.

"Now see what you done!" Cody protested.

"Can I kiss as good as Clara?"

Cody was flustered. He got up quickly, stammering, "We've— we've gotta get home."

Laughing, Lolean got to her feet. She reached out and gave Cody a hug. "Well, that Evening in Paris works pretty well. I'll tell you what. When I come in the morning I'll be sure to bring the bottle."

"What do you mean 'come in the morning'?"

"I'm going to drive you tomorrow. Aunt Kezia won't be well, and somebody has to stay with Corliss. I'll bring my Evening in Paris with me." She gathered up the remains of the picnic and marched off toward the bus.

Cody watched her go, reached up, and touched his lips tentatively with his fingers. "Well, I'll be dipped," he muttered and shook his head in awe and wonder.

⟶ CHAPTER 9 ⟵

Maeva twisted her head to look at the backseat of the car, and as she expected, Thelma was curled up, sound asleep. The woman had not slept peacefully, but always seemed to be troubled with dreams. She would whimper and sometimes scream out, and Maeva had often had to wake her and comfort her.

This time as Thelma cried out, Maeva waited to see if she would wake up, but when the woman seemed to go back to a fitful sleep Maeva turned and looked out the window. The air was cool for they had climbed into the mountains east of Bakersfield. The mountains were barren with little vegetation, and the two-lane highway bore little traffic.

She gazed down the highway in front of them. The desert lay ahead somewhere, but she was not good with maps. Logan had shown her on a map where they were and which direction they were going. He had said, "We were lucky to get across the mountains without having a breakdown." He had also warned her, "When we get to the desert, if we break down there, it's going to be bad news."

A whimper from Thelma caught Maeva's attention, and she saw that Thelma had pulled herself up into a fetal position and was crying with great choking sobs. Logan pulled over, and Maeva went around to the backseat, got in, and pulled Thelma to a sitting position. She held her as she would a small child and whispered, "It'll be all right, Thelma. You're doing fine."

Still trembling, Thelma opened her eyes. "I'm scared, Maeva! I'm scared of everything."

"You don't need to be afraid. Logan and I are going to take care of you, and when we get home, you can stay with my family. It'll be like you're my sister."

A faint hope touched the woman's eyes, and she whispered, "I never had a sister, not one that I knew, anyhow."

"Well, you'll have three now. Me and Lanie and Corliss. And you'll have two brothers, Davis and Cody. And Logan, he'll be like a brother to you too. You'll have a family to take care of you." For some time, Maeva sat there talking, and gradually the tremors left the woman's body. "Now, I'm going to get out and make some tea and fix us something to eat."

She got out of the car and went back to the small two-wheeled trailer. With Thelma using the backseat for a bed, there had been no option but to buy a small trailer. Logan had fixed the trailer hitch, and now all of their belongings were there, including a tent Logan put up for the two women at night. Opening the box, she looked at the pitiful supply of food and shook her head doubtfully. All they had left was a half-empty jar of peanut butter, a few saltine crackers and five slices of cheese, two cans of soup, and two Baby Ruth bars.

"We're going to starve to death at this rate." Maeva lifted out a can of soup and a saucepan, then at the side of the road, she found enough dead branches to start a small fire. Logan got out a folding grill, and soon the soup was boiling. She filled a soup bowl, added several crackers, then poured a cup of boiling water into a cup and dropped in a tea bag.

She turned a wooden box upside down for a table, then stepped back over to the rear of the car. "Come on, Thelma. Time to eat."

Thelma got out of the car and came over to the small fire. She looked both ways, shivered, and said, "There ain't much traffic on this road."

"Just a few trucks and a car every now and then. I guess people don't have the money for gas."

The two women sat down at the makeshift table. Maeva watched Thelma take her first spoonful of soup. She closed her eyes as she swallowed and quickly spooned another into her mouth. "I always like Campbell's tomato soup."

"We'll get you some more the next time we stop." As Maeva said this, she wondered if there was enough money for another can of soup. Logan kept their money, but she knew it was about gone.

While they ate, Maeva kept up the conversation, trying to keep Thelma's spirits up. But Thelma once again brought up how afraid she was to testify. "They'll kill anybody that speaks up against them," she said.

"They won't hurt you. You know Pardue Jessup?"

"You mean the sheriff?"

"Yes, you know what a tough man he is. If those Bigginses even look at you sideways, Pardue will put the run on them. You can depend on it."

Thelma stared at her with disbelief. "I was never friends with no law man."

"Well, you can be friends with Pardue. He's a good man. Here, eat some more soup."

"No, you eat it."

"I'm not hungry," Maeva said, although she was.

The two women sat there after the soup was gone. In the distance, they heard the rumble of a truck coming toward them. The truck grew larger and came to a grinding halt just short of where the car was parked.

"It's Logan," Thelma said. She had grown very dependent on the big man, and now her whole face lit up. "He came back."

"Of course he came back. He just went to get a part for the car."

The two women watched as Logan thanked the truck driver and gave him a salute. He looked over at the women, a big grin on his face. "Well, I found a junkyard and got a used part. Only cost forty cents. It would have cost five dollars at least at a parts store. You ladies having lunch?"

"Let me fix you something, Logan."

"First things first. I need to get the car to running."

Maeva fixed two sandwiches, which finished off their last loaf of bread, and opened the jar of dill pickles. Only one was left. She put the sandwiches and pickle on a paper plate.

"It ought to work fine now." Logan wiped his hands on a rag as he headed to the table.

"Sit down and eat, Logan."

Logan sat down beside Thelma, put his arm around her, and gave her a hug. "How you doing, little sister?"

"I'm all right, Logan." She smiled for he had started calling her little sister from the beginning, and it seemed to give her some kind of confidence.

After Logan had eaten, keeping up a running conversation, he said, "Well, let's get as far as we can before dark. You want to lie down again, Thelma?"

Still looking weary, she nodded, then headed to the back of the car. When Thelma had gone, Maeva turned to Logan and said, "How much money do we have left?"

He took a few bills from his pocket and handed it to her. "Nine dollars and forty-five cents."

Maeva knew a moment of bleak despair. "That won't even buy gas to get us anywhere."

"No, it won't."

"Well, what will we do?"

"I guess we'll go as far as we can." He turned his head to one side and said, "If Lanie were here, she'd say we'd have to trust God."

"I've been trying to do that," Maeva said, "but I can't go to God. I've ignored Him all my life, Logan. Now I can't ask Him for help."

"I don't think it would bother Him if you did, Maeva. He's used to people that can't help themselves calling on Him. I've been thinking about it myself. Well, get in the car. We'll go until we run out of gas and money."

"There's not much food left."

Logan laughed, reached out, and ran his hand over her hair. "Well, the Bible talks about fasting so I reckon we're about to try it."

❦

"This is Ash Flat," Logan said pointing to a sign. He slowed the car down, adding, "Not much of a town, is it?" He looked down and shook his head. "We're running on the fumes. We've got to have gas."

"Is there any money at all left?"

"Not enough to fill the truck with. I guess we've reached the end of the line." He shut the engine off and said, "I'll pitch the tent. I don't reckon it's going to rain, but you two can sleep in it tonight." He pitched the tent quickly and said, "I'm going in and look around and see if I can get a job, enough to pay for some gas anyway. I'll try to find something to eat too."

Maeva watched him go off, and then she went over and sat beside the tent. Thelma came over and sat down close to her. "He'll come back, won't he?"

"Logan? Of course, he will. You're his little sister, aren't you?"

"I like him. He takes care of us, doesn't he?"

"Yes, he does. He's a fine man."

The two sat there for nearly an hour, and then Maeva said, "Look, there he comes."

Logan came up at a fast walk and held out a sack. "Supper," he said.

"What is it, Logan?"

"Hamburgers. I cleaned out the kitchen for a bunch of them. Got some coffee here in this jar—probably pretty cold by now. Let's heat this coffee, and we'll eat and drink and be merry."

Maeva made a small fire, and soon the coffee was bubbling in the percolator. They waited until it was hot, and then she filled three cups and passed the hamburgers around. "I got two hamburgers for each of you and three for me."

"Oh, these are good!" Thelma cried. "I was so hungry."

"So was I," Maeva said. "How come they let you have these hamburgers?"

"Like I said, I cleaned the kitchen up."

Maeva suddenly laughed. "I bet you charmed the waitress, didn't you?"

"Well, I did have to turn on a little bit of charm. Not full force or the poor girl would have fainted."

"I'll bet! Well, I forgive you this time."

They ate the hamburgers, and for the first time in a couple of days they were filled. They drank the coffee, and night was falling quickly. After they had eaten, Logan got his guitar from the trailer. He sat down and said, "Let's have a little music. Good for the digestion." He began playing, and he and Maeva sang a few songs. He looked up, saying, "That old car looks to be in as bad a shape as ours."

A car almost as old as their own was coming down the road. It slowed down to a stop after pulling off the road. An elderly woman got out. She was in her sixties at least but was strong looking, and her hair was in a bun at the back of her head.

The woman stopped and looked down on them. Logan nodded pleasantly and took off his hat. "Howdy, ma'am. How are you this fine evening?"

"I'm as good as gold," the woman said. "I'm Sister Smith. What are your names?"

"I'm Logan Satterfield. This is Maeva Freeman and Thelma Mays."

"Where you folks bound for?"

"Trying to get all the way back to Arkansas. We got some urgent business there."

"What kind of business?"

Maeva smiled at the woman's curiosity. "You're not a sheriff, are you?"

"No, I ain't no sheriff. I'm a preacher. Have you got troubles? Let's hear it."

For some reason Maeva trusted the woman. She quickly traced the problem and how that they needed to get Thelma back to testify to get her father out of prison.

Sister Smith looked over at Thelma and said, "You look peaked, daughter. What's wrong?"

"I been a little bit sick."

"We need to get her to a doctor," Maeva said, "but we don't have any money."

Sister Smith laughed. She had a robust laugh and said, "Well, we got Doctor Jesus, ain't we? Let me get my healing oil, and we'll just anoint this dear sister and pray for her."

As the woman went back to the car, Thelma said nervously, "What's she going to do, Maeva?"

"Oh, she's just going to pray for you," Maeva said. "I might ask her to pray for me too."

Sister Smith came back with a bottle of oil and without pause upended it, poured her palm full. She rubbed it on Thelma's forehead and prayed in a voice that could be heard all the way to the center of Ash Flat.

Maeva smiled. She was a great deal like Sister Myrtle Poindexter, the Pentecostal preacher back home in Fairhope.

"Well, now. That'll do for now. We might catch up with some praying later." Sister Smith turned her light blue eyes on the pair. "Are you a-playing that there guitar, young man? You know any church songs or just devil's music?"

"I know quite a few church songs."

"Are you a man of God, then?"

"No, ma'am, I'm sorry to say I'm not. My granddaddy was, though. He was a Methodist preacher."

"Well, you got good blood in you then. What about you, young lady? Are you born again?"

"No, I'm afraid not."

"Well, it ain't too late. Can you sing any of them church songs?"

"Oh yes. I know quite a few of them."

"Let me hear one of them."

Logan winked at Maeva and began playing "When the Roll Is Called Up Yonder." Maeva began to sing, and her clear contralto voice filled the silence of the evening. Logan's fingers ran up and down the guitar, and when they were through Sister Smith said, "I reckon you'll have to do."

"Do for what, Sister Smith?" Maeva asked, puzzled.

"We done lost our music musicians for my meeting tonight at the Pentecostal church, but you two are going to come along and provide that."

Logan blinked at the woman in surprise. "But I told you, Sister, we're not even saved."

"Well, I aim for you to get in the middle of the Gospel and hear some good preaching, and you can start singing about the blood of the Lamb. This may be your day to get saved. Come on now. I haven't got time to fool with you. I don't want to be late."

Maeva began to giggle. "I don't think it would be seemly. I know that because my brother Cody's a fervent Christian. If he was here right now, he'd say it's not seemly."

"It's seemly enough. We've got to have some good church music, and you two are sitting here on the side of the road. God put you here waiting for me, so don't argufy with me. Let's go."

Maeva got to her feet and said, "Come on, Thelma. We're going to church."

"I don't have any gas for this car," said Logan. "We'll have to go with you."

"Well, get yourselves in. We're going to have the Gospel served hot tonight!"

⊂══⊰⊱

The church was an old timer, and as Maeva got out, she knew she had seen many just like it — white-framed with a small steeple on the front. People were filing in, and one man came rushing forward. He was a tall, gawky man with gray eyes and an Adam's apple that moved up and down when he talked. "Sister Smith, we was afraid you couldn't make it."

"Couldn't make it? Didn't I tell you God wanted me here tonight? Of course I'm going to make it."

"Well, like I told you on the phone we ain't got no guitar players tonight. We'll just have to sing without no picking."

"That's where you're wrong, Brother Ramsey. God had this guitar picker and this fine Gospel-singing woman right here. They're going to provide the spiritual music for our meeting."

Brother Ramsey's eyes flew to the three guests. "You tell me that! My, ain't that fine!" He came forward at once and introduced himself to all three of the newcomers. "You all come right in. It's time to get started."

They went inside the building, which was packed. The women were all on one side and the men on the other side, which puzzled Maeva. "Why is it like that?" she whispered to Logan.

"It's an old-time church. It was the same way in my grandpa's church. In fact, they had a board right down in the middle of the pews. The men sat on one side, the women on the other. I didn't know there was any of that left though."

Sister Smith marched right to the front, and her voice boomed and filled the building. "Praise be to God! Blessed be the Lord God and the Lamb forever!" The room was filled with amens, praise the Lords, and hallelujahs.

Sister Smith's voice rang out. "We're going to see the wall of Jericho fall tonight. We're going to see miracles, folks. We're going to see people healed of sickness. We're going to see devils cast out. Wouldn't surprise me a bit to see the dead raised." An amen or a similar exultation from the congregation punctuated every sentence.

They were all poor people, Maeva saw, many of them dressed in their best overalls, and the women in their best print dresses. They looked to her just like the farming people in Arkansas. She looked at Thelma who had been placed on the front row by Sister Smith, and then Sister Smith said, "The first miracle's already done took place, beloved. We didn't have no picker, and we didn't have no tune heister, but as I was on my way, God told me He would have one. I seen this car parked by the wayside, and there was this tall man picking the guitar, and there was this young woman belting out a song. I knowed God had come through again. God sent 'em. They ain't in the family of God yet, but they're gonna be."

An overweight woman sitting on the front row raised her voice. "You're not letting sinners play in our church, are you, Sister Smith?"

"Certainly, I am. God told me to use them. Are you too holy to hear singers sing? Then you need a touch of salvation, Sister Diffy. Now we're going to pray, and then we're going to sing, and then I'm going to preach, and then the glory's going to fall!"

❦

The prayer time was long and noisy. People fell on their knees on the altar, some in the seats in front of them. Some walked around, praying and lifting their hands.

"I never saw anything like this, Logan."

"You never went to a Pentecostal church then. Grandpa's church was like this. Methodist folks were different in those days. They were called 'shouting Methodists.' I think they've calmed down in lots of churches."

"I think you're right."

"Well, might as well get ready for a long service. Grandpa's meetings always had a beginning but no end, at least so it seemed."

Finally, Sister Smith concluded the prayer and said, "Now, this young fellow's name is Logan Satterfield. He's a sinner, but he's going to get saved. Maybe tonight. But until he does, he's going to sing in the glory of God and the glory of Jesus, and this young woman too. Jesus sent her and her name's Maeva. She's a pretty little thing, but she's heading straight for hell, but that could change in a moment's notice. Okay, let's have some good old Gospel music."

Logan began to play church songs. The first one again was "When the Roll Is Called Up Yonder," and Maeva had sung it practically every Sunday of her life. She had a strong, powerful voice, and it filled the place. The two had not gotten halfway through before the crowd was singing at the top of their lungs with a spirit she had not seen in church ever.

Logan played one song after another. Some of them Maeva did not know, but Logan knew the words to all of them, especially the old camp meeting songs.

As they sang, Maeva found a peculiar thing was happening to her. She had never been particularly moved in her spirit by the singing at church, but then she had been running from God most of her life. But when Logan sang, "Are You Washed In the Blood?" and she joined in, she found something tugging at her heart. She could not explain it, but she suddenly was filled with a sense of fear mixed with hope. It was the strangest feeling she had ever had in her life.

The next song was "What a Friend We Have in Jesus." She knew that one and sang as Logan played, but as she sang the song, she suddenly found herself thinking of Jesus in a way she never had before. She had heard a thousand sermons about Him, but none had ever taken root, or at least so she felt. But as she sang, she found to her shock and amazement that tears had come into her eyes. Maeva was not a crying young woman, never had been, and to cry over a church song seemed amazing to her. The words seemed to go right into her soul, and by the time the song was over, she could barely speak.

As the song service continued, Maeva found herself less and less able to sing. She saw that Logan was staring at her with some sort of concern, and as for Thelma Mays, she was sitting there with her eyes wide open, taking it all in.

Sister Smith came over and put her hand on Maeva's shoulder. "The Lord is dealing with you, my dear young friend. Jesus is standing at your heart's door, and He's asking you to open it and let Him in. Tonight's your night to meet Jesus the Savior."

Sister Smith lifted up her voice and said, "We're going to do things different tonight. I ain't preached the sermon yet, but I'm going to ask you all to come to the altar. If you've got a lost daddy, a lost child, son or daughter, or a lost friend, I want you to come, and I want you to pray especially for this dear young woman here, Maeva Freeman. God's doing something in her life tonight."

There was a rush to the altar, and Maeva, who had never responded to an invitation in her life, felt herself trembling. She felt Sister Smith's hands on her shoulder, looked up into the woman's eyes, and saw the compassion and kindness she had longed for. "It's time for you to pray, honey, and I'm going to pray with you. Just kneel right where you are."

Maeva had never knelt in her life, and she found herself kneeling with Sister Smith beside her. Sister Smith put her arm around Maeva and began to pray, not loudly but in a sweet voice, speaking to God as if He were right before her eyes visibly. "Lord, you know this young woman is hungry. She's had a bad life, but you're the friend of sinners, and I'm praying, O God, that she would just open that door that you said we must open. You said, 'I stand at the door and knock. If any man will open the door, I will come in and sup with him and him with me.' So, I'm praying that this dear young woman will find her place in the Kingdom of God tonight."

Later Maeva did not remember a great deal of what happened, but she did remember Sister Smith's warm urgent compassion, and she remembered beginning to weep openly as she never had, and she did remember she had called out loudly, involuntarily, "Oh, God, I'm a sinner. Help me. Come into my heart, Jesus!"

As she cried out like this, there were others crying out calling on God. She felt Sister Smith's hands over her forehead and on the back of her head, and Sister Smith was saying, "Fill this young lady with your Holy Spirit. Let her give her whole life on the altar for you, Lord Jesus, as you gave your life for her."

As Sister Smith prayed, all of the urgency and tumult Maeva had known seemed to fade. A silence, peaceful and sweet and pure, came into her heart and into her mind. She slumped there and when Sister Smith released her, she lifted her head. Sister Smith was smiling. "Jesus come in, didn't He, honey?"

"Yes," Maeva Freeman whispered. "He did."

That was not the end. She looked at Logan who was staring at her with the oddest expression she had ever seen on his face. She smiled at him, and he put his guitar down and came over. "What are you doing, Maeva?"

"I asked God to forgive all my sins, and He did. You need to do that too, Logan."

Logan stared at her. "I don't know how."

At once, Sister Smith was beside him. "Well, *I* know how, young man," she said, "Get on your knees, boy. You're fixing to get ready for heaven!"

For a moment, Maeva saw resistance in Logan's face. She reached out, put her hand on his arm, and said, "Please, Logan, you need God just like I do."

Logan stared at her and then without another word dropped to his knees. Sister Smith got on her knees on one side and Maeva on the other side. They had their arms around his shoulders and for the first time in her life Maeva prayed for someone and knew that God was hearing her.

Sister Smith prayed and then Maeva heard Logan praying. It was a broken prayer. "God, I ain't no good. Never have been. You know all that. I'm just a sinner, but if you can help me, I need it. Have mercy on me, a sinner, and save me in the name of Jesus."

Sister Smith let out a piercing cry. "Glory be to God, he's in—he's in! He's in the Kingdom!"

Maeva never forgot the look on Logan's face. It was a mixture of awe and wonder and joy and confusion. All those things swept across his face, but she reached out, hugged him, and said, "We're saved, Logan! We're saved!"

Logan stared at her and shook his head. "I reckon we are," he said. "What do we do now?"

"I'll tell you what you do now, boy. You serve Jesus ever waking moment. Whether you eat or drink or whatsoever you do, do all to the glory of God." Sister Smith grabbed them both and cried out,

"You take that young woman back, and she's going to help you. She's going to get your pa out of prison and make your family whole again. God's going to do great things for you."

The woman's words flowed into Maeva like a soothing ointment, and all she could say was, "Thank You, Jesus!"

◯━◁━

They were back at the tent now, and Thelma was asleep already. The two of them sat in front of a small fire, and finally Logan looked up and said, "I wish my grandpa could have been here. He prayed for me every day of my life, I think. He'd have been happy. I bet he would have done some shouting."

"And I wish my daddy could have been here."

"You think it's real, Maeva? Will it last?"

"Yes, it's real. We're going to serve God. Whatever He says, we're going to do it."

Logan shook his head. "I didn't expect Sister Smith to take an offering for us. Here, she put it in this sack. She said she didn't know what it was, but it was whatever God wanted. She sure gave instructions. She told everybody to put all they had in there and God would pay them back. Never heard of an offering like that. Let's count it, Logan."

Logan opened up the sack and began counting. He looked up and said, "Why, Maeva, there's over a hundred and fifty dollars here! That's enough to get us back to Fairhope if we watch it and don't have car trouble."

Suddenly a voice came. "You think God did all this?" Thelma had come out of the tent, and now she looked at the money and shook her head. "God never did anything like that for me."

"Of course, God did it. He's going to do a lot more too, Thelma. You're going home and get my daddy out of prison, and God's going to take care of you." She looked up at the stars, rose, and put her arms around Thelma. "I'm going to have to sing different kinds of songs from now on."

Logan grinned up at her. "I reckon I will too."

Maeva Freeman lifted her arms. "Won't they be surprised back home when they hear how Maeva Freeman and Logan Satterfield hit the Glory Road!"

⇒ CHAPTER 10 ⇐

Dawn had come, bringing the first thin line of light in the east. Lanie sat by the window with her tablet on the small table and stared at what she had written. She scratched out a line and wrote another then sat back and considered the poem. She had always been fascinated by the woman taken in adultery that Jesus forgave, so she decided to call the poem simply "The Adulteress." As always, when she wrote a poem, she tried to put herself in the place of the central figure, in this case the nameless woman who the Pharisees had brought to be stoned. She read the poem in a whisper:

So short my breath — my heart pounds harder
Than old Simon's hammer on his anvil!
They meant to stone me,
Yet some of them I've seen before
(Less concerned with Moses and the Law!)
Old Eleazar — see how blue and bruised
My arm where he struck me —
Him with his pious talk, **Adultery!**
In the very act!
I could tell a thing:
His hot eyes glittering
When he came scratching at my door — at night!

Still, it was not me they hated, but **him,** *the Rabbi*
They brought me to.

Round him they circled — hungry-eyed, crying;
Like a pack of angry wolves!

When they snapped at him, **Moses said to stone her;**
What say you? *I squeezed my eyes in fear.*
One word from him — one little word —
Well, I'd be meat for wild dogs right now!
But then so quiet and still it got.

I raised my eyes, to see him stooping,
Writing in the dust — right here, you see these marks?
Since I cannot read I only guess
What sent them flying, guilt in every face.
The names, perhaps, of those who pray so loud
On Sabbath — then whisper in my ear by night?

But still I couldn't move until
He said, **I don't condemn you:**
Go and sin no more.
I saw him smile, and then —
He went away.
Now I sit and wonder at it all.

If I am to do as he commands,
O God of Israel,
You'll have to push and shove me to another life!
But if this man can save me by a few remarks
In a dusty street,
Somehow I feel my life is safe
For all my days!

After she read the last line she stopped, and a troubled light came into her eyes. She put the tablet away and for a time, she sat there praying. It was a simple enough prayer but one that she had trouble speaking.

"Lord, I know you are not pleased when your servants are filled with worry and doubts. You want us to have faith—and I wish I did, but O Lord, you know my heart, and you know that I'm so concerned about Aunt Kezia. She seems so frail, and I don't want to lose her. I worry about Maeva. She's so far away, and she's not a strong Christian. She's a lost girl, and anything could happen to her out in that place. You know my heart, and my faith isn't even as big as a mustard seed, it seems. So, I ask you to increase my faith. Help me, Lord, never to doubt You but just simply believe that Aunt Kezia will be strengthened, and Maeva will find her way into the family of God. Forgive me for my little faith, Lord Jesus."

The sound of the rooster crowing broke her concentration. Corliss had named the rooster Judas. She simply liked the name, she said, and everyone had laughed. But Corliss had said, "He's a good rooster, and I like that name."

Lanie rose and looked over to where Cap'n Brown was lying on her bed, his eyes half open as she moved.

"I wish I didn't have any more worries and troubles than you have, Cap'n Brown. All it takes to make you happy is a saucer of warm milk or a nice fat juicy mouse and some rubbing on your tummy. That's some life you got there."

It was time to make breakfast and get started on the day's work, but Lanie was strangely reluctant. It was Saturday, and Davis had a baseball game, so there was no one to take the Rolling Emporium on the rounds. Saturday was always a good day, but she could not leave Kezia or Corliss. With a sigh, she put her writing materials away and left the room. Cap'n Brown watched her go then closed his eyes and went instantly to sleep.

⚔

"I was on my way out to the Carter house, Lanie, and I thought I'd stop by and see how Aunt Kezia's doing."

Lanie had answered the door and had been surprised to see Owen there. Saturday was usually a busy day for him. The people who worked all week seemed to take that day to catch up with their doctoring. "Come in, Owen. Have you had breakfast?"

"Yes, I stopped in at the Dew Drop Inn and got my usual ham and eggs with a liberal dose of wisdom of the world from the customers."

Lanie smiled. "You can get whatever you want in the way of advice from the Dew Drop Inn. A lot of those men that go there every day don't even have a job, but they know exactly how to run the country. I'm not sure Aunt Kezia's up yet. Come along and we'll see."

The two went upstairs, and Lanie opened the door gently. "Are you awake, Aunt Kezia?"

"'Course I'm awake. What would I be doing, sleeping this late?"

Owen came in and grinned. "Some people wouldn't call six thirty in the morning late."

"What are you doing here, Merritt?"

"I was on my way out to doctor up the Carter kids."

"What's the matter with them younguns?"

"Probably chicken pox, but you know Mrs. Carter. She gets scared to death every time one of them sneezes. Here, let me listen to that ticker of yours."

Owen took out his stethoscope, sat down on the chair beside the bed, and listened to Kezia's heart. She watched him with her sharp black eyes, and when he nodded and removed the stethoscope, she said, "Back when we were on the Oregon Trail there wasn't no such thing as them stethoscopes. A doctor just laid his head on your chest and listened." She grinned wickedly and said, "I got to ailing once, and there was a good-looking young doctor. My first husband brought him by to look me over. He laid his head down on my chest, and I guess he got to liking it because he stayed there a mite too long to suit my husband. He jerked the doctor up and said, 'I didn't bring you here to get familiar with my wife.'"

"What'd the doctor do?"

"Oh, he turned red as a beet, stammered something, and then he left."

Lanie smiled. "Were all your husbands jealous of you, Aunt Kezia?" She was on the other side of the bed looking down at the old woman.

"Well, of course they was! They all thought I was as pretty as a speckled pup under a wagon."

"I saw that picture of you when you were first married. You were some pumpkin." Owen grinned. "I'll bet you gave those husbands a hard time."

"That's part of a wife's responsibility. You'll learn that one of these days, Merritt, if you ever talk anybody into marrying you."

Owen grinned and looked down at the old woman. "Well, I don't have any new medicine to give you."

"Don't need any. I ordered some of Doctor Tompkin's Native Oil from Australia. It'll be here tomorrow. It'll set me up fine."

"Aunt Kezia, I don't want you taking that awful stuff," Lanie protested.

Aunt Kezia stared at Lanie. "If it comes from Australia, it's got to be good, don't it now?"

Lanie gave a despairing look at Owen who winked at her. "Probably as good as some of the stuff we get from the drugstore. Are you sleeping all right?"

"No, I ain't. Are you?"

Owen was taken aback by the question. "Very well, I guess. Why aren't you sleeping?"

"Because I'm getting old, and old people don't sleep as much as young people. I'd thought a doctor would have knowed that."

Owen stood there, listening to Kezia fuss, then he took her hand and said, "Your heart sounds fairly good. I don't want you putting any strain on it though."

"You think I'm going to get up and wrestle a bear? Take him out of here, Lanie. He's like all them other doctors. He just looks at a body and makes some kind of guess."

Owen laughed and squeezed her hand. "I'll stop by later. You can tell me some more about the Oregon Trail."

The two left the room, and Lanie whispered, "How is she really, Owen?"

"Her heart's very irregular and weak. Don't let her do anything very strenuous."

"I won't."

"You're not going out on the Rolling Emporium, are you?"

"No. Davis has a ball game so Cody's going again."

"Has he got his driver's license?"

"No, Lolean Oz has been coming by to drive. She's seventeen and has a license." They had reached the kitchen now, and she said, "How about some fresh biscuits and blackberry jam?"

Owen's eyes lit up, and he sat down quickly. She poured them both some coffee, then sat down across from him. As they talked, he studied her face and noticed she was not as animated as usual. "Are you worried about something?"

"I'm worried about Maeva. We haven't heard from her in a long time. She was never one much for writing."

"I haven't heard from my brother Dave for a while. But the last letter I had said that he was working hard to find Thelma Mays. He thinks he will but it'll take a while."

"Maeva and Logan are singing in one of those awful nightclubs. You know what they're like. I wish she'd just come home."

"Maeva's a pretty firm young woman."

"Firm? Stubborn is what you mean, and you're right. She never gives up on anything."

Owen tarried as long as he could, enjoying his time with Lanie. Finally, he got up reluctantly and said, "The biscuits were good, and the blackberry jam was first class. Send for me if you need me, Lanie."

"I always do, don't I?"

⊶⋆⊷

Lolean had shown up wearing a pair of her brother's blue jeans and a white shirt that she had almost outgrown. It was warm for

September, and she put aside the light jacket she had worn. Cody had begun at once, as soon as they pulled out of the house, saying, "You ought not to be wearing those forked pants."

"What's wrong with them?"

"They're not fittin' for you to wear."

"They're my brother's old jeans. They're comfortable too."

Cody struggled to find some way to get Lolean to understand and wound up by giving her a lecture on the behavior of young women. He went into great detail as Lolean sat there driving slowly, listening, and nodding every once in a while.

"So, don't you see, Lolean, young women have to be careful because some young men aren't to be trusted."

"What do they do, Cody?"

Cody gave her a sharp look. "Why, you know what they do."

"You don't think I'd put up with improper advances from a man, do you?"

"Well, you wouldn't mean to, but women are weak. They are especially vulnerable where snakes are concerned."

"You mean Eve in the garden? That was a long time ago."

"Well, girls don't have much sense when a good-looking man shows them attention. They're just weak, Lolean."

Lolean had enjoyed her time with Cody immensely. She found herself highly amused by his rather puritanical views. During this year, she had filled out and grown up to young womanhood, so young men had been pursuing her. She found it humorous that Cody was as careful with her as if she were something very fragile.

Cody talked for a while about the importance of knowing the Bible, and Lolean said, "I love the Bible, Cody. You know what part I like?"

"Why, you like all of it."

"Well, there's one particular place that's extra good. It's the part that says that when a man takes him a wife he doesn't go anywhere for a year. He just stays at home and makes her happy, does everything she wants."

Cody's eyes flew open wide, and his jaw practically dropped. "Why, there's nothing like that in the Bible!"

"Well, of course there is. I'm surprised you don't know it. It's in Deuteronomy 24:5."

Cody scrambled to get his Bible out, but he discovered that he had torn out that page to give to someone. "I don't have that part of the Bible with me, but it don't say what you just said."

"Oh, yes, it does. I liked it so much I memorized it. It said, 'When a man hath taken a new wife, he shall not go out to war, neither shall he be charged with any business: but he shall be free at home one year, and shall cheer up his wife which he hath taken.'" Lolean turned to look Cody in the face. "You see? That's what a man's supposed to do. For a whole year, he's supposed to cheer up his wife. That means make her feel good and say sweet things to her and bring her presents."

Cody had fallen into shock. He had no memory of that verse, and he muttered, "I'll have to look that up when I get home, but it don't mean what you say."

"But, Cody, you always say the Bible always means exactly what it says. I've heard you say it a hundred times."

Cody struggled desperately to extricate himself. "Well, that's probably symbolic."

"No, I don't think so. I think it means just exactly what it says. Oh, Cody, I'm sure looking forward to that first year of marriage. It's going to be so wonderful." Cody said nothing, but at the very next stop at a house inhabited by a widow named Libby Pardue, he asked, "Mrs. Pardue, have you got a Bible?"

"Well, of course I've got a Bible."

"Could I look at it for a minute please?"

Mrs. Pardue stared at Cody and smiled. "I'll go get it, Cody."

Lolean had gotten out of the Rolling Emporium, and she stood now beside Cody, a smile playing around her lips. She said nothing and neither did Cody, but when Mrs. Pardue brought the Bible out he took it and thumbed through it until he got to the book of Deuteronomy. Lolean leaned forward and put her finger on the verse. "That's the verse right there, Cody. Verse five."

Cody's lips moved as he read it, and Mrs. Pardue said, "What does it say?"

Cody said, "Oh, you wouldn't be interested."

"I guess I would if it's in the Bible."

"It's the verse that says that when a man gets married he stays home from work for a year and pleases his wife, Mrs. Pardue."

Mrs. Pardue stared at Lolean. "Well, I sure missed out on that one. I was married twice, and neither one of my husbands stayed home a week to please me.'"

"Well, they just didn't know the Scripture, but Cody knows it, and I'm sure he's looking forward to having that year off."

Mrs. Pardue laughed. "Have you got her picked out yet, Cody?"

"No, I haven't got her picked out." He gave Lolean a scandalized look. "But I'll tell you one thing," he said grimly, "she's not going to be older than I am."

Lolean shrugged her shoulders. "I've tried to explain to Cody that when I get married it will be to a younger man so I can help him get rid of all his bad habits."

"And I've told you I don't *have* any bad habits," Cody said.

"Mrs. Pardue," Lolean said, "we got some new material here. It sure would look nice if you could make yourself a dress with it. It's just your color."

Mrs. Pardue went with Lolean inside to look at the material. She came out with a length of it and paid Cody, saying, "You've got a fine young saleslady here, Cody. You should have brought her around a long time ago."

"Oh, I'll be coming pretty regularly now," Lolean said.

"No, I'll get my driver's license."

"The Bible says two are better than one. Did you know that, Cody?"

"Of course, I knew it."

"Well, two of us are better than one of us. Thank you, Mrs. Pardue."

When they got back late that afternoon, Lolean told Lanie all about their adventures and giggled. "Cody's so cute. He thinks he knows everything, but he's really green as grass."

"You work on him, Lolean. You see if you can stop him from this foolishness of trying to convert everybody he meets."

"He didn't do it today. He was too busy trying to defend himself. I showed him the verse in Deuteronomy that said a man, when he takes a new wife, he's not supposed to work for a year to stay home and please his wife. To cheer her up, the Bible said."

"I don't remember that verse."

"Cody didn't remember it either, but I bet he won't forget it now. Well, school's started now, so I guess it will just be Saturday when I go with Cody, but you can depend on me."

"I'll do that, Lolean."

Maeva, Logan, and Thelma looked ahead, all of them tired of the flat, arid Texas prairie. The scant grass was brown and the trees were twisted.

"Them mesquite trees are awful looking," Logan said. "I reckon if hell has trees, that's about what they'll look like."

Finally, they came to what appeared to be a very small town and Maeva said, "What town's that?"

"I don't know. Not much of a town." They passed a small sign that said Bushland, Texas.

Maeva looked at the map and said, "We're almost to Amarillo."

"Well, if we're that far along, we'll be home before you know it."

"Look, there's a café," Thelma said. "I sure would like to have a good hamburger."

"Well, let's just go get one."

"Do we have enough money, Logan?" Maeva said.

"The Lord provides what we need."

Maeva laughed. "You're talking more like a preacher every day."

Logan gave her a fond look. "It's getting to be downright entertaining to be a Christian. I should have done it a long time ago."

The three entered the restaurant with the name of the Horned Steer Café. There were several men in there, a rough-looking sort, and they kept eyeing Maeva.

The hamburgers came, and they ate hungrily. When they were almost through, a burly man with red hair and bright blue eyes came over and leaned over Maeva. "Well, ain't you a pretty little thing."

Maeva shot a glance at Logan, for when a man approached her with this kind of talk it usually set Logan off. He looked up lazily at the big man and said, "She is pretty, isn't she?"

"She your wife?"

"No, she's my sister."

"Your sister! You don't look alike."

"Well, she's my sister in the Lord, I mean to say."

Maeva's eyes danced. "Sit down here. I want to ask you about your soul. Have you ever been born again?"

The big man stared at her. "What?"

"I asked you if you had ever been born again. You know. Have you ever been washed in the blood of the Lamb? Are you on your way to heaven? Have you hit the Glory Road? You understand any of that?"

The big man backed up, his eyes wide with shock. "Get away from me. I don't need no woman preacher!"

Maeva and Logan began laughing. Maeva said, "For years I've been trying to figure out a way to get rid of dumbos like that, and now I found it. All you have to do is ask them if they know the Lord. That puts the run on them, it looks like."

Logan winked at her and grinned. "Just keep it up, girl." He pulled the wrinkled map out of his pocket and unfolded it. "Here we are right outside of Amarillo. You know, we'll be in Oklahoma pretty soon. When we get across Oklahoma, we'll be in Arkansas first thing you know."

The two talked with excitement about what was going to happen, and Thelma was watching them. Her health had improved, and the bruises were fading. She had been amazed at how the two had changed. "You two really believe we can do all this stuff? That we can get home and find some judge that will listen to me and get your daddy out of jail?"

Maeva reached over, put her arm around Thelma, and hugged her. "God can do anything."

"That's right, and He's going to. Well, let's hit the road. I'm anxious to see some good old Arkansas territory."

⊷⇒ CHAPTER 11 ⇐⊷

Y ou've been cooking all day, Lanie." Davis had popped into the
kitchen to check on a snack. "We got company coming?"

Lanie turned. She was wearing an apron over her pale blue pat-
terned dress. There was a smudge of flour on her right cheek. "Roger's
coming tonight."

"Well, it looks like we're not going to run short of food. Can I
help you in any way?"

"No, it's about under control. I was trying some new things
tonight. Why don't you go help Corliss wash up? She's been outside
wallowing in the mud. She looks like a pig."

"I'll take care of it."

As soon as Davis left, Lanie checked the oven and nodded with
satisfaction. She was pleased that Roger was coming. He had asked
her to the movies, but instead she had insisted he come over for a
home cooked meal. He was doing some surveying work and was away
from home a good deal of the time so home cooking was just what
he wanted.

She had just taken the biscuits out of the oven and put them in
the heater at the top of the stove when Cody came in, followed by
Roger. "I found this fellow hanging around the front porch. Do you
want to let him in the house?" Cody grinned.

"Don't be foolish, Cody. You go get cleaned up."

"There's nothing wrong with me."

"You go take a bath."

"But I didn't fall down all day."

"I'm not arguing with you. Go take a bath or you don't get anything to eat."

"Women have gotten uppity, haven't they, Roger? I knew after we taught them to count money and let them eat at the table with us things would go downhill!"

Roger laughed at this, and Cody left the room. "I like Cody. He's a fine young fellow."

"I'm surprised he let you in the house without making you show your baptismal certificate."

"Well, he straightened me out on that the last time I saw him. Made me tell him how I got saved. I think he's giving the same treatment to everybody he meets. Doesn't sit too well with some." Roger came over and sniffed the air. "Something smells good. Is that you or your biscuits?"

"It's the biscuits. Now you behave yourself, Roger."

Roger reached out, put his arms around her, and kissed her on the cheek. "I've missed you, Lanie," he whispered. "Did you miss me?"

"Yes, I did. Now, you sit over there and behave yourself and tell me what all you've been doing."

Roger sat down and began recounting his activities, but he had barely gotten started when a knock sounded at the front door.

"Excuse me, Roger. Let me go get that."

"Oh, I'll get it. You finish up on your cooking there."

Lanie was working on her new casserole, which she called Company's Coming Casserole. She loved to try new dishes, and this one had been given to her by Nelson Prather. He claimed he had made it up himself. She had cooked up ground beef until it was brown, put in tomato sauce, then layered cottage cheese, cream cheese, sour cream, green onions, and green pepper with noodles, and covered it with melted butter. She pulled it out of the oven, poked it with a straw, and muttered, "I don't know if it's any good or not. Nelson swears it's the best thing he's ever eaten, but I'm not sure he's the best judge."

She suddenly turned and saw Owen come into the room. "Why, Owen, what are you doing here?"

"Well, I want to see Aunt Kezia. I've got something that might help her."

"What is it? A new medicine?"

"No, not new exactly. It's nitroglycerine tablets."

Roger stared at him. "Nitroglycerine! Why, that's an explosive."

"Yes, it is, but they've done a lot of experimental work, and they found that in small doses it's good for heart patients. What it does is open up the arteries real quick. You see this little bottle? I want you to be sure that Aunt Kezia carries this bottle everywhere she goes. If she ever has a heart attack, or you think she's about to, have her take one of these. If it doesn't work, give her another one in five minutes. That ought to do it."

"It sounds dangerous, Owen."

"I think it's all right as long as she follows the instructions. I'll just go up, give it to her, and explain it. How are you doing, Roger?"

"All right. And you, Doctor Merritt?"

"Staying busy." Owen left the room.

Roger said, "Are you worried about Aunt Kezia?"

"Yes, I am. Her heart's not good at all. I hope she doesn't have to take any of this medicine. It sounds terrible."

The two sat there, and the meal was ready when Owen came back. "Well, she's okay. I explained it to her, and as usual, she's always excited about some kind of new patent medicine, but you don't take this unless you really need it. I preached that to her, and you do the same thing, Lanie."

"All right, Owen." She hesitated and then said, "It's fairly late. Would you care to stay for supper?"

"Why, that would be fine. I'm as hungry as a bear."

"Well, then I'll just set another plate. There's plenty of food."

The whole family, along with Owen and Roger, sat down, and Cody asked the blessing, a rather long involved one. As soon as he said amen, there was a knock at the door.

"Who is that coming at supper time?" Davis said. "I'll get it." He got up and soon returned with Brent Hayden. Hayden was wearing a suede jacket, a white shirt, and a tie. He was one of the neatest dressers that any of them had ever seen. "I didn't mean to interrupt your meal, but I have some good news for you, Lanie. You want to hear it in public or in private?"

"Oh, just say it, Brent."

Brent stepped around the table where Lanie was sitting, reached into his pocket, pulled out an envelope. "Read that."

Lanie opened the envelope and said, *Poetry?* Is that a good magazine?"

"It's the premier poetry magazine of America, and they are taking three of your poems. There's the check that goes with it."

Everybody began to babble at once, and Corliss came around to look over her shoulder. "Is that money, Lanie?"

"The same thing as money."

"Will you buy me something pretty with it?"

"I expect I will when we go to town." Lanie looked up at Brent, and her eyes were shining. "This is wonderful news, Brent."

"It is good news. This is not just some little magazine. It's the top. The best. You're on your way up, Lanie."

"Oh, Brent, sit down and eat. I want to hear more about this magazine."

Hayden hesitated. "Oh, I wouldn't want to interrupt."

"I've got plenty of food. Davis, get a chair for Brent, and I'll get another plate."

There was a brief flurry of activity, and then Cody said, "Now I got to say the blessing all over again."

"Oh no, you don't," Davis said. "This food's already been blessed."

"Well, Brent wasn't here."

"Well, the food was so you just start eating. Brent, don't pay any attention to Cody. Just lay your ears back and plow right at it."

Brent laughed. "I think I will. This looks good."

Lanie held up the platter of fried chicken and said, "I bet none of you ever had anything like this."

"Why, it looks like fried chicken," Davis said.

"It's buttermilk fried chicken."

"You fried this chicken in buttermilk?" Cody said. "Why, that won't do."

"Then you don't have to eat any, Cody."

"Well, I'll just try one, but it couldn't be good."

Cody plucked a leg off and bit into it. He chewed at it and then said, "You know, this ain't at all bad. Give me some more, Davis."

"No, you don't like buttermilk fried chicken," Davis said. "That's all you get."

"I tried something new tonight," Lanie said. "I got the recipe from Nelson Prather. I call it Company's Coming Casserole." She explained all the ingredients, and then Owen said, "Let me try some of that. If it doesn't kill me, Roger, you can have some."

Owen took a big spoonful of the Company's Coming Casserole and put it in his mouth. "This is downright good! I thought Nelson specialized in superstitions."

"He's a good cook too," Lanie said. "I didn't know what that would taste like."

The table was covered with cat head biscuits, collard greens, corn on the cob, fried squash, deviled eggs, and for a time the dining room was filled with the sound of laughter. Lanie said, "I hope you saved room for blackberry cobbler with fresh cream."

"I wish you had told me," Roger said. "I would have saved more room."

"You always find a way for dessert."

The blackberry cobbler was outstanding, and afterwards they all insisted on helping do the dishes. It was a little crowded in the kitchen, and Corliss insisted on singing for them while they did the dishes. She sang several songs, and finally she amused them all by asking, "Do you want to hear a song about a chigger?" Of course, everyone did, and she began to sing in a clear voice:

There was a little chigger
And he wasn't any bigger
Than the wee small head of a pin.
But the bump that he raises
Well it itches like blazes
And that's where the rub comes in.
Comes in, comes in, and that's where the rub comes in.

"That's the best chigger song I ever heard in my life," Roger said. "Did you make that up?"

"No, I heard somebody singing it, and I liked it."

Finally the dishes were done, and Lanie waited for the company to leave. She had invited Roger for this was to be his night. But neither man showed any inclination, and finally Corliss said, "Let's go in the parlor, and we can make some music."

"That sounds like a good idea," Owen said quickly. "Nothing like music after a good meal like that."

They all went to the parlor, and soon the room filled with music. All the Freeman children played. Davis played guitar, Cody played on the mandolin, and Lanie could play almost any stringed instrument. The music continued for quite a while, and all the time Lanie kept expecting Owen and Brent to leave.

Davis whispered in her ear, "You got three fellows here, and they're all determined to be the last one here with you."

She gave him a warning look, but as the evening wore on, it was obvious that the three men were doing exactly what Davis had said.

Corliss had the finest time of all. She went from one visitor to another pumping them with questions, some of them rather embarrassing, but Corliss was never shy with anyone.

Finally, Lanie knew something had to be done. "Well, I hate to be the one to call a halt to a musical, but I've got to go take care of Aunt Kezia, and we've all got to get up early in the morning."

Roger shot a look at Owen, but there was nothing for it. He got to his feet and said, "That was a fine meal, Lanie."

Lanie went over and whispered to him, "You'll have to come again, Roger, and next time we'll keep it a secret."

Roger laughed and said, "That sounds good to me." He left, and Owen waited for Brent to leave. Brent caught the look and smiled. "Well, I just came over to give you the good news. How's the new project coming, the novel?"

"I feel like I don't know what I'm doing."

"Well, I want to take a look at what you've got. I'll meet you at the library tomorrow."

"All right, Brent."

Brent left, and Owen stood there looking somewhat ill at ease. "I didn't mean to butt in and stay all evening."

"Didn't you, Owen?"

"No, I didn't. I hope you don't think —"

Lanie laughed. "It's all right. We're always glad to see you here, and that's good news about the medicine for Aunt Kezia."

"The meal was fine," Owen said, and he stood there making small talk. Finally, Davis came in and said, "You still saying good night, Doctor Merritt?"

"I was just on my way." Owen left and Davis came over, and his eyes were filled with fun. "Well, that was quite an evening."

"It was fun, wasn't it?"

"Three suitors in your parlor. That's as good a show as I've seen. Next time let's sell tickets."

"Oh, go to bed, Davis."

Lanie waited to put Corliss to bed and was cajoled into reading a chapter of *The Wizard of Oz.*

"I like Owen, don't you?" Corliss said sleepily.

"Yes, I do."

"And I like Roger especially. He always plays with me, and Mr. Brent's a nice man too."

"They're all three nice."

"If you could marry all three of them, it would be good."

Shocked by this remark, Lanie leaned over. "What do you mean?"

"Well, Owen's a doctor. We wouldn't ever have to pay any doctor's bills. Roger's got money so that would take care of that. And Mr. Brent helps you with your writing."

"A woman can't marry three men."

"Oh, I know it," Corliss said. "Which one do you like the best?"

"Good night, sweetheart." She left the room hurriedly, and the question stayed with her all the time she was preparing for bed. She took a bit of time to write in her journal.

September 22, 1932

Well, we had quite a time at supper. Roger, Owen, and Brent were all here. They wouldn't leave until Davis practically shoved them out the door. It was funny and yet I was embarrassed. Davis says not many girls have three suitors sitting around waiting on her.

She looked at what she had written and then scratched it out. "I don't want such a foolish thing in my journal," she said. She got into bed; Cap'n Brown hopped up and curled against her, purring like a small engine. "Good night, Cap'n Brown."

Cap'n Brown did not answer. He was already asleep.

CHAPTER 12

"I reckon if I'm able to breathe, I'm able to go to church." Aunt Kezia shot a hard look at Lanie and then added petulantly, "Never done nobody no harm to go to the house of God, did it now?"

Lanie was concerned by Kezia's request. She had announced her intention of going to church, and Lanie had tried to persuade her that it was too much of a strain.

"Well, I got these pills Merritt gave me. If I have any trouble, I'll just pop one down."

"I'm going to keep those pills. You're too quick to take medicine, and these are very dangerous."

"You can keep them if you want to, but I'm going to church and that's final."

Lanie knew that when Aunt Kezia got her mind made up there was not much anyone could do to change it. At the same time she thought, *Well, if she had a heart attack, a church would be a good place to have it.* "All right," she said, "you can go. Let me help you get dressed."

When they reached the church, it was somewhat later than usual. Lanie said, "Do you want to stay out in the auditorium or go to children's church, Corliss?"

"I want to stay at the big church."

"All right. Davis, you hang onto her now. Don't let her do anything embarrassing."

"Why, she wouldn't do that." Davis grinned. "Would you, Corliss?"

"I don't know. I might."

Lanie smiled and turned to Kezia. "Now, you sit right here, Kezia, with Cody. If you want anything, he'll get it for you."

"Let me have them pills. You'll be up in the choir. I might need one in a hurry."

"You don't need them. If I see you're having a problem, I'll come out of the choir. Now behave yourself."

"You sure are getting to be an uppity female, Lanie Freeman."

Lanie left and made her way toward the choir room. Colin Ryan stopped her and asked, "How is everybody?"

Lanie hesitated. "I guess I need a special touch from God, Pastor, an encouragement of some kind."

"You worried about Maeva?"

"Yes, I am, and Aunt Kezia's heart is very weak."

"You know, the old Methodists had people who called themselves exhorters. It's too bad we don't have them here."

"Exhorters? I never heard of that. What did they do?"

"Well, they went from church to church, and they encouraged the saints."

"Well, I wish one were here today," Lanie said. "I need one."

"God's going to honor your faithfulness, Lanie. I know sometimes we get a little low in spirit, but God's always there."

"Thank you, Pastor. I'll remember that." She went to the choir room where she put on her robe. She spoke mechanically to those about her, but she was thinking about all the difficulties that lay ahead. Finally, it was time for them to go, and they filed into the sanctuary. As Lanie took her place, she looked out over the congregation. These were people she had known all of her life, and the church had been a source of strength to her. Her eyes fell on her own family, and she was pleased to see that Kezia had more color in her cheeks.

The song leader, Wayne Dixon, came forward and started the service. He gave a brief prayer and then said, "We're going to sing an old favorite of all of you, I'm sure. I've always thought this hymn sums up all I believe about serving God. You all know it—"Jesus Paid it All."

Lanie had sung the song hundreds of times, probably, but somehow as she sang the words, they began to sink down into her heart.

There were other songs, but Lanie could not get the words of the chorus out of her mind. *Jesus paid it all. All to Him I owe. Sin hath left a crimson stain. He washed it white as snow.*

Brother Colin Ryan got up to preach. As usual, he was dressed rather casually, but the congregation was used to this by now. He opened his Bible. "We all know that David was a man after God's own heart. That's quite a tribute. I wish it would be said of me, of you, of all of us. There was something special in David, and I think Psalm 3 gives the answer to why David was a man after God's own heart."

He opened his Bible and said, "You know, this psalm was written, as your heading tells you, when Absalom attempted to kill his father David. What a terrible time! Absalom was his favorite child, and now David is running for his life with Absalom dead set on killing him. You can read for yourself the history in the book of Second Samuel, but you know the story. But there's one thing about this psalm that never ceases to amaze me. I want to read the first four verses."

> *Lord, how are they increased that trouble me!*
> > *many are they that rise up against me.*
> *Many there be which say of my soul,*
> > *There is no help for him in God. Selah.*
> *But thou, O Lord, art a shield for me;*
> > *my glory, and the lifter up of mine head.*
> *I cried unto the Lord with my voice,*
> > *and he heard me out of his holy hill. Selah.*

"Now this is a prayer," Brother Colin said, "that any of us might pray. To cry unto the Lord, as the verse four says. But the verse that always makes me see David in a new light is verse five. Remember now nothing has changed. He's still a fugitive running from his son—a son he loved more than life—who was trying to kill him. What would you do if you had a problem like that?"

Colin Ryan looked out over the congregation. "We know what David did because verse five tells us. It said, 'I laid me down and slept.' Isn't that marvelous? With death at his right hand and betrayal at his left, David went to sleep. How could David do that? Because he had just called on the Lord. 'I cried unto the Lord with my voice,' and he knew that the Lord had heard him. "He heard me out of his holy hill."

"That's what I want to speak to you about. Look at verse six. 'I will not be afraid of ten thousands of people, that have set themselves against me round about.' That's the sermon this morning—do not be afraid."

Brother Ryan began to preach, but he had not gotten far when his message was interrupted. There was the sound of automobiles roaring up and horns blowing. Lanie looked out with astonishment. She could not see through the stained-glass window, but there was something going on. Everyone was turning around to look.

Suddenly the door burst open, and Sister Myrtle Poindexter appeared. Lanie could not believe her eyes as to who was trailing the sister!

There Sister Myrtle was holding onto Maeva with her right hand and holding Logan Satterfield with her left. She was shouting, "Glory to God—glory to God!" Without really meaning to, Lanie pushed her way past the other choir members and ran forward to meet Maeva. She grabbed her and cried out, "Maeva, you're back!"

"I sure am, sister." Maeva's eyes filled with tears.

"What are you doing here?"

Sister Poindexter heard this. "Pastor, I apologize for breaking into your service, but I saw this young couple come in with another young lady right by our church, and I ran out and stopped them. They told me what had happened, and I brought our whole congregation here.

I don't want my flock to miss no miracle. Now," she said firmly, "you two tell the church what's happened."

Maeva took Logan's hand and Thelma's. She pulled them to the front and turned to face the congregation, two congregations actually, and her voice was at first strong as she said, "You all know me. I've been nothing but trouble to my family, as a girl and woman. It wasn't my daddy's fault or my mama's or any of my brothers and sisters. I was mean and low-down." She looked straight at Lanie and smiled. "They put up with me when anybody else would have put me out. Well, I put myself out. I always knew my daddy didn't kill that man Duke Biggins like the witnesses said, so I went to find Thelma Mays. We knew she had seen the whole thing but she never testified. This is Thelma. She's going to tell the truth to the judge, and my daddy's going to get out of prison."

There were sounds of hallelujahs and "Praise the Lord." Most of Sister Poindexter's flock was Pentecostal, though a few were Baptist in origin.

"I want to tell you something now. We found Thelma because Doctor Merritt's brother Dave helped us. We left California with no money and no food. We were sitting beside the road. Logan was playing his guitar, and I was singing. This car stopped, and a woman got out. She was a Pentecostal lady, I could tell. She had her hair in a bun and sleeves down to her wrists and no jewelry. Her name was Sister Smith. She lit right into us and told us that God had sent us. We were going to sing and play at her meeting that night. Logan tried to tell her we weren't even saved, but she said that didn't matter. So, she just about made us go to church, didn't she, Logan?"

"I'd be afraid to argue with Sister Smith," Logan said. He smiled and looked out over the congregation. "None of my family is here. None of them are saved, but they're going to get saved. I'm believing God for that."

"What happened was we got to church, and Logan played and I sang, and then there was an altar call, and Sister Smith prayed for me—" Tears came then to Maeva Freeman's eyes. She had never cried in public. She was not a crying young woman, but she dashed the tears away and in a tremulous voice said, "Sister Smith prayed for me, and I prayed for myself, and Jesus came into my heart."

There were loud shouts of amen, praise the Lord, and glory to God from the whole congregation.

"And the same thing happened to Logan. Logan, you tell them how you got saved."

Logan gave his story, which was simple enough. "My granddaddy was a Methodist preacher. I should have been saved years ago, but praise the Lord I'm saved now."

Maeva turned and said, "Have you given the invitation yet, pastor?"

"No, not yet."

"Well, if you'll give one, I'll be the first to come. I want to be baptized and serve the Lord."

"So do I, Preacher," Logan said.

Colin Ryan was well acquainted with the Baptist tradition that anyone who came had to be voted into the fellowship of the church by the membership. "Everyone in favor of welcoming Maeva Freeman and Logan Satterfield into the family of God shout amen."

Everybody in the congregation, Pentecostal and Baptist alike, shouted loudly their amens.

Davis leaned over to his brother. "That's the first time Pentecostals have ever voted in a Baptist church." He grinned. "You going to say it's unseemly?"

For once Cody Freeman was not argumentative. "No," he said. "If God wants to do it this way, that's fine to me."

The next thing was to welcome the two new believers into the fellowship of the church, and everybody wanted to shake their hands. When the lawyer Orrin Pierce came to Maeva, he said, "I'm happy for your decision."

"You've got to hear what Thelma saw. It'll get my daddy out of jail."

"I believe it will. The law is slow moving, but I want to talk to her as soon as this service is over. If she's willing to testify, I'll start tomorrow morning to get your daddy a new trial."

People were talking and hugging Maeva, and suddenly Lolean came over to Cody. "I'm downright happy because of your sister Maeva, and I know God's going to get your daddy out of prison." She leaned over suddenly, hugged Cody, and kissed him on the cheek.

"Are you crazy?" Cody gasped. "You can't kiss fellows in church! The Bible says!"

"No, it doesn't." Lolean was ready. She opened the Bible and said, "It's right here in Romans 16:16. It says, 'Salute one another with an holy kiss.' You see here—I got it underlined."

Cody stared at the verse and swallowed hard. He looked confused, which was unusual for him. Finally he whispered, "Lolean, are you sure that was a holy kiss?"

"Well, sure it was."

"Okay. I guess it's all right then."

Davis had been standing close enough to catch this interchange. He came over and said, "Cody, I never thought I'd see you kissing a girl in church."

"I didn't kiss a girl. She kissed me, and it was a holy kiss."

"Well, it looked like a regular kiss to me, Cody."

"You don't understand these things, Davis. The Bible says salute one another with a holy kiss. I'm surprised you don't know that."

"Well, come on. I guess it's all right. If you'll excuse me, I'm going to find some pretty girl to salute."

That was a night to be remembered at the Baptist church. People would date things by the occurrences, and if something important happened, they would say it was right after or right before Maeva and Logan came to the Lord in the church.

As for Lanie, she was holding onto Maeva, and her heart filled with joy. She whispered, "Lord, I'm sorry I doubted you. I hope I never will again!"

PART THREE

A Free Man

⤙ CHAPTER 13 ⤚

September had swept in with a frigid breath sweeping the mountains, and soon, Lanie knew, the trees would lose their green hue. They would turn to red, yellow, and gold, and the woods would be clothed with glorious colors. It was a time of year she loved perhaps more than all the rest. The hot summers were leaving, and winter lay ahead, but the fall was the time when the air was like wine.

Sitting in her bedroom beside the window, Lanie stared out. She watched Corliss who was playing a game with Beau and Booger; the child made up games and incorporated the animals on the farm as well as those humans she could enlist to act them out. Lanie smiled as Corliss spoke something to Booger, and the big bloodhound lifted his head and howled. It was a mournful sound, and Booger had a mournful face, and yet he was, all in all, a happy dog.

I wish I knew what was going on in Corliss's head. She's so smart. There's no telling what she'll do as she grows up.

She shifted her gaze then and watched Davis throw baseballs at a target he had made from a box with a hole not much larger than the ball. He wound up and threw with a strength and power that amazed Lanie. Time after time, the ball made a white streak and disappeared into the hole with a loud thump. Even those that didn't go into the hole didn't miss by much. She thought then of his offer to play professional baseball and knew her dad had advised against it. Still, Davis had not made up his mind.

The grandfather clock downstairs struck ten times, and Lanie turned her attention back to the sheets of paper spread out on the table. She picked up her Bible and read again the story of the Last Supper. She had been writing a poem trying to incorporate some of the events of that night, and she read again the verse that she had put at the top of the poem:

Jesus riseth from supper, and laid aside his garments; and took a towel, and girded himself. After that he poureth water into a basin, and began to wash the disciples' feet, and to wipe them with the towel wherewith he was girded.

She had been puzzling over the title for days, and now it came to her: *Footwashing.* She wrote it down firmly over the verse.

She had worked hard on the poem, staying up late and rising early. Somehow, the Last Supper had always had a tremendous effect on her. Every time she took communion at church, it was a time of self-examination for her and a time when it seemed that Jesus revealed Himself to her very clearly.

"What must it have been like," she murmured. "All the disciples were thinking about Jesus as a king, and here He washes their feet—the act of the lowliest servant in anybody's household. What must they have been thinking?"

She had worked hard on the poem, and now she read it aloud, trying to capture the disciples' thoughts:

When Jesus stooped, Bartholomew thought,
To wash my feet, the sight of him kneeling there went through
My heart! He's in some kind of prison;
Almost it seems his soul is sick to death.
Quiet he is tonight, as if some fatal vision
All but stopped his living breath.

Have we grown tired of daily wonders?
Too many miracles numb the heart (as thunders
startle first, then petrify the fragile ear)

And yet when first I saw a milky eye
So sudden as his word turn dewy clear,
Remember my wild cry?

This miracle we've seen tonight
(God's Messiah kneeling humbly in our sight,
Washing grimy feet) I never can escape —
A love so strong it dares to don humility,
To make of it a royal cape,
Why — that's miracle enough for me!

Lanie was not entirely pleased with the poem and knew it would need more work. She looked up and saw Dorsey Pender, the mailman, coming down the street. She had been expecting to hear from a publisher she had sent some poems to, so she quickly put away her writing materials and ran down the steps. She went outside and greeted him, a tall lanky man with a face tanned from years of delivering the mail in rain or sleet or snow. "Hello, Dorsey."

"Why, hello there, Miss Lanie."

"Do you have any mail for me?"

"Well, we got a new Monkey Ward Catalog." He handed her the bulky catalog, and as usual, began passing along information. He did not consider himself a gossip, just a bearer of tidings to the town of Fairhope.

"I suppose you heard about Mamie Hardesty." Without waiting for an answer, Dorsey nodded and said, "Yep, she's going to marry up with Ralph Taylor. The two of them are going to have a hard time of it. You know how Mamie is, stubborn and willful, and that fellow she's marrying ain't much better."

Lanie stood there waiting while Dorsey went over the news of what people in Fairhope were doing, and finally he said, "Everybody's talking about how your sister Maeva and that Satterfield fella come back from California. There's quite a bit of talk about that pair going off together, them not being married and all."

"I'm sure there was, Dorsey. Did you have any mail for me?"

But Dorsey was not through yet. "Where is Miss Maeva? Is she on the place today?"

"No, she and Logan have gone to see my dad."

"I reckon they've gone to tell him about bringing Thelma Mays back."

"I expect they will tell him that."

"Well, I don't know how much it'll do to have her as a witness. She's no better now than she was then, you know, back when she was here."

"She's a changed woman, I think, Dorsey. Now please. Do you have any mail?"

"No, no mail today. Did you hear about Willie Summerlin?"

"I'm sorry, Dorsey. I don't have time. You're going to have to tell me about Willie the next time."

Pender gave her a sorrowful look then shrugged his thin shoulders and shuffled off toward the next house.

"That man is just a gossip factory," Lanie said. She walked over to where Corliss was digging a hole in the ground with a spoon. "What are you digging for?"

"I'm looking for buried treasure."

"Well, if you find any, I get half."

"All right," Corliss agreed.

"What kind of a game were you playing with Booger and Beau?"

"We was playing that I was a princess, Beau there was the prince, and Booger was a wicked, evil king."

"Booger's not very wicked."

"He has to do what I tell him," Corliss said cheerfully. She looked up and Lanie said, "What's that dirt around your mouth?"

"I ate some of it."

"You ate dirt? Why'd you do that?"

"I wanted to see what it tasted like."

"Well, did you like it?"

"No, it's awful. I spit it out. I'm not going to eat dirt anymore. When will Maeva and Logan come back?"

"It'll probably be pretty late. Now, you go ahead and dig for your treasure. I've got to go wash clothes."

⊶

"This prison always gives me the creeps," Maeva said. She glanced at Logan who was pulling the old car up into the prison parking lot. "Do prisons bother you?"

Logan turned and smiled at her. "Not as long as I'm on the outside. Well, come on. Let's go see your dad."

The two of them entered the front gate and went through the process of visiting one of the inmates. They were taken to the visitors' room and saw that there was only one other inmate there talking to an older woman. The two of them waited impatiently. Finally, the door opened and Forrest came through. He took one look at Maeva, smiled, and came toward her opening his arms.

She hugged him hard and said, "Daddy, it's so good to see you!"

"Wonderful to see you, Maeva." He reached out his hand and said, "Logan, you brought her back."

"I sure did, Mr. Freeman."

"Daddy, we've got the most wonderful news."

"Well, what is it?"

"It's about Thelma Mays."

"I've heard a little about that. I got a letter from Lanie, but I want to hear all about it. Here, could you drink some coffee?" He poured three cups of the rank coffee in mismatched mugs, and they all sat down. "Now, tell me all about this business."

Maeva started, her eyes flashing as she told how Doctor Merritt's brother Dave had helped them find Thelma. She related dramatically how Thelma had been unwilling to come back and testify until her boyfriend had beaten her up and abandoned her.

"We didn't have any money to get back, but God worked a miracle."

"He sure did, Mr. Freeman. A preacher lady came by. I was plunking on my guitar, and Maeva was singing. Her name was Sister Smith. She almost forced us to go sing and play at her meeting."

"We told her we weren't even Christians. She said God was going to use us anyway."

Forrest sat back and watched the two. His heart was full, for he'd had this story already in a letter from Lanie, but he wanted to hear them tell it. He waited until they were through, then said, "So, the two of you got saved right there in that meeting."

"That's right, Daddy. I know you been praying for me all my life, but I'm a Christian now and so is Logan."

Forrest was smiling, but he said almost sadly, "I wish your mama could have known about that."

Maeva said, "I wish I'd been a better girl."

"Well, you can't change the past, but you can do something about the future."

"Orrin is working to get you a new trial, Daddy, and I just know God is going to get you out of this place."

"Well, it will take a miracle, but it can be done."

"Thelma's story ought to do it. She says all that stuff that the Bigginses said about the shooting was lies, and she's willing to go before a judge and tell the truth."

"Well, you two have done fine, and I know God's going to reward you for it." He hesitated and then said, "What are you going to do now?"

"What do you mean, Daddy?"

"Well, I mean are you going to go on singing?"

"You mean in saloons and bars? No, we're not going to do that, neither one of us."

"Well, I'm glad to hear that. God's given you both wonderful talents, and somehow I know He's going to use them."

Forrest Freeman sat there, his heart crying out thanks to God. *Thank you, Lord, for bringing this girl into the family of God, and thank you for this man who's been faithful without much encouragement. Put your hand on them, Lord, and touch their lives.*

☞

It was late on Wednesday afternoon before Orrin Pierce finally was able to see Judge Lawrence Simons. Pierce was a handsome man of thirty with premature silver hair and piercing blue eyes. He drank more than he should, but he'd had nothing to drink at all on this day for he wanted his mind to be clear.

"The judge will see you now."

"Thank you, ma'am." Orrin made his way past the receptionist into the judge's inner chamber.

Simons glanced up and said, "Hello, Mr. Pierce. What can I do for you?"

"It's about the Forrest Freeman case, Judge."

Simons had presided over the trial of Forrest Freeman and had been the one who had pronounced sentence on him. Somehow, the judge had never felt comfortable with that decision, but the evidence that came before the court was incontrovertible. Two witnesses had sworn that Forrest Freeman had walked in and without provocation had shot Duke Biggins dead.

"That's kind of ancient history, isn't it, Orrin?"

"There's something new, Judge. Did you ever hear of Thelma Mays?" When the judge shook his head, Orrin quickly laid out the case. "She was there the night of the killing."

"She never testified."

"No, she was in the next room, and she was scared. But she saw the whole thing. I've taken a deposition for you to look at."

Judge Simons took the folder but shook his head. "Just tell me what it says."

"It says that the two witnesses lied. She says that Forrest came into the room and tried to reason with them, and they threatened to kill him. He had a gun that he used mostly for snakes out in the woods. He pulled it to keep them away, and Duke grabbed his arm. The two struggled, and the gun went off. She says it was purely an accident. She also said that she heard them boasting to friends later how they were going to put Forrest in the penitentiary forever."

"Well, that does make a little different story."

"I need to talk to you about a new trial, Judge."

Simons shook his head and doubt crossed his face. "Orrin, you know something about politics. Governor Matthews is in a dogfight with Carleton Hobbs in the race for governor. I suppose you remember Hobbs."

"I sure do. He was the prosecuting attorney at Forrest's trial."

"Well, he's the attorney general now, and he would have to agree to a new trial. Frankly, I think you'd be wasting your time, but you'll have to try."

"Thank you, Judge. I'll go see."

Simons got up and shook hands with Orrin Pierce. "I've never felt right about the way that trial went. It just didn't feel right, and I think you've got something of the truth here, but I don't think you'll get around Hobbs. He'd have to admit he was wrong, and he's not likely to do that—not in the middle of a race for governor with Big Bill Matthews."

Carleton Hobbs was a small man, rather fierce-looking, and his voice was sharp as he said, "I don't see anything in this deposition that changes things, Pierce. I can't agree to a new trial."

"But it directly contradicts the evidence of the two witnesses who claimed it was cold-blooded murder."

"It's Thelma Mays's word against theirs. I'm sorry, but it's just not enough for me to order a new trial."

Orrin tried everything he could, but he could not get Hobbs to change his mind. He left the office depressed and went at once to the Freeman house to give the bad news to the family. He went into the living room, and they all gathered around him.

"It's not good news, is it, Mr. Pierce?" Maeva said, watching the lawyer's face.

"It's a political matter. The prosecuting attorney is running against the sitting governor. He's not about to admit that he made a mistake of any kind."

"But isn't there anything we can do?"

Orrin shook his head. "I'll be thinking about a way."

Maeva threw her head back and said, "I've found out that God's able to do anything He wants, and if He wants Daddy to have a new trial, He'll find a way."

Orrin Pierce stared at Maeva. "You're right about that, Miss Maeva. We just have to get God activated somehow."

After Orrin left, Lanie said, "We've all got to be praying that Orrin will find a way."

"He didn't sound very encouraging," Davis said doubtfully. "Isn't there something else we can do?"

"Sometimes," Lanie said slowly, "we do all we can with our own strength—and when that doesn't work we know that we just have to pray and leave things up to God. Let's all join hands right now and pray that God will give Daddy a new trial."

Lolean Oz had been driving the Freeman Rolling Emporium on Saturdays—which did not exactly please Cody. He had protested vehemently to Lanie that he was able to drive, but he had no license and could not get one until he was seventeen.

Lolean and Cody had said little on their route, and finally Lolean asked, "What's the matter, Cody? You seem all depressed."

Cody hesitated then blurted out, "It looks like unless God does a miracle, Daddy's not going to get out of jail."

"But I thought Thelma Mays was going to be able to change that, with her testimony, I mean."

"Mr. Pierce says he can't get a new trial because of politics."

Lolean moved closer and put her arm around Cody's shoulder. She was a very affectionate girl and not adverse to showing it. She squeezed him hard, and he gave her a startled look. "Why are you hugging me?"

"Why, I just wanted to show a little sympathy."

But Cody was vitally aware of Lolean's figure as she pressed against him. "Don't be hugging on me."

Lolean dropped her arm and looked hurt. "I was just trying to be nice." When he didn't answer, she said, "Cody, there's a dance over at Benton Springs next Saturday. If you'd ask me, I'd go with you."

"You know I don't go to those dances."

"Why not? They're fun."

"Well, there'll be people drinking there, and there'll be some liberties being taken."

"Well, we don't have to do any of that. We could just go over and listen to the music and dance and have a good time."

Cody hesitated, and then, for some reason he couldn't understand at the moment, he said, "All right, Lolean. If you want to, we'll go over."

"Good. I'll borrow my daddy's car. We'll have a good time."

Cody shook his head. "Somehow, it don't seem right going out dancing and having a good time when Daddy's in prison."

"Life has to go on, and besides, you told me you believe God's going to get him out. So, you just have to keep on believing that. If you're going to be a preacher, you got to have faith."

Cody had never told anyone he was going to be a preacher, but Lolean had made up her mind that he was. He also knew she had made up her mind that she was going to marry a preacher, and he was waiting for an opportunity to talk to her about those wild sayings.

Maybe a dance would be a good time to do that. He nodded and said, "Okay, we'll go, but I ain't promising to have a good time."

∝━⊷

The highlight of the Sunday morning service at the Baptist Church was the baptismal service. It was held before the preaching service, and there were nine candidates to be baptized. Colin Ryan, as interim pastor, had been an effective preacher, and many had been converted and had joined the church since he had taken the helm.

The whole Freeman family was there, of course, and when Maeva moved out into the baptismal tank where Colin Ryan waited for her, Lanie's heart seemed to swell. "I wish Daddy could be here to see this," she whispered to Davis who was on her left hand.

"So do I, but Maeva's right. She wanted to be baptized as quick as possible. Gosh, I'm proud of her."

Brother Ryan took his position and put his hand on the back of Maeva's neck. She was wearing a white robe, and there was a sweet, angelic look on her face. "You all know this young lady—Maeva Freeman. Part of one of the finest families in this world. She has taken Jesus Christ as her personal savior. Maeva, would you like to say a word?"

Maeva turned, and she was calm, but there were tears in her eyes. "Brother Ryan's right. I have given my life to Jesus. I wish I had done it years ago. I'm sorry for all the pain I caused my family, but from now on I'm going to serve Jesus the best I can."

Amens and praise the Lords rose from the congregation, and then Colin turned Maeva around and raised his right hand. "And now in obedience with the commands of our Lord and Savior Jesus Christ, I baptize you, my sister. In the name of the Father, in the name of the Son, and in the name of the Holy Ghost."

He lowered Maeva down into the water, and when he brought her up, he was startled at the response. People were applauding, and he suddenly laughed. "Well, Sister Maeva, you're on your way as a Christian."

Maeva waved out at the congregation, and as soon as she left, Logan came out. He was a tall man, much taller than the pastor was, and when he took his place Brother Ryan said, "Logan Satterfield has also given his life to Jesus Christ. Is that right, Logan?"

"It sure is. I've wasted a lot of my life, but I want to serve the Lord all my days."

Brother Ryan spoke the words over Logan then lowered him into the water, and when he brought him up there was the same response.

Corliss said loudly, "I want to be baptized."

"You will be one day," Cody said. "As soon as you get saved, you can be baptized."

The curtain closed over the baptismal tank, and the service continued. After Maeva and Logan came out, their hair wet and wearing fresh clothes, they took their places in the pews, Brother Ryan preached a fine sermon.

At the end of it he was about to dismiss when Maeva rose. "Could I say a word, Brother Ryan?"

"Of course you can, Maeva."

Maeva turned and faced the church. "I want to ask the church to pray for my daddy. We know he's innocent, but Mr. Pierce hasn't been able to get them to order a new trial for him. So, I'm asking you all to pray hard that this will happen."

Pastor Ryan spoke up then. "I think this is a time for fasting and prayer, and we believe that we're going to see Forrest Freeman walk out of those prison gates, and it will be God's victory."

⇒ CHAPTER 14 ⇐

For two weeks, Lanie had waited impatiently for word to come from Orrin Pierce concerning a new trial for her father. She had awakened every morning filled with hope and gone to bed at night filled with doubts that she could not seem to shake off. Orrin reported faithfully, but he had not had any success whatsoever in getting a new trial scheduled.

Lanie dressed and glanced at the calendar. Monday, October 17. She crossed the previous day off with a pencil and murmured, "1932 is almost over. God, you've got to get my daddy out of prison. You've just got to!"

Going downstairs, Lanie started fixing breakfast. Davis was going to take the Rolling Emporium, and Cody had been strangely silent. When she entered the kitchen, she found him fully dressed and seated at the table. "Why, what are you doing up so early, Cody? You're usually a sleepyhead."

"I couldn't sleep."

Instantly Lanie went over and sat down beside him. She knew that Cody usually slept like a rock. "What's the matter?"

Cody shook his head. "Nothing," he said but could not seem to meet her eyes.

"You can tell me, Cody."

"Well, Lanie, I'm afraid I'm nothing but a sinner."

"What in the world makes you say a thing like that? Why, you're a fine Christian."

Cody squeezed his hands together and was silent for a moment. When he turned to her, he had misery written on his face. "You know that dance I took Lolean to last Saturday?"

"Yes, I remember that. What about it? Did something happen?"

Cody cleared his throat and ran his hand through his hair. "Yeah, something happened. It's hard to talk about, though."

"You can tell me," Lanie said quietly. "I'm your sister."

"Well, I felt kind of guilty going to that dance anyhow, and just like I told Lolean there was drinking going on, and there was stuff going on between the men and the women that embarrassed me. But what happened was I got to dancing with Lolean, and it was one of them slow dances where you hold on to the woman, and she holds on to you, you know?"

"Yes, I know. It wasn't a square dance then."

"No, it would have been better if it was. But I hate to tell you this, Lanie, but Lolean's a real affectionate girl. She is always patting on me and hugging me, and when we was dancing she put herself right up against me real tight." Cody's face suddenly went dull red. "And I had impure thoughts. Ain't that awful?"

Lanie was not certain how to answer Cody. He was such a moral young man, and here he found himself trapped in a temptation that she suspected came to all young men, no matter how moral they were.

"Dancing is a temptation, and maybe you shouldn't have gone, Cody. But I know you didn't mean to do wrong."

Cody's face twisted in misery. "Shoot, here I am passing out tracts and trying to be a good Christian, and I go acting just like a sinner."

Lanie put her hand over Cody's. "You know the good thing about this?"

"No, I don't see nothing good about it."

"The good thing, Cody, is that you didn't just pass it by and keep on with what you were doing. You felt that you'd done wrong and you told me about it, and now you know what 1 John 1:9 says. It says if we confess our sins He's faithful and just to forgive us our sins and to cleanse us from all unrighteousness."

Cody was totally still. "That's right. It does say that, don't it?"

"It sure does. Why don't we just pray that you will be able to overcome all temptations of this kind in the future."

"Let's do that."

Lanie prayed fervently for her brother, and when finally she said amen, she looked up and saw Cody's face was relieved. "I ain't hardly slept a wink since that dance, but I'm going to be more careful from now on. I'm going to tell Lolean if she wants to dance with me, she's got to stay at least six inches away."

"Well, that'll be a sight to see. I don't think—"

A sudden knock came at the front door.

"Who could that be? I haven't even started breakfast yet." She went to the door and was surprised to find the woman the town knew as Butcher Knife Annie. "Why, Annie," she said, "what are you doing out and about?"

"I've got to talk to you, Lanie."

"Why, come on in. I was just fixing to make breakfast."

Annie followed Lanie into the kitchen. Cody had disappeared so the two women had it all to themselves.

"I haven't even made a fire yet to heat coffee."

"I don't want no coffee," Annie said. She was a frail woman with pure silver hair and a face worn by a lifetime of trouble. She had been known as Butcher Knife Annie because she had lived in a tarpaper shack inhabited by numerous cats and had hauled a wagon through the alleys of Fairhope gleaning for junk—and some said she carried a butcher knife. She had become friends with the Freeman family, and they had all learned to love the old woman. She still was not the cleanest person in the world, and the cats still inhabited her house, leaving a terrible aroma, but now as Lanie got her to sit down, she saw that the old woman was worried. "What's the matter, Annie?"

"Do you believe God speaks to people, Lanie?"

"Why, you know I do."

"I figured as much. Well, I ain't been much of a Christian, but God's been putting something on my heart. It ain't like He spoke to me, you understand, with a voice, but it's something I know has got to be done."

"Can you tell me about it, Annie?"

"God wants me to talk to the governor."

"You mean Governor Matthews?"

"That's right. I've got to talk to him, God says."

Lanie was stunned. Governor Matthews was engaged in a fierce fight for reelection, and she hardly thought he would have time to talk to someone like Annie. "Why do you think God wants you to do this?"

"I can't say no more. All I knew was to come to you. It's God telling me to do it. That much I know."

Lanie hesitated but the thought came to her that God worked in strange ways. He had used Logan Satterfield, one of the wilder young men of the county, to help her sister Maeva bring Thelma Mays back and make a trial possible. Still, this seemed highly unlikely.

"All right, Annie. I'll talk to Orrin. Maybe he'll know a way."

"I think it's important, Lanie."

"I'm sure it is. I'll see what can be done."

❦

Orrin Pierce came to the house at Lanie's urgent call, and Owen Merritt arrived a few minutes later to check on Aunt Kezia. Lanie had just gathered the family to tell them about Annie's visit, and because the men were both good friends of them all, Lanie invited them to join the family in the kitchen. Even Aunt Kezia was feeling well enough to sit up and drink her sassafras tea while the others had coffee.

Lanie began at once by telling them about Annie's visit. As she told the story in detail, a look of despair touched her face. "I know it sounds impossible, but Annie is sure that God wants her to talk to Governor Matthews."

"I doubt if it would be possible to get her in to see him. He's so busy these days," Orrin said.

"Besides that," Owen said, "she's in bad health. She's in no condition to make a trip to the capital in Little Rock."

Kezia slammed her mug down on the table. "He ain't in Little Rock."

"Not in Little Rock? What are you talking about?" Orrin said.

"He's out begging for votes!" Kezia said sharply. "Don't you never read the paper? It says he'll be speaking in Fort Smith day after tomorrow."

"I did read that," Owen said, "but even that's a hard trip for a sick woman. Besides, I can't imagine walking up to the governor of the state of Arkansas and saying, 'An old woman says that God wants you to talk to her.'"

"Well, Big Bill's been a good governor, but he's not very religious," Orrin said doubtfully.

The four of them sat around the table trying to think about a plan, and all seemed doubtful—except for Aunt Kezia.

"What's the matter with you people? The woman says God told her to do it. If God told her, He'll make a way. Stop listening to your fears."

"All right," Orrin said. "We'll make the trip, but you'd better go with us, Owen. She might need a doctor on the way."

"We've got to do it," Lanie said, finally convinced. "It may be a door that God has opened."

"Well, we'll take my car," Owen said. "We'll need to leave pretty early, and I'll get us some rooms at a hotel there."

"It's going to be hard to see the governor," Orrin said doubtfully, "but we'll do our best."

Annie made the trip to Fort Smith better than any of them had expected. Owen watched her carefully, but by the time they reached

Fort Smith, she was tired and they took her at once to the room she was going to share with Lanie.

"You see that she gets some rest, Lanie," Orrin said. "I'll go talk to the governor."

"Do you know him at all?" Owen asked.

"Oh, sure. I've been a supporter of his for a long time. I think he'll listen to me, but I don't know if I can talk him into this."

❦

Orrin Pierce had a stunned look on his face when he showed up late that afternoon at the hotel. He found Owen up in Annie's room, and when he stepped in, Lanie and the others turned to look at him.

"Well, I don't believe it," Orrin said, "but I've got to because it's true."

"What happened, Orrin?" Lanie cried. She saw something different in Orrin's face, and she decided it was hope.

"It's the governor. He's coming here."

"You mean here to the hotel?" Owen demanded.

"I mean right here to Annie's room."

"How did you do that?" Lanie exclaimed.

"I didn't do anything. I finally got to see the governor, and I explained the situation, and he laughed. He made fun of me at first. 'You want me to go see an old woman that God's talking to saying she wants to see me?'"

"Wasn't much I could say to that and the idea seemed to amuse the governor. I think he's pretty tired of the campaign trail so he said, 'Well, I'll go see this lady, and we'll just see what God's telling her about me.'"

"When's he coming?"

"He ought to be here any minute. He came in his own car, and I came in ours."

Ten minutes later Lanie looked out the window and said, "Look, there's the governor getting out of the car."

"I'll go down and meet him," Orrin said. He looked flustered as he left, and Lanie went over to sit beside Annie who was resting quietly in a chair.

"You feel like talking?"

"That's what we came fer, girl."

Five minutes later the door opened, and William Matthews, better known to the citizens of Arkansas as Big Bill Matthews, entered the room. He was, indeed, a big man with a thatch of silvery hair and a pair of snapping dark eyes. "Well," he said, his voice booming, "where's this woman that's got a word for me from God?"

"Right over here, Governor," Lanie said. "Annie, this is Governor Matthews."

Annie took the big hand that Matthews held out to her. "It's good to see you again, Governor."

Matthews stared at her. "We've met before?"

"A long time ago."

"Here, sit down, Governor," Owen said quickly.

Matthews sat down and said, "I'm afraid I don't remember, Annie."

"Well, you wouldn't remember me. It was a long time ago. I was married to a man named Tom Toliver. Do you remember that name?"

"It does sound familiar. How long ago was it?"

"You were just a boy, and you stole a horse from Tom Toliver."

Big Bill's eyes flew open. "Stole a horse!"

"That's right. You remember that?"

Big Bill stuck his hand under his collar as if it had grown too tight. "Well, I remember a little bit about that."

"Do you remember what happened when you were caught with that stolen horse?"

"I guess I do," the governor said. "A policeman was taking me to jail. I knew I was going to be charged and sent to the reform school."

Annie smiled sweetly. "And do you remember why you didn't go to jail?"

"I remember it all now. I guess I kind of buried it in my mind. Your husband talked the policeman out of arresting me. He said it was a mistake. He got me off."

"I'm Beulah Ann Toliver, Governor. Thomas Toliver was my husband. He's been gone for years now, but he never forgot what happened with you and that horse."

"I never forgot it either. I don't think I ever really thanked him."

"Well, while he was alive he kept up with your career. He always thought he was a part of your success. He kept clippings on all the things you did, the elections that you won. He was so proud of you, Governor."

Big Bill Matthews stared at the frail woman. "Why are you here, Mrs. Toliver?"

"I'm here because God told me to come, and I'm hoping that you're a man who understands how important a second chance is — because that's what my husband got for you."

"He did. If I had been tried and had gone to reform school, I don't think I would have ever been able to have any success in the public life."

"Let me tell you. This young lady here is Lanie Freeman. Her daddy is Forrest Freeman. You may not remember, but he was sent to prison for killing a man."

"I'm afraid I don't remember."

Orrin broke in quickly and gave the governor the details of the trial and conviction of Forrest Freeman. He said quickly, "We've got new evidence, but Mr. Carleton Hobbs is adamant. He won't have any mercy on Freeman."

The room was silent, and everyone seemed to be holding their breath. All the governor had to do would be to walk away and it would all be over.

But Governor Matthews suddenly smiled. "I guess you folks know that Mr. Hobbs and I don't see to eye-to-eye on most things."

"How's the election going?" Orrin asked.

"Neck and neck. I need all the help I can get. I know you've been my supporter, Orrin, and I appreciate it. It's going to be a close race. Hobbs is clever." He thought a minute. "I'd like to get involved in this case. Let me do some checking around, and I'll get back to you as soon as I make a few plans."

"Thank you, Governor," Annie Toliver said. "Tom was always proud of you, and I was too."

"I thought about stealing that horse for many years, and maybe now I can do Tom Toliver's family a service."

⚮

Matthews stepped outside the door and motioned to L. C. Thomas, the governor's aide. Thomas was a tall, lanky man with a sour face but a pair of bright, intelligent dark eyes. "L. C., come on. We got to talk."

Thomas was a man of few words. He followed the governor downstairs, and they got outside and stepped into the car. As soon as the door slammed, Governor Matthews told L. C. what he had just heard.

"So, you want to do something with the case, Governor?"

"You know, there might be an opportunity here."

Thomas grinned. "You'd like to hang Hobbs's hide on the wall, wouldn't you?"

"Yes. Check the woman's story, L. C. Here's the deposition from this woman Thelma Mays. If she's telling the truth, Freeman never should have been convicted. She wasn't there to testify—but she is now."

L. C. Thomas looked thoughtful. "You know, this could be good copy, Governor. The papers will eat it up. Just imagine the headlines in the *Arkansas Gazette* and the *Democrat*: BIG BILL MATTHEWS FREES INNOCENT MAN."

Matthews grinned back at Thomas. "And in the story it could say that Hobbs doesn't give a dead rat for a poor man."

"I'll look into it, Governor."

"Better act quick. We need to take action on this."

＊

The two witnesses against Forrest Freeman responsible for sending him to the penitentiary were Alvin Biggins, the brother of the slain man, Duke, and Ethel Crawford, Duke's live-in girlfriend. The two of them were met by officers with subpoenas and had been ushered unceremoniously to the Hotel Majestic where they were taken to the second floor. Biggins stared at the two men and knew Orrin Pierce, although he did not know the other man, and said, "What's this all about, Pierce?"

Orrin said, "This is Mr. L. C. Thomas. He's the governor's right-hand man. He has a few questions to ask you."

"We don't have to answer any questions."

L. C. Thomas grinned wickedly. "All right. We'll just send you right on to jail then."

"Jail! What are you talking about?" Alvin Biggins said, turning pale.

"Do you know what perjury is?"

"Telling a lie, ain't it?"

"Swearing in court to a statement that isn't true. Judges don't like things like that. They send people who perjure themselves to prison for as long as they can."

"We ain't lied about nothing. We told just what we seen, didn't we, Ethel?"

"That's right, we did," she said aggressively. "I heard about this witness Thelma Mays. She was there that night, but she was drunk in the next room. She didn't see nothing."

"That's not Miss Mays's story. She tells about the shooting in a completely different light."

"Why, she's lying."

"We got three witnesses," L. C. Thomas said loudly. "You talk too much, both of you. These witnesses will swear that you told them you fabricated the evidence in order to get even with Forrest Freeman. They'll tell the truth on the stand because they don't want to go to jail for perjury."

Orrin Pierce stared at the two. "Mr. Thomas and the governor are determined to get a new trial. If they do, and it comes out you were lying, they'll put you so deep under the jail they'll have to pipe sunlight to you."

"That's right. The governor's behind this, and he's going to hit you hard."

Ethel Crawford had turned pale. "I don't want to go to jail. It wasn't my fault. Alvin, you made me say those things."

"Shut up! I didn't make you say nothing."

"Alvin, you've got one chance," L. C. Thomas said. "Admittedly you were drunk that night. You said you saw a lot of things, and you denied pulling a knife on Forrest Freeman. If you'll give us the truth of that, maybe being drunk will be enough to get you off."

"Anyone can make a mistake," Orrin put in. "Your big mistake would be in taking on Big Bill Matthews, Governor of Arkansas, head-to-head."

For the next half hour, the two poured out their story, which had changed considerably. L. C. Thomas had them dictate it to a secretary and then signed the deposition. "Maybe you'll get off," he said. "It depends on how merciful the judge is."

As soon as the pair was shown out of the room, Thomas picked up the phone and dialed a number. "Governor, it's okay. They admitted they were lying. I promised them some leniency so I don't know if we can put them in jail where they belong. What now?" He listened carefully and then said, "I'll take care of it."

"What did he say?"

L. C. Thomas grinned. "He said he's calling a special meeting of the parole board to consider the case of Forrest Freeman."

"You mean there wouldn't have to be a trial?"

"Not with what we've got. We've got Thelma Mays with the new testimony, and we've got the depositions that the main witnesses lied, and we've got the governor behind this. I think it looks mighty good."

"I've got to get out to the Freemans and tell them. They're going to be one happy family."

❦

Indeed, the Freeman family pranced and hugged each other when Orrin Pierce gave them the results of the meeting with Alvin Biggins and Ethel Crawford.

"But does it mean Daddy's going to get out of jail?" Cody said.

"That'll be up to the parole board. They can turn it down, but I don't think they will. They'll know the governor's behind it, and they're responsible to him. Besides, the evidence is as strong as any I've ever seen. No, I don't think there'll have to be another trial."

"Then Daddy will be coming home?" Lanie whispered.

"Yes, he'll be coming home," Orrin said.

"And Annie was right. God did speak to her," Maeva whispered.

"I think He did," Orrin Pierce said. "Indeed, I think He did."

❦

The special meeting of the parole board at the prison was not the normal assembly. The governor himself had come, which made all the members of the board apprehensive. L. C. Thomas was there, and he laid the evidence before the board. "We can go get a new trial, and I think that wouldn't be too hard with the governor's help, but the simplest thing is to simply grant this parole."

The board looked solemn, but they listened as Thelma Mays gave her version of the shooting. As soon as she was out of the room, L. C. Thomas handed out written copies of the deposition taken from the two witnesses Biggins and Crawford. He allowed them to read it and said, "The governor feels strongly about this, and so do I. There's been an injustice done here. These two witnesses perjured themselves. That was the only real evidence against Forrest, and now we have three other witnesses who will swear in a court of law that Biggins and Ethel Crawford told them they were out to get Forrest, and they'd see to it that he'd go to the pen no matter what they had to say."

Finally, the visitors left, and the parole board was left to make their decision. The door stayed closed for only five minutes. When L. C. went inside he looked over at Forrest and then at the chairman of the parole board.

The chairman's face was bland, and he said, "By unanimous consent we're granting a full pardon to you, Forrest Freeman."

Orrin Pierce let out a yelp but managed to control himself. "Get yourself ready, Forrest. We're taking you out of here."

Forrest Freeman could not say a word, but his face worked with emotion, and tears ran down his cheeks. A sense of joy filled his heart as he thought of being free to walk his land, to laugh, and to enjoy his precious family. He tried to pray, but could only whisper over and over, "Thank you, God! Thank you, God!"

The reporters had been waiting outside, and now they swarmed the governor, demanding a story.

"Well, boys, justice has been done. An innocent man has been set free. That's what I believe about our justice system, that the little man deserves a break."

"What about Carleton Hobbs? He was the prosecuting attorney at the trial, wasn't he? Couldn't he have done something about this?"

"Well, Hobbs was responsible, in my view, for a miscarriage of justice. He's a hard man. He has no compassion for the little fellow."

L. C. Thomas was standing there, grinning. He winked at Big Bill who winked back. Thomas turned to Orrin. "This will put Bill in office for another term. It might even make him senator."

Lanie and Owen had come to Annie's house. They had given her the good news, and Lanie's eyes were swimming with tears as she embraced the old woman. "You saved my daddy, Annie."

Annie took the woman's embrace and held on to her hand. "God let me do something for you and your family—before I go home."

·❧ CHAPTER 15 ❧·

Forrest walked down the hallway beside the burly guard. Odd feelings coursed through him, and somehow he found it difficult to believe that at the end of this walk he would be free of prison life. He had slept little all night, thinking instead of the miracle that God had done to use a frail old woman to influence a powerful governor.

As they passed several guards, each smiled and spoke to him. "Good luck, Forrest. Don't come back. Take care of yourself."

His guard stepped aside to let him go through the final door, and Forrest found Warden Gladden waiting for him. The warden's face was beaming, and he held a newspaper in his hand. "Well, you're a famous citizen, Forrest. Look at this."

Forrest took the newspaper and saw on the front page the story of his release. "Can I keep this?"

"You'll want to frame it. The governor came out on top of this. He'll win the election for sure now." A smile creased the warden's broad lips. "The governor also said to tell you if you need anything, you come to him."

Forrest tucked the newspaper under his arm and stuck his right hand out. When the warden grasped it with a viselike grip, he said, "Warden, you've been a good friend to me. I'll never forget you."

"I'm happy for you, Forrest. Not many feel-good stories in this place, but you're one of them. You take care of yourself. Drop me a line and let me know how you're getting along."

"I'll do that."

As they strolled outside the prison, the October sunlight was bright, but there was a nip in the air. "There'll be some good hunting when you get home, Forrest," Gladden said.

"I've missed that. I'll miss your dogs and your horses too. You be sure you get a good man to take care of them."

"He won't be as good as you, but I'll see to it."

When they reached the gate, a grinning guard opened it and shook Forrest's hand. "God bless you."

"And you too, Mr. Hardin." As soon as Forrest stepped out, he saw a crowd had gathered. There were vehicles everywhere, and his eyes lit instantly on his family. They were all there—Lanie, Maeva, Davis, Cody, and little Corliss. They all moved toward him. Corliss was the first one there, and Forrest knelt down and grabbed her, holding her in his arms.

"Daddy, I'm so glad you're coming home!"

"Me too, honey." He rose to his feet, while the rest of his family crowded in to embrace him.

The reporters were there with their cameras, and Forrest was swamped with questions. He managed to fend them off, and finally one reporter said, "Not many men walk out of here with a full pardon. How do you account for it, Mr. Freeman?"

"I account for it by saying that it's all a blessing from God. Now, if you don't mind, I'd like for us to get on our way."

But a second wave of greeters—all from Fairhope—surged forward: Phineas Delaughter, the mayor; Myrtle Poindexter, the pastor of the Fire Baptized Pentecostal Church; Orrin Pierce, of course; Harry Oz, the owner of the hardware store; and many others. Delaughter came to grip his hand. "We're all jumping up and down, Forrest. We're going to make a parade all the way back to Fairhope!"

⌖

Indeed, it was a parade. Cars blew their horns every time they passed through the small towns. One town had put up a banner that said, BLESS GOVERNOR MATTHEWS. HE LOVES THE LITTLE MAN!

Forrest sat between Davis, who was driving a borrowed car, and Corliss, who peppered him with questions. As soon as they got into the city limits, they heard the sound of music. As they pulled up into the town square, it seemed everybody in Fairhope had gathered there. The high school band had donned their uniforms and were playing either "Hail to the Chief" or one of their fight songs from the football season. He couldn't tell which.

"Look, Daddy, they've all come to welcome you," Maeva said. She leaned forward from the backseat, put her arms around him, and kissed him. He reached back and ran his hand over her smooth hair.

"I could do without all this."

"No, you deserve it," Lanie said. "And you'll have to make a speech."

"Oh, I can't do that."

But as they got out of the car, Forrest found himself greeted by people that he had known all of his life. The band played on as cheers rose in the air, and finally he made his way to the platform. Mayor Delaughter raised his hand for quiet. "Believe it or not I'm not going to make a speech, but I'm going to ask Forrest to come and say a few words or as many as he pleases."

"You'll have to go say something, Daddy," Lanie said. "Everybody expects it."

"Where's Thelma?"

"Right here," Maeva said. She brought Thelma to meet Forrest, who didn't remember her. "I owe you a lot, young lady."

"I'm so happy for you, Mr. Freeman."

There was no time for more. Forrest mounted the steps, turned to face the crowd, and a lump rose in his throat. The crowd fell silent. He looked out and said, "I don't think any of you know what this means to me, but I'm going to tell you right now that I give God all the glory along with this young lady here, Miss Thelma Mays, and this other young lady, Miss Annie Toliver." He went over to where Butcher Knife Annie was sitting in a special chair, leaned over, and kissed her cheek.

"Thank you, Annie," he said. "You brought the miracle." He straightened up and gazed out over the crowd again. "I can't say any more except I thought about all of you people and my family every day that I was in prison, and I know that it was God who got me out. I pray that He will make me a faithful servant as long as I live. Now, I want to go home."

There were cheers, and the band again broke into music. Forrest went back, got into the car, and Davis started it up. They pulled out slowly to avoid people who crowded around, and finally they were on the road home. Corliss chattered like a magpie, but Forrest was drinking in the sights. As they pulled up to his old homeplace, he said, "There's Booger and Beau."

As he got out of the car, Booger came at once and reared up on him. Beau did the same thing, and he embraced the two big dogs. He looked down and saw that Cap'n Brown had come out to join the other four-legged greeters. He bent over and stroked the big cat's back. Finally, he turned and looked up at his family. "Home again."

Aunt Kezia came up, pulled Forrest's head down, and kissed him on the cheek. "Now you behave yourself, Forrest Freeman."

"I plan to do that, Aunt Kezia."

"You come on in. I made one of your favorite dishes. Pigtail soup."

Forrest laughed. "Nothing better than pigtail soup. I thought about that a lot while I've been gone."

⌖

For two days, Forrest did not get far from the house. He spent the two days simply walking around, mostly with Corliss at his side, often with either Cody or Davis, listening to them. At nights, he would gather the family, and they would sing the old songs. The house was filled with music, and on the second night, they played some hymns. He looked over at Maeva and said quietly, "Daughter, you're a different woman."

"I guess I am," Maeva said. "And I needed to be, didn't I?"

Forrest grinned. "Well, you always made life interesting."

"That's a nice way for you to put it, Daddy."

"Let's play some fast songs," Davis said. "How about that new gospel song, 'Turn Your Radio On'?"

"I don't think I know that one," Forrest said.

"Aw, you'll pick it up, Daddy," Davis said. They all began, and after they had played through it once and sung the lyrics, Forrest found that he could indeed pick it up. "You know," he said when they ended the song, "we could go on the road. The Famous Freeman Family Singers."

"You reckon anybody would pay to hear us?" Cody asked with astonishment.

"They'd pay to hear worse than us," Maeva said. "You should have heard some of the sorry pickers and singers out there in California! Couldn't even carry a tune!"

They stayed up late, and Forrest got up before dawn. On his third day home, he shaved and walked into town. By the time he arrived, the morning crowd was beginning to filter into the Dew Drop Inn. As soon as he walked in, Sister Myrtle shouted, "Well, praise God, it's Forrest Freeman! Come in, Brother Forrest. The meal's on the house."

"I missed your cooking, Sister Myrtle. Charlie, what can you make for me this morning?"

Charlie stuck his head up through the window in the wall that separated the kitchen from the restaurant. His grin was infectious. "Anything you like. How about some scrambled eggs with squirrel brains mixed in?"

"I don't think there could be anything better."

For the next two hours, Forrest sat there. He finished his breakfast quickly, but the townspeople were coming in, and he knew they all wanted to talk. He drank cup after cup of coffee, and finally Doctor Oscar Givens limped in and grinned at him. "Back again, Freeman. Glad to see you."

"Glad to see you, Doc. You're looking well."

"That Owen Merritt's doing all the work, and I'm taking most of the money."

The doctor sat down, and Sister Myrtle came over and said, "I wish you'd stop feeding Louise Simpson all that medicine. The Lord done healed her, and you keep pumping medicine down her throat."

"Sister Myrtle, I don't tell you how to cook. Please don't tell me how to practice medicine."

"Practice! That's what you do. You *practice* on people. I know what you doctors say," Myrtle sniffed. "You just say 'Let's *try* this.' Ain't that a fine thing now as if we were a bunch of guinea pigs."

Everyone could hear Sister Myrtle, for her voice was strident. Doctor Givens looked around and asked with some irritation, "Did it ever occur to you, Sister Myrtle, that I might not like to have all my conversations heard by everybody in Fairhope?"

"If you ain't got nothing to be ashamed of, there ain't no harm in it. Now, what do you want to eat?"

"I want flapjacks and sorghum."

"We're all out of sorghum."

"Well, what have you got?"

"Got maple syrup and molasses."

"Mix me up some of that. One will kill the taste of the other."

Givens sipped his coffee, leaned back, and studied Forrest. "You look good, Forrest."

"Well, I got lots of fresh air and sunshine after my operation."

"I heard it wasn't exactly an operation."

"No, it wasn't. It was a miracle. They're still shaking their heads over at the hospital. Claim there was something wrong with the X-rays." Forrest grinned and shook his head with amusement. "They just don't know how the Lord operates."

The crowd kept coming in, and Forrest found himself answering all sorts of questions about what it was like in prison. He didn't really want to talk about it, but these were his townspeople and he knew he might as well get it over with. Finally, Owen came in and joined them. Doctor Givens said, "This young man's going to be taking over my practice. What he needs to do is get married."

"Don't start preaching at me, Doctor Givens," Owen warned.

Sister Myrtle said, "He needs to marry up with your oldest daughter, that's what, Forrest."

Owen's face turned beet red. "Sister Myrtle, did you ever think of anything you didn't come out and say out loud?"

"Not that I know of. If I think it, I got to say it."

"Well, stop talking about Lanie like that."

"Well, you wouldn't get a better girl."

Owen refused to comment, but when Forrest got home, he hunted Lanie up at once. After a while, he managed to mention what had happened.

"Owen would never marry me."

"Why not?"

"He thinks he's too old. Besides, he still thinks of me as the little fourteen-year-old girl I was when I first met him."

"All he has to do is open his eyes and see that you're not."

"I don't want to talk about it."

"What about Roger?"

"Well, what about him?"

"You told me he asked you to marry him."

"He did, but Roger's so young. I don't think he's ready to take on a wife yet."

"Well, I might as well get them all in," Forrest said. Cap'n Brown came over, leaped up in his lap, and he began stroking him. "What about this writer fellow, Brent—Brent Hayden?"

"He's just—a friend, Daddy. He's helped me a lot."

"And no romance there, huh?"

"I don't think so."

"You don't sound very sure, Muff."

Lanie was glad when suddenly Cody came in. "Daddy, I got to show you my new invention."

"I heard about the one where you nearly broke the world up with those dynamite caps. That didn't work too well."

"Well, it's got a few bugs in it, but I still say it'll work."

"What are you inventing now?"

"An automatic chicken plucker. You know what a pest it is to pluck them chickens and geese and turkeys. Well, this thing will pluck them automatically."

Forrest Freeman was used to his son's so-called inventions. "Well, let me see it, son," he said.

"Oh, I haven't started it yet, but I got a drawing of it." He pulled a piece of paper out of his pocket and unfolded it. "You see, it works on sort of a drum thing here that I hook up to a motor, and these things here. They're some kind of rubber fingers. They hit the feathers and just knock them off."

"What's to keep them from knocking the meat off?"

"Well, I'm working on that, Daddy. Come on and let me show you what I've done to the Rolling Emporium. I made some improvements on it."

The two went outside. Forrest, who had never seen the Rolling Emporium, was filled with praise for it. "Why, this is a fine idea, and it's brought enough income to help the family. I'm hoping I get a job, and you won't have to work so hard."

"Oh, we don't none of us mind, Daddy."

Cody finally fell silent, and Forrest gave him a close look. "What's the matter?"

"Oh, it's Lolean Oz."

"Lolean? What's she done?"

"Well, she's taking it on herself to drive me around in the Emporium. I don't have my license yet, but I'm going to get it when I have my next birthday. But she gets on my nerves. Wonder why she does that?"

"I expect she likes you."

"Well, she bothers me." He hesitated and then said, "I told this to Lanie because you weren't here." He repeated the story of how at the dance Lolean had pressed herself against him and it had troubled him. "It gave me impure thoughts, Daddy. How do I keep from having those things?"

Forrest didn't smile, although he wanted to. "Well, some men become monks. They go hide out, but I don't think that would work. Jesus didn't tell us all to leave the world, did He?"

"No, He didn't. Well, you're going to have to help me with this, Daddy."

"I'll be glad to help all I can."

⊂══◆══

Later that afternoon Forrest talked to Lanie. They were out picking up pecans from under the big pecan tree in the backyard.

Booger did not get far away. The big dog loved the pecans. Every once in a while Forrest would crack one in two in his hands and give the dog a big pecan half.

"Cody told me about his impure feelings about that Oz girl," Forrest said, "but I didn't know what to tell him."

"Oh, he'll outgrow that. He's so holy he wouldn't eat an egg laid on Sunday, Daddy. You know he considers himself the spiritual head of the family now for some reason. Did you hear about his witnessing?"

"No. What's that all about?"

"He goes around with a Bible, and everybody he meets he tears a page out and gives it to them. It doesn't make any difference what's on it. He says it's all the Bible, and he's written a tract that's just awful. It's called *Turn or Burn!* Trying to scare people into becoming Christians. I'll be glad when he gets a little sense about that."

As they continued to pick up the pecans, Forrest questioned Lanie about Davis and Corliss, and then Maeva.

"Do you think she's interested in Logan?"

"They got awfully close on their trip, and of course they got saved together. I'm very proud of Logan. He's a good man."

"What about you?"

193

"Well, what about me?"

"Well, what do you want for yourself? You've been so busy taking care of this family you haven't had time to make any life for yourself."

"Why, Daddy, I want what all girls want, I guess. I want a home and a family."

Forrest turned to face her. "Well, I hear there's a line of young men waiting up to help you with that."

Lanie stared at him. "You've been at the Dew Drop Inn. They're just a bunch of gossips. Next thing they'll be taking bets on who I'll marry."

"Well, which one do you favor?"

Lanie was disturbed. "I don't know, Daddy. They're all fine men. Of course, Roger's the only one who's actually asked me."

"Well, I'm glad to see you're not in a hurry. You deserve just the man God's got picked out for you."

Lanie did not answer. She looked off into the distance at the faint haze of the mountains, then she finally turned to him and smiled brilliantly. "I'm glad you're home, Daddy. Now when I have problems I can just bring them to you."

⇥ CHAPTER 16 ⇤

As Lanie stopped pedaling her bicycle and guided it in toward Brent's cabin, she involuntarily gave a glance over her shoulder. The sun was almost down and it was growing darker, but still she was acutely aware of the gossip concerning her visits to Brent Hayden's place. Feeling somewhat guilty, she moved her bicycle around to the side of the cabin, leaned it against the wall, and then plucked the manila folder out of the basket. Clutching it, she paused for a moment and felt a strong inclination to leave. She halted there caught between two desires, and finally thought, *I'll just drop this new work off for him. I won't have to stay.*

With this resolution in mind, she went to the front door and tapped. She heard the sound of footsteps, and then the door opened. Light sprang out at her, and Brent said, "Why, Lanie, what a pleasant surprise! Come in."

"Oh, Brent, I won't come in. I just wanted to leave some new work that I had done."

"Nonsense. I've just made some stew. Come in and help me eat it."

Lanie opened her mouth to protest, but Brent simply laughed, took her arm, and guided her in. "I'm getting to be quite a cook." He took the folder from her, surprised at the heft of it. "Well, you have been busy."

"It's part of what's going to be my novel."

"Well, here. Let's sit down and eat this stew, and you can tell me all about it."

Lanie was very hungry, and the aroma of the stew tantalized her. "All right," she said, "but I can't stay long."

Brent pulled the chair out, and Lanie sat down. He went to the cabinet, pulled out another soup bowl, put it on a plate then came over and put it in front of her along with a soup spoon. He ladled the stew out into the bowl, added some to his own, then he sat down. "Taste it. See what you think of my cooking."

Lanie took a spoonful of the stew. "Oh, this is delicious, Brent! I didn't know you were such a cook."

"Oh, I'm not really, but a bachelor gets tired of eating sandwiches all the time. Here, have some of this cornbread. Mrs. Jennings dropped it by. I told her I was making stew. It goes with it very well, I think."

Lanie took a slice of the cornbread, added some of the creamy butter, and tasted it. "She makes good cornbread."

The radio was on, and an orchestra was playing some piece of classical music she didn't know. "I wish I knew more about that kind of music that you listen to."

"We'll educate each other. I need to know more about the mountain music that you and your family play. I like it very much indeed. It's so down-to-earth."

The two sat there talking about various kinds of music, and as always, Brent knew so much that Lanie was amazed. He had been to college, she knew, had been an editor, and the shelves that he built and fastened to the walls were packed with books of every sort. Her gaze went around the room, and she shook her head. "I wish I had read as much as you have, Brent."

"I wish I could sing and play like you do. To each his own." His face glowed with pleasure as he continued to talk about music.

Lanie could not help noticing how neat he was. Even without company he was well dressed with a pair of rust-colored slacks and a pure white shirt. His hair was neatly combed. It had a slight curl, and he had an English cast to his features she found very appealing.

"Mrs. Jennings brought me a pie too. She takes pity on me pretty often." He got up, busied himself, and soon came back with two thin slices of chocolate pie. "You can have anything you want as long as you want chocolate pie." He grinned at her and set the pie before Lanie, then sat down, and the two plunged in. Lanie finished her pie, and then Brent said, "Now, to polish it all off with some fresh coffee."

Lanie opened her mouth to say that she had to go, but the coffee did smell good.

He poured it from a small percolator and came back with two small china cups. "These don't hold very much. You have to fill it up several times."

Lanie sipped the coffee and looked around the room. "You've done such a fine job of decorating this place, Brent. It's so cozy."

"Well, you were the one who found it for me. Come on. Let's sit before the fire. Take the chill off. It's getting colder."

He drew up a couch in front of the fireplace, and the two sat down. Lanie balanced her cup and watched as Brent placed two more small logs on the fire, jabbed it with a steel poker, and the sparks went swirling up into the chimney. He replaced the poker and came to sit beside her. "Did I tell you I'm cutting my own firewood now? Got real blisters on my hands. I've really gone native."

"I love fireplaces. Sometimes I get anxious for summer to end so that fall can come, and we can build fires again." She watched the yellow blaze of the flames as they leaped higher, and the popping of the logs made a counterpoint to the ticking of a mantel clock.

When he had come to Fairhope he had planned to stay only for a brief time, but the time had stretched on, and during that time, she had become more and more aware of what a brilliant man he was.

"Tell me about your family. How's your dad fitting back in?"

"Oh, Brent, it's so wonderful having him home!" Lanie exclaimed. "It's like a new world. You know, all the years he was in prison I went around with a weight on my back almost like Pilgrim in *Pilgrim's Progress*, but it's all gone now."

"What's your dad going to do?"

"He'll probably go to work in the woods. He's done that all of his life."

"That's a hard job, cutting timber."

"Yes, it is. I wish there was something else, but with this Depression it's hard to make a living at anything."

"Yes, it is. Well, I'm happy for your family and especially for your dad. I haven't met him yet, you know."

"Well, you come by the house tomorrow. I think he'll be home."

"Fine. I'll do that. Now, tell me about this work you've done."

Brent sat there listening as she began to talk about her work. The flickering light of the fire changed her appearance as it touched her face. Her lips were gently set, and her shoulders were square and definite against the couch's back. There was a current of vitality in this young woman that caught at him. She had a steadfast quality, but now as she spoke of her writing, her features seemed to shine, somehow giving her a dreamy depth. She had on a simple dress, the color of dark roses.

Finally, she laughed self-consciously. "It's hard to talk about the writing I do. It's so very personal."

"All writing should be personal."

Brent started to speak, then hesitated. He had been thinking much about this young woman. The long hours in the cabin alone had given him time such as he had never had before. He found himself even waking up at night and thinking of something that she had said, or the way that her eyes danced when she was secretly amused.

"I want to say something, Lanie."

"What is it, Brent?" She looked at him curiously. He had turned to face her. He reached out suddenly and took her hand, and she was surprised and somewhat disturbed.

"I'm not a very romantic fellow, but I've been thinking about you for some time now. Let me ask you: Have you ever thought of me as a man you might marry?"

Confusion rushed through Lanie. She had, of course, thought of this. Any young girl would have had thoughts like this. Her face grew flushed. She was acutely aware of the pressure of his hand.

"I don't have to tell you, I think, how much I admire you. I don't have much to offer. I'm not a rich man, but I care for you, Lanie."

He suddenly pulled her closer, putting his arms around her, and drawing her in. His kiss was gentle. It was not the first time she had been kissed, but somehow Brent's words had taken her off guard so that she was unable to act. He lifted his head and bent to catch a better view of her face.

"It could be a very good marriage, Lanie. We could move to Chicago or New York where all the editors, publishers, and other writers work. I know a great many, and I could help you with your career." He hesitated again, then said gently, "Do you think you could ever learn to care for me?"

"I don't know, Brent. I'm so confused." One thing she knew, however, was that this was no place for her to be. She rose and said, "I shouldn't have come here, Brent. I planned just to leave the writing off."

"Is that all you have to say, Lanie?"

Lanie hesitated. "I never thought you would want to marry a girl like me. I mean, you're educated, and you're used to big cities. I think we're too different."

Brent shook his head. "That's no barrier. When a man and woman love each other, they learn to reconcile those differences. Think about it, will you, Lanie? That's all I ask."

"I'll—think about it, Brent." She felt a sudden urgency to leave and hurried toward the door. "I'll see you later."

"I'll read your material tonight. When I come by your place tomorrow, I'll bring it back. I'll get to meet your dad, plus I can give you my opinion."

"Thank you, Brent. Good night."

She pedaled furiously away from the cabin, wanting to put as much distance between them as possible.

Brent wants to marry me! His proposal both pleased and frightened her. She thought of Roger. He loved her, but he seemed so young. There was much she admired in Brent, and in truth, he was different from any man she had ever known, but she couldn't imagine fitting into his life. By the time she pulled up in front of the house, she still had not regained her composure. She parked the bicycle and went inside.

Cody was sitting on the floor in front of the fire reading *The Wizard of Oz.* "Where you been? Maeva's almost got supper cooked."

"Oh, no place in particular." She quickly headed to the kitchen to get away from his questions.

〰〰

Lolean arrived to drive the Rolling Emporium and was rather shy when Cody introduced his dad.

"Oh, I remember you, Mr. Freeman. I saw you pitch the time you beat Springdale in a doubleheader."

"Well, I'm glad somebody remembers that, Lolean." He smiled and turned his head to one side. "You're taking this son of mine around with the Emporium?"

"Yes, sir. I've really enjoyed it. It's been a lot of fun."

"Well, it's been a great help to the family."

"I'll go out and load the rest of the stuff, Lolean. We'll go in a few minutes." Cody scurried out of the room, and Lolean turned to face Forrest Freeman. She was an honest girl and said, "I guess maybe somebody told you how much I like Cody."

"Yes, I did hear about that. Does he like you, Lolean?"

"He's scared of girls, I think. He's kind of mixed up, Mr. Freeman."

"Well, at his age I was kind of mixed up myself." He stood there talking to the girl who he remembered vaguely as a leggy teenager, but she had grown into a fine-looking girl now with all the exuberance and joys of youth. "You watch out for Cody. He's going through kind of a hard time."

"Oh, I'll take care of him."

Forrest went to the window and watched as the two got into the Emporium. Lolean was laughing about something, and she reached over and pulled Cody's hair. He caught her wrist and began laughing.

"They make quite a pair, don't they, Daddy?" Lanie said, coming to stand beside him.

"They sure do," he said. "What do you think?"

"Well, she's a little bit forward, but I think Cody really likes her. He pretends not to, though. She says she's going to marry him, and he's going to become a preacher. She teases him all the time because he's younger than she is—about six months, I think." She laughed at the thought, and her eyes danced. "She says she wants to marry a younger man so she can get all of his bad habits worked out of him. Of course, Cody says he doesn't have any bad habits."

The two watched the Rolling Emporium leave, and he turned and said, "Well, Maeva will be getting married soon, I think. I expect you will be one day. It's hard to think about being a grandfather."

Lanie hesitated then said, "Brent is coming by today. He's looking at something I've written, and he wanted to meet you."

"I'm anxious to meet him. He's a pretty interesting man, from what you've told me."

"He knows so much. Makes me feel ignorant."

"Don't you ever say that, Muff. You're smarter than a tree full of owls." He hugged her and as the two turned away from the window, Forrest wondered what Lanie really thought of Brent Hayden.

⚬═⟨⟩⟩

Forrest and Lanie pulled up in front of Annie's house. They had decided to stop there on their way to the store to see if she needed anything. Four large cats came strolling by looking at them curiously, and Forrest shook his head. "Annie's always loved cats. I wonder how many she has now."

"Not as many as she used to have. Only five, I think." She knocked on the door, and they waited, but nobody answered. "That's strange," Lanie frowned. "She must be home. It's too cold for her to be out."

"Try again."

The two stood on the porch, knocking, and finally Lanie tried the door. "I worry about Annie. Let me see if she's all right."

The two stepped inside the house, and Lanie walked through it. It smelled strongly of cats as it always did, but that didn't bother her. The clutter of years of collecting and not throwing anything away filled the room. She had to pick her way through it, and when she opened the bedroom door and called out, "Annie?" she saw Annie was still in bed.

"Annie, are you all right?" She went over and saw that Annie's eyes were closed. For a moment, her heart seemed to stop for she thought the woman was dead, then she saw her chest rising and falling.

She turned quickly and went out. "Daddy, go get Owen. I think Annie's in poor shape."

"All right. I'll get back with him as quick as I can."

Lanie pulled up a chair beside Annie's bed. The old woman's breathing was very faint, and more than once, Lanie was afraid that it had stopped. Finally, Annie's eyelids fluttered and then opened. At once, Lanie leaned over and said, "Are you all right, Annie?"

Annie moved her lips, and then the words were faint, but she cleared her throat and said, "I don't think so. I had a spell with my heart."

"I sent for Owen. He'll be here soon."

"I'm glad you're here." Annie lay quite still, making a thin form beneath the coverlet.

Lanie took her hand and held it. "You'll be all right."

"I'm glad you came. I've wanted to talk to you . . ."

Twenty minutes later Lanie heard the car stop. Owen came in followed by her father. "How is she?"

"She's not very good. She said she had a spell with her heart."

Lanie moved away, and Owen sat down. He pulled his stethoscope out of his bag and listened to Annie's heart. Something in his expression warned Lanie. "Is it bad, Owen?"

"Very bad."

"Can you hear me, Annie?"

Annie was lying still, and her face had lost color. She opened her eyes, saw Owen, and whispered, "I've been telling Lanie something."

"What did you tell her, Annie?"

"It's a secret."

Owen said nothing, but Lanie went around and pulled a chair up to the other side of the bed. Annie's breathing grew erratic, and Lanie was alarmed. "Can't you do anything, Owen?"

Owen looked at her and shook his head. "I don't think I can this time."

Annie lay still for ten minutes. The old clock in the other room clicked loudly. Then she opened her eyes, looked around, and smiled. "You've been a precious daughter to me, Lanie. You tell Davis and Cody and Maeva and Corliss how much I love them."

"I'll tell them, Annie."

Annie seemed to sink deeper into the covers. "Don't forget what I told you, Lanie."

"I won't, Annie. I won't forget."

Owen searched Lanie's face, but she did not look at him.

The room grew quiet, and thirty minutes later Annie Toliver slipped away from earth. Lanie could not stop the tears from rolling down her cheeks. Owen folded Annie's hands, came around, and put his arm around Lanie. "Come along, Lanie. I'll take care of Annie."

She stumbled out of the room, and Forrest said, "She was a good friend to you, wasn't she?"

"Yes, she was, Daddy."

Owen looked at her curiously. "What did she tell you?"

Lanie turned and said, "I can't tell you, Owen. It was—it was something very private."

The funeral of Beulah Ann Toliver was far more impressive than anyone had expected. The church was packed, and Colin Ryan asked people to give their testimonies about what Annie had meant to them.

Davis Freeman stood up, and his face was pale. "When I first knew Annie she was called a witch by a lot of people. Me and Maeva and Cody stole some pears from her. Annie came out, and I was up in the tree. I fell down. They called her Butcher Knife Annie, and I thought she had a knife, and I threw a pear at her and it hit her, and as soon as it did, I saw the hurt in her face." Tears gathered in Davis's eyes. "I never could get away from that so me and Cody and Maeva came the next day, and Lanie too, and we brought her cake, and I told her how sorry I was. After I got to know her, I saw what a kind heart she had, and I've never forgotten that."

Lanie listened as others spoke, and finally she said, "Back when Daddy first went to prison we kids were all alone. We did everything we could to get money to pay the payment on the mortgage, and every month we'd be short, and there'd be money out on the porch in a jar with a note saying 'I love you.' We found out later it was Annie who left the money there."

Forrest rose to speak. "If it hadn't been for Annie, I'd still be in the penitentiary." He looked down at the still form of the woman in the casket and said, "I didn't know her as well as I should have, but she got me out of prison, she and Thelma Mays, and every day of my life I'll thank God for Sister Annie."

That night Lanie wrote for a long time in her journal:

We buried Annie today. She was such a dear person. I remember how some people were afraid of her and some didn't like her, but I loved her and so did all my family.

She went on for some time writing about Annie and how much the old woman had meant to her. Finally, she closed her journal, put it away, and went to bed. Cap'n Brown was waiting for her, and as she burrowed down under the covers, he shoved close to her. She reached down and stroked his fur. He said, "Wow!" just as he always did.

I'm going to miss her, but I'll see her one day. The thought was both sad and triumphant, and Lanie went to sleep thinking about what Annie said before she died.

◆ CHAPTER 17 ◆

November came to the Ozarks, painting the trees a glorious color. The maples were the most colorful—their red, yellow, and golden leaves adorning the earth with a brilliance that almost hurt the eyes. There was a snap in the air and a hint that cold weather was just around the corner.

Forrest had eaten an early breakfast, and Lanie came down just as he was finishing up.

"Why, Daddy, I would have cooked your breakfast."

"I thought I'd be gone by the time you got up," Forrest said.

"Where are you going?"

"I'm going to try to get a deer. Some venison would go down pretty good."

"It would be good, but don't you want to take the boys with you?"

"No, they're both busy. Besides, I just want to be alone for a while today. You get that way, don't you?"

Lanie laughed ruefully. "I don't have time to be alone much, not in this house."

"You've had a hard time, Muff. I want to make it easier for you somehow."

"Don't you worry about it, Daddy. Let me fix you something to take with you."

"That wouldn't go bad. Just some sandwiches maybe."

Lanie hurriedly put together a quick lunch of three thick sandwiches and an apple and handed it to him. "Where do you think you'll go?"

"I think I'll head south and go down along the banks of the river. I seen lots of tracks down there."

"Well, don't try to drag the deer home by yourself."

"I won't. I'll come back and get the boys to help me."

She kissed him again and watched as he left carrying the rifle in the crook of his arm. A wave of thanksgiving went through her as she watched him head south toward the river. She had missed him every day he had been gone, and just having him back in her life again had made life different.

For Forrest the air was soothing as wine although he was not a wine drinker. "I got to stop having those poetic thoughts," he said aloud, then laughed. As he walked along old paths through the woods, the thought of his years in prison came to him. Despite the beauty of the world around him, a shudder ran through his body. He had left prison, but his nights had been troubled with dreams of bars and chains.

Even now as he moved in perfect freedom, a tiny thread of fear touched his spirit with a chill that frightened him. *A man never knows what's in store for him. One day the birds are singing and everything is fine—but the next day monsters creep out of the closet.* He shook off the grim thoughts, determined to enjoy the day.

For the next hour he traipsed along the bank of the Singing River, but the only tracks he saw were old, and he stopped finally and shook his head. "Nothing much going on this way." He turned and looked up to the north where the dark foothills were outlined now by the rising sun. He knew there were deer there, for he had hunted them all of his life. He turned and hurried along, wanting to get deep into the hills before noon.

As he moved quickly, he thought about his family, and a prayer of thanksgiving came to him. "Lord, I'm grateful for Maeva, that You brought her into Your kingdom, and I'm thankful for Cody. He's a handful, Lord, but he's a good boy. And Davis, and Lord, I do thank You for that baby girl of mine. I pray You'll keep her safe. And I thank You for Lanie who's held everything together."

As he walked, he found himself filled with such a fullness that it was like joy overflowing. He found that he was able to walk at twice his usual rate, and soon he entered the foothills, and the land began to slope up. The farms were more spaced out, for the sides of the mountain did not make good farming country. He passed what he thought was the last, and as the country lifted sharply, he found himself reaching for his breath.

I must be getting old. Back when I was sixteen I could run up this mountain and never take a breath.

Two hours later, he was deep in the woods. He was not familiar with the country, but he saw several deer signs and looking up, he saw a peak ahead. "I'll find a spot around that peak."

Soon he came to a large creek. The rains had filled it up, and he saw deer sign there. He saw a likely looking spot on the far side where he could make his stand and decided to cross. Fallen trees created a latticework pattern on both sides, and one decaying tree trunk spanned the creek. He stepped onto the log, his balance precarious, and started to move slowly across.

He had taken only a half dozen steps when the log shifted. Forrest waved his arms wildly, trying to catch his balance, but the log gave way, and he plunged into the cold water. Before his feet struck the bottom, the log shifted and rolled. Before Forrest could move out of the way, the log settled deeper into the water, pinning his legs against the silty bottom of the creek.

Frantically he tried to pull free, but the heavy log settled even more firmly, now pressing down against his legs, the water chest high. He had dropped his gun when he lost his balance, but could not see it in the murky water.

What a mess this is! He was not overly alarmed except it was bad weather to be submerged, and even if he did find a way to dig himself out, he had no way to dry his clothes or even make a fire. The matches in his pocket would be soggy for days.

He began some serious efforts to get out from under the log. It was no more than a foot in diameter and was broken off across the creek, but he could not get a firm grip. He struggled and strained, but when he put his arms under it, he could get no leverage. It was impossible to lift.

A thread of fear ran through Forrest then as he considered his predicament. *I wish I hadn't told Lanie I was going south. They'll send somebody to look for me, but they'll never think to come up into these hills.*

The sun was high now and the murmuring waters made a sibilant sound, but Forrest Freeman knew he was in serious trouble. If he could not free himself, someone would have to help him. But these were isolated hills, and he was off the beaten track. He had followed the logging road, but it showed little sign of use. He called out, "Help, somebody! Can you hear me?"

His voice sounded hollow and thin, but he called out again and again, though with a growing sense of futility. No one was likely to hear him.

For two hours, Forrest sat there growing colder and his legs now growing numb. He leaned forward, put his arm over the tree, and began to pray, "Lord, this is something I can't help myself with. I'll ask You to get me out of this somehow or other. You didn't get me out of prison, I don't think, just to let me die in this creek."

Time passed, and Forrest would call out, but only a faint echo returned.

The minutes passed slowly. The water seemed to grow colder, and his left leg hurt even though it was growing numb. The sun was going down rapidly, and he knew soon it would be nightfall, and the thought of spending all night in the cold waters of this creek pinned like an insect was more frightening than anything Forrest had ever known. He cried out, "Oh, God, help me! I can't help myself." But his words seemed to float back to him instead of rising up.

⚬━⊷

By the time the first light appeared over in the east, Forrest was almost unconscious. His lower body was completely numb, and the water was as cold as ice. His voice was hoarse now, but still, from time to time, he would call out, "Help!" Thoughts of death came to him as they had been all night long, and he feebly shoved the tree but knew that it was useless. He was exhausted, and finally he went to sleep leaning on the tree that was pinning him to the bottom of the creek.

He woke up with a start for he thought he heard something. He cried out hoarsely, "Help me! Somebody please help me!" He waited, but the only sound was the sound of his own voice. He listened hard and thought he heard a sound, but he was so numb and pierced with the cold he could not be sure.

⚬━⊷

The wagon bounced over the old logging road, and the woman who sat in the seat rolled with the motion. She was a big woman wearing a man's overalls and a man's old felt hat pulled down almost to her ears. She was not old, but there was a strength to her, and the hands that held the lines to the horses were strong and tanned.

A big bluetick coonhound was lying in the seat beside her. The woman reached over and ran her hand over his head. "Well, Blue, we caught ourselves some fish, didn't we?"

The big hound licked the woman's hand, and she laughed. "You're an affectionate rascal, I'll say that." She glanced back at the catfish that were flopping in the bed. "That'll make some good eating, Blue — that and those hush puppies you love."

She sat loosely on the seat, strong bodied, and balanced against the wagon's jolts. She was surprised when the big dog suddenly lifted his head and jumped from the wagon seat before she could move.

"Whoa, you critters!" She pulled the horses to a stop and watched as Blue covered the ground toward a stand of trees to her left. "What's got into that fool dog? There must be a deer there." She tied the horses, reached down, got a gun from where it lay in the bottom of the wagon, and moved over toward where the dog had disappeared. She moved carefully for there were panthers still in this wild and woolly part of the county.

"Blue, where are you?" She heard a faint baying sound. It was not like the noise he made when he treed a coon or caught a deer scent, and the woman was puzzled. She moved forward and had to press through some heavy brush. She saw the dog standing beside the creek and said, "What's wrong with you?"

The dog barked sharply, focused on something down in the creek.

"What is that—a beaver?" Moving quickly, she came to the edge of the creek and then stopped dead still. "Lord above, it's a man!" She put the gun down and moved to the very edge of the creek. "Mister, are you all right?" She saw the man lift his head, but his voice was so weak she could not make it out. "Can't get out," she finally heard him say.

For a moment, the woman thought about going for help, but there was no one close. Taking a deep breath, she put the rifle down then waded out into the creek. The cold water chilled her, but she paid no attention. When she got to the man, she saw that he was pale and shivering violently. "What's the matter?"

"The tree ... fell on me. It's got my legs pinned."

Bending over, the woman reached into the water and felt around. "You're pinned all right. Got to get that tree up."

"It's too heavy."

The woman said, "I'll be right back."

She ran back to the wagon for the ax she always carried. Quickly, she felled a sapling four inches in diameter, trimmed it until it made a pole some twelve feet long, then hurried back. She waded out, shoved the thick end under the log, and found there was another tree she could use for a fulcrum. "I can't lift the log and pull you at the same time, mister. When I lift that log, you'll have to drag yourself out."

"All right."

The woman put all her weight against the sapling and at first, nothing seemed to happen, and then the log that pinned the man down began to rise. "That's it," she cried out. "Pull your legs out!"

Forrest threw himself backward, and his head went under water. His legs were numb, but he dragged himself out with the strength of his arms. He came up gasping and sputtering.

The woman dropped the sapling, came to him, and grasped him under the arms. She dragged him to shore and said, "Are you hurt?"

"Leg's broken, I think."

"That's a bad one. You wait right here. I'm going to get the wagon as close as I can to this place, then we'll have to get you in it."

She hurried back to the wagon, drove the horses until they were at the very edge of the brush. Tying them off, she went back and said, "We got to get you to the wagon. You're going to get pneumonia out here. Can you stand up?"

"I'll ... try." For Forrest it was like a dream. He was shaking so violently, and the leg was hurting so intensely he could barely stand it. He felt the woman's strong arms pulling him up, and he did not cry with pain.

The two struggled through the brush until they got to the wagon. She led him to the back and said, "Here, back up to it. I know it'll hurt, but I've got to shove you onto the bed."

"Go ahead." Forrest gritted his teeth. The woman leaned over, grasped his legs, and with one strong motion lifted until he slid on to the back of the wagon. She got into the wagon, pulled him further in, and threw the catfish in the front so they would not get the man with their spines. She saw he was trembling violently and shook her head. "We've got to get you warm quick, mister."

Forrest did not hear this, for he had passed out with the pain from his injured leg and the freezing cold.

The sound was of a fire crackling, and Forrest was aware of a warmth. He tried to move, but his leg gave him such pain he grunted and had to bite his lips to keep from crying out.

He opened his eyes and was shocked to see the face of a woman bending over him.

"Well now, you didn't die after all. How do you feel?"

"Not too good."

"I guess not. You'll be lucky if you don't get pneumonia. You had a fever."

"How long have I been here?"

"Since yesterday. I had a time getting that fever down. What's your name?"

"Forrest Freeman."

"I'm Dakota Jones."

"Mrs. Jones, I've got to get word to my family. They'll be worried sick about me."

"You got a family, wife, and young ones?"

"My wife is dead, but I've got five children. They'll be worried."

"Well, I can't leave you, but Ike Jennings will be by first thing in the morning. I'll send him by to get your folks. Now, we've got to get something warm in you." She reached down and pulled him up into a sitting position. He saw that his leg was bound up with a splint. "My leg broken?"

"No, it ain't broke, but it's going to be mighty stiff."

The woman named Dakota moved over to the stove. Forrest found he was lying on a bed in a large room that evidently served as a kitchen, dining room, and bedroom. There was a door leading off into the other part of the house. It was a tight, well-made cabin, and weak as he was, he wondered where the woman's husband was.

When she came back, she carried a bowl full of broth. "Here, you want me to feed this to you?"

"I guess so."

She took the large spoon, scooped up some of the broth, blew on it, and then gave it to him. "We need to get something inside of you. You gave me quite a skeer there."

"Is your husband here?"

"I lost my husband four years ago." She kept feeding him the broth, and it seemed to go clear down into the nerves and bones. The leg was painful, but finally he finished the broth.

"We'll give you a little more later on. Better do it in little bits than in one big one."

"I'm grateful to you, Miss Jones."

"Just call me Dakota. Everybody does."

"Were you born in Dakota?"

"No, my pappy was though, and he wanted to name me after the state he was born in."

The woman sat there, leaning over his bed. She was, Forrest saw, a large woman, and she had the most direct blue eyes he had ever seen. He marveled at the strength she must have to get him out, but her figure was fairly well concealed by the bulky men's overalls she wore. "I'm much obliged to you. I think you saved my life."

"Well, the Lord sent you, Forrest."

Forrest thought he had not heard her right. "I don't understand that."

Dakota Jones was smiling. There was actually a prettiness about her when she did. "Well, I've been praying for God to send me a husband, and He's done it."

Forrest did not grasp her meaning for a moment, and then shock ran through him. "Why—you don't mean *me!*"

"You're the one He sent."

Forrest was getting sleepy. The food had warmed him, and he felt himself dropping off, but he managed to say, "I've got no idea of marrying anybody, Dakota."

Dakota's voice came clear and steady.

"You've got to, Forrest. God's already decided that."

CHAPTER 18

Pardue Jessup stood listening as Lanie spoke nervously. He had been out searching for her father, and had brought the news that they could find no trace of him.

"Pardue, he's *got* to be out there somewhere," Lanie said, twisting her hands together nervously. "He's been gone all day and all night."

"Well, we couldn't hunt during the night. If he's lying hurt somewhere, we'd miss him, but I'm raising a big bunch to go looking just now. By ten o'clock we ought to have a hundred men and boys out looking along that river."

"What could have happened to him, Pardue?"

Jessup was a big man, six-feet-two with black hair and rough good looks. "A lot of things can happen in the woods. You know that, Lanie. He might have shot himself in the leg. That happens to hunters some times trying to cross a fence with a loaded gun, things like that."

"Well, he couldn't just be lost. He knows this country."

Jessup had fears that the situation was at least as bad as Lanie feared. Forrest Freeman knew this country well. He had hunted Singing River all of his life, and now it appeared that something had happened and this something could not be good. "We've got to keep our heads. I'll call in the National Guard if I have to so we can cover more ground."

The door opened then, and Owen stepped inside. "Is there any news, Pardue?"

"No, there's not," Lanie said.

Owen said, "I'd like to help. I don't know the country very well."

"You can help, Doc," Pardue said. "We're going to string men twenty feet apart and cover both sides of the river. I think there's enough light now we can start."

Pardue turned and left and Owen came over and saw the misery in Lanie's face. "I'm sure we'll find him, Lanie."

"Owen, I'm so afraid, and I feel so helpless."

Owen put his arm around her and held her tight. "I know God did a miracle with your dad's tumor, and he did another one getting him out of the penitentiary, and now we need another miracle. I don't know what God's doing, but it's bound to be something."

Lanie suddenly felt weak. She leaned forward and put her cheek down on Owen's chest. She could feel his heart beating strong and steady, and when his arm went around her, she just wanted to stay there and not return to the harsh reality of life. But she knew she had to. She straightened up and said, "You go help look. I'll cook up something for the men."

Owen gave a quick nod, turned, and left the room. Lanie moved slowly toward the kitchen. She felt numb. "Oh, God, where is he? Where is my daddy?"

⚬

"Well, this here leg don't look too bad."

"It hurts."

"I reckon you twisted it when that tree fell on you." Dakota smiled. "When a tree falls on a man that's enough to give him a little ache, but it ain't broke."

Forrest was sitting up in bed, and he had just finished a bowl of scrambled eggs and sausage and fresh biscuits. He had found himself ravenously hungry, for the fever had drained him, and now he said petulantly, "Dakota, we've got to get word to my family. They'll be worried sick. Couldn't you go?"

"Ike Jennings will be along any time now. He comes along every week on Saturday. He rides to town, and he always stops to ask me if I need anything. You want anything else to eat?"

"No, I've had plenty."

She took his plate, moved over to the cabinet, and put it down. She came back and drew up her chair. It somehow made Forrest nervous when she did this—which was often. She had very dark hair and dark blue eyes, and he could only guess her age at somewhere between thirty and forty. Her face was smooth and unlined, and he sensed that there was strength in her body covered by the bulky, shapeless overalls.

"Tell me about your children."

"What about them, Dakota?"

"What are their names? How old are they?"

Forrest named his children, and Dakota listened intently.

"Do they look like you?"

"Some of them do. Some of them look like their mother. That's a good thing."

"How old are you, Forrest?"

Forrest stared at her. "I'm thirty-eight."

"Is that a fact? Well, I'm thirty-six myself."

She continued to ask questions until finally she lifted her head. "There comes Ike. I hear him whistling. You want to write a note to your children?"

"Yes, I'd better do that."

She got pencil and paper, handed it to him, then went to the door and called, "Ike, come in here."

A tall, shambling man wearing a faded green mackinaw and a wool cap stepped inside. He hadn't shaved lately, and his whiskers were white although his hair was darker.

"Ike, this here is Forrest Freeman. He done hurt himself, and you got to take a note to his family saying he's all right and tell them how to get here."

Ike studied Forrest and said, "I heard about you. You're the fellow that was in jail."

"That's right, I was."

"What were you in jail for, Forrest?" Dakota asked.

"I was accused of murdering a man, but I was pardoned. I just got out a few weeks ago."

"Just in time," Dakota said with satisfaction.

"In time for what?" Ike said.

"Why, time for me, Ike."

Hastily, before Dakota could announce her marital intentions, Forrest folded the paper and said, "If you'd take this into Fairhope, anybody can tell you where the Freeman place is. I've got the street address written down there. I wish you'd hurry. My family will be worried. I'd be glad to pay you."

"I don't reckon I'd take money for a thing like that, and I'll hurry as much as that mule of mine will take me."

After he left, Dakota said, "Ike's a good man. Knows how to find beehives. Brings me honey every year. Got arthritis so he lets them bees sting him, and he says it cures it all up. Mighty hard way to get cured, I'd say."

"I'm real grateful to you, Dakota, for what you've done for me."

"Well, I'm anxious to meet your family. If we're going to get married, I want to see what kind of children you were able to produce."

Forrest opened his mouth to argue, but when he saw the determined look on Dakota's face, he knew it was useless. He settled back, and she said, "I'll bring you some coffee. That'd go down pretty good, wouldn't it?"

⚓

Roger had been involved in the search for Forrest, and he had come back to bring word that they had found nothing. "I'm going to take Booger with me. Give me some of Forrest's clothes. If he found me, he can probably find your daddy."

"I doubt it. The rain probably washed all the scent away, but you can try."

Even as she spoke, a knock came at the door, and she went to find Brent Hayden there. "I came as soon as I could. I just heard."

"Thank you for coming, Brent. You already know Roger Langley ..."

The two men shook hands, and Roger eyed the older man warily. "You're the writer."

"That's right. I've come to help with the search. I don't think I'll be much good in the woods, but I've got to try."

Roger said, "I don't think we need any more help. We've got it pretty well covered. I'll see you later."

Brent stared at the young man. "What's he mad about?"

Aunt Kezia had been taking it all in. "Why, he's jealous, boy. He's been trying to get Lanie to marry him for a long spell."

"I didn't know that." Brent turned to Lanie and said, "You never mentioned it."

"I guess I didn't."

Kezia said, "Come on in. You can help us cook the food for the men."

"I'm afraid I'm not much of a cook."

Kezia cackled. "Well, what are you good for then?"

"Not much of anything, I'm afraid."

"Oh, this is my Aunt Kezia. You didn't meet her the other day."

They went into the kitchen and began fixing fried chicken for those who were searching. While they were cooking, Cody and Davis came in, looking discouraged.

"These are my brothers, Brent." She introduced the boys, and Cody said gloomily, "We've gone ten miles down river. I guess we'll go another ten."

"I'm real worried about Daddy," Davis said. "He couldn't be lost. He must be hurt somehow, but we just can't find him."

"You boys sit down and eat something."

"I'm not hungry," Davis said.

"You've got to eat!" Kezia snapped.

The boys sat down to eat. They had almost finished the fried chicken when a dog barked outside. Corliss ran over to the window. "It's a man on a mule."

Lanie went to the front door, and the tall lanky man pulled his hat off. "I'm looking for the Freeman place."

"Yes, I'm Lanie Freeman."

"Well, I got a note from your daddy."

A great sense of relief washed through Lanie, and she said, "Is he all right?"

"I guess he'll tell you in the note."

She opened the note, and the others had come crowding out. "What does it say, Lanie?" Davis cried.

Lanie read, *I had an accident and am unable to walk to get back home without help. I am at the home of a lady named Dakota Jones. The man who brings this will show you how to get there.*

"How was he hurt? I don't know your name," Lanie said.

"You can just call me Ike. I don't know how your pappy was hurt. He was in bed though. Dakota Jones is a good woman with sick folks."

"Will you take us there, Ike?" Maeva asked.

"Sure will. It'll be a little bit slow on that mule though."

"We'll go in the Emporium," Cody said. "Then we can make a bed for daddy, and he can lie down on the way back."

Maeva said, "I'll get some blankets and a pillow."

Five minutes later, they were ready. They had put Ike's mule out in the pasture with the cow, and Ike was fascinated at the Rolling Emporium. "It's just a store on wheels, ain't it now?"

"That's what it is." Davis was driving. Almost at once Lanie began questioning Ike, but he appeared to know little.

"I don't believe I know anyone named Jones. Where do they live?"

"Up in the hills." He pointed north. "You take old State Highway 27. Ain't been used for years now, and you turn off on a logging road. It's kind of hard to get through."

"And the family's name is Jones?"

"Well, there ain't no family to it," Ike said. "Is this Vienna sausage?" He reached over and pulled a can off the shelf.

"Yes, would you like some?"

"I am partial to Vienna sausage."

Cody grabbed a can and opened it, saying, "Here, help yourself." Ike fished one of the sausages out and popped it into his mouth. "Oh, that is purely good."

"About the Joneses—"

"Oh, well, it's just Dakota. She's a harb woman, you know, and good at healing. Lost her husband a few years ago. She's kind of a preacher woman too, at times. Got a fine farm, but she don't farm it now. But she does raise fine hosses."

"Does she have children?"

"She had two girls, but they married and moved away off in California or somewhere. Like I say, she raises fine hosses and goats. Does right well for herself."

Ike ate three cans of Vienna sausage as he gave them a complete history of Dakota Jones. Finally, he said, "There's the logging road. It's kind of rough. Can't turn this here bus around until we get to Dakota's house."

Davis slowed down, for the road was indeed rough, and it was barely wide enough to accommodate the Emporium.

Finally, Ike said, "Well, there she is. That's Dakota's house." He pointed at a log cabin that was set in a clearing, smoke rising from its chimney. Davis pulled the Emporium up and opened the door. They all began piling out, Lanie first, and she saw a woman wearing a man's overalls step outside the door. "I see that Ike found you."

"Yes, I'm Lanie. Is Daddy all right?"

"I'm Dakota Jones. Come in. Your pa's been fretting about you."

Dakota moved inside, and the whole family, except for Ike, came in. Lanie saw her father sitting in a bed, his leg splinted somehow, and he looked pale. "Daddy, are you all right?"

She ran over and threw her arms around him, Maeva came to the other side, and Corliss shoved her way in. The boys edged closer, and they all began to pepper him with questions.

Forrest raised his hands. "Well, I made a bad mistake. I told you I was going south, and instead I changed my mind and came up here in the hills. I was crossing a creek, and a freak accident happened. I was on a log, and it shifted, and I fell in, and the blasted log fell right across my legs. So there I sat, the whole tree holding me down. I was out of the water from the chest up, but that water was cold."

"Couldn't you get out, Daddy?" Davis asked.

"Couldn't pull my legs out. Hurt my left leg real bad when that tree pinned me."

"How awful!" Maeva said. She was holding Forrest's hand, reached out, and ran her hand across his hair. "How long did you have to stay there?"

"About twenty-four hours, I reckon. It was pretty cold."

"What happened?" Cody said. "What did you do?"

"Well, son, mostly I prayed, and I'd call out every once in a while but nobody answered. Finally, this lady here, Miss Dakota Jones, she had a hound dog with her in the wagon. He must have heard me call, so he jumped out, she says. Is that the way it happened, Dakota?"

"Sure is. Old Blue went right to where your daddy was trapped under that log."

"How'd you get him out?" Cody asked.

"I cut down a four-inch tree and used it as a lever. I lifted the log up that was holding your daddy down, and he managed to pull himself out. He was pretty far gone though. He passed out by the time we got him in the wagon. I was afraid he was going to get pneumonia. He had a mighty high fever."

"Dakota just about saved my life."

"Well," Dakota said, smiling, "it was the Lord who led me that way. Usually I don't have old Blue with me. He was the one that really found your pa." She looked around at all of the children and studied each face carefully. "Forrest, you sure do have handsome children."

Cody grinned. "Well, that's right nice of you to say so, Miss Jones."

"Nothing more than the truth, and since I'm going to be your new ma you can call me Dakota for a while — then later after your pa and me are married, you can call me ma."

Everyone stared staring at Dakota, openmouthed. "Our ma?" Davis said. "What do you mean?"

"Why, I've been praying for God to send me a husband, and He sent your pa."

Forrest's face was flushed. "I've tried to tell you, Dakota, I don't intend to marry again."

"Well, that's what you think now, Forrest, but God's promised me, and I didn't tell you the rest of it."

"What's the rest of it?" Maeva said. She found the whole situation rather amusing, and there was a wicked curiosity in her question.

"Well, God promised to give me a new husband, and He promised me we'd have our own children." Dakota looked with satisfaction at the Freeman children. "I was a mite worried that my new husband wouldn't give me handsome children, but I see now that Forrest is plum able to do that."

Forrest threw up his hands. "I've tried to explain to Dakota that I'm not a candidate for marriage."

"That's what you say now, but God ain't through talking to you yet."

"How'd you get here?" Forrest said.

"The Emporium," Lanie said.

"Well, make me a bed. I want to go home."

The boys helped Forrest to get out of the bed and hobble on one leg to the front door. He turned and said, "Dakota, I want you to know I'll never forget you. You saved my life."

"No, you won't forget me," she said cheerfully. She came over and put her hand on his cheek. "You go get that leg healed up. I'll be coming to visit you."

Forrest stared at her and then shook his head. "We'll be glad to see you," he said shortly. "Boys, get me out of here. Put me to bed."

Ten minutes later the Emporium was winding its way down the logging road, Davis driving carefully. Forrest was on the floor, and Corliss was sitting beside him asking questions as usual. "Daddy, am I going to have a new mama?"

Forrest tried to laugh. "Dakota was just joking."

Maeva winked at Lanie. "I don't think she was joking, Daddy."

"Well, she saved my life, and I'll always be thankful. But she's wrong about marrying me."

Corliss took Forrest's hand. "I like her, Daddy. If you married her, I'd have a mama—I'll bet she'd give me a pony all my own, and I could name it Pepper."

Forrest laughed. "Well, we'll see about the pony, but don't count on getting a new mama."

PART FOUR

A Time to Embrace

❧ CHAPTER 19 ❧

Forrest Freeman sat listening to the radio, staring moodily into the fireplace, watching the yellow flames lick around the white oak logs. The fire made a pleasant crackling sound, and a log shifted, sending a myriad of fiery sparks up the chimney. Forrest loved fireplaces; as a matter of fact, he loved everything about wood fires. He even loved the task of going into the woods, cutting down the trees, bringing them home to saw into lengths, and then using a splitting maul on them.

The radio announcer sounded excited, but then Forrest supposed that newscasters were always supposed to be like that. He slumped deeper into his chair and dropped his chin onto his chest as the announcer said:

> *Today, November the eighth, 1932, Franklin D. Roosevelt won a landslide victory for president of the United States. He carried all but six states by promising to "restore this country to prosperity."*
>
> *His stunning defeat of President Herbert Hoover comes at a time when the nation is in a deep Depression, a time of growing bread lines and soup kitchens, of bank failures and farm foreclosures and soaring unemployment.*
>
> *Despite the fact that Roosevelt is badly crippled from polio, he was buoyant, joyous, and confident as he spoke of what he called "a new deal" for Americans.*

"The country needs, the country demands, bold, persistent experimentation," he said early in the campaign. "It is common sense to take a method and try it."

Roosevelt has vowed to revive prosperity on the farms, to rehabilitate the railroads, to regulate the banks and security exchanges. "I am waging a war in this campaign." he said, "a frontal attack, an onset, against the four horsemen of the present Republican leadership: the four horsemen of destruction, delay, deceit, and despair."

Forrest rose and stared at the radio as if it were a mortal enemy. "That's lots of promises, Franklin Roosevelt, but I doubt if you can live up to them." He turned the dial, and the strains of the song that had caught the mood of the country, "Brother, Can You Spare a Dime," made a tinny sound in the room. He changed the dial again, and a smooth syrupy orchestra played "I'm Getting Sentimental Over You."

"What are you listening to, Dad?"

Forrest turned to put his eyes on Lanie who had come into the room with a cup in her hand. "Just the news."

"I brought you some hot chocolate."

"Thanks, Muff." Taking the chocolate, Forrest sipped at it and then stared moodily into the fireplace. He sat down in the chair, and Beau came over and tried to sit on his lap.

Forrest shoved him off. "You're too big to be a lap dog, Beau. Go somewhere else."

As always, Beau's sensitive feelings were hurt. He gave Forrest a sad look then went over to the corner and plunked himself down staring at the wall.

"That's the only dog I ever saw that could pout," Lanie said.

Forrest shook his head and gave her a strange look. "That's what I'd like to do—go somewhere and pout."

Maeva came hurrying in and said at once, "I'm expecting Logan. He told me that he might have some good news, but he wouldn't tell me what."

"He hasn't found work, has he?" Forrest said. "I sure haven't been able to find any."

"Just day work, but we know God will give us something to do." She went over and suddenly sat down on Forrest's lap. "You can hold me like you did when I was a little girl."

Forrest laughed and put his arms around her and gave her a squeeze. "You're a little bit bigger now, Maeva."

Maeva kissed his cheek, got up, and said, "We've got breakfast fixed. I'll go call the boys."

Ten minutes later, they were seated around the table, eating, and Corliss suddenly said, "There's Beau barking. Somebody's coming."

"It must be Logan." Maeva got up and went to the front door. She opened it and smiled. "Come in, Logan. You're just in time for breakfast."

"I can use some." Logan pulled a chair up to the table and Maeva heaped his plate up with scrambled eggs.

"I mixed some squirrel brains in with these. I know you like that."

"It gives me the creeps," Cody said gloomily, "eating squirrel brains."

"I notice you didn't shove away from it," Davis grinned.

Logan ate heartily, then took a big swig of the coffee out of the large mug. He grinned and said, "I've got some good news for a change."

"Well, I reckon we can use some. What is it?" Forrest asked.

"Do you remember a fellow named Charlie Bailey?"

Maeva frowned. "I remember meeting him in California. He was an agent, wasn't he?"

"Yeah, he's the agent for several country western singers. Well, he heard us sing when we were at Ozzie Williams's place in L.A. I got a letter from him, and he told me to call him collect, so I did. He wanted to talk about putting us under contract as our manager."

"You mean you'd go back to California?" Lanie asked quickly.

Logan shook his head. "I told him we weren't interested in that life anymore. I told him Maeva and I both had given our lives to the Lord. That kind of set him back."

"I don't guess he gets that kind of response from many people," Maeva said. "Was that all of it?"

"Well, not really. I told him we weren't going to sing anything but gospel, and he got a little bit huffy about that and that was it. But he called me back just yesterday and said he had second thoughts." Logan leaned forward, and his face was alight with excitement. "He told me there's room for gospel music, and he wants us to make a record."

"Make a record!" Maeva echoed. "You mean a gospel record?"

"Yes, we'd go over to Fort Smith. Bailey owns half that recording studio over there. He says his partner will push it if it's any good. If it goes well, he said he could get us bookings as gospel singers."

Maeva jumped up out of her chair and ran around to Logan. She threw her arms around him and Logan grinned. "It may come to nothing, but it won't cost anything to try—just gas money and a hotel for one night in Fort Smith. I don't even have that though."

Aunt Kezia said firmly, "I'll pay for that." She grinned and added, "Then you'll have to give me some of that money you're going to make off of that record."

"What song will we do?" Maeva said.

"I think we'll do the one I wrote myself. You haven't even heard it yet. Come on in the living room, and I'll play it for you."

"What's the title of it?"

"Heaven's Only a Step Away."

"That sounds like a mighty good title, Logan," Kezia said. "You play so pretty, and Maeva sings so good."

"We're going to make a duet out of this." Logan suddenly laughed. "Wouldn't it be something if we had a hit record and got on the Grand Ole Opry?" He shook his head and said, "It'd take a miracle though. There's lots of records out there in the world."

"When will we leave, Logan?" Maeva demanded.

"As soon as Aunt Kezia gives us the money we'll be on our way."

Roger noticed the big new Oldsmobile parked out in front of his house. He didn't recognize the car and wondered whose it could be. As soon as he stepped inside, he was met by his father, who was smiling broadly. "Come on in, son. I've got some people I want you to meet."

Roger accompanied his father down the hall, and they turned into the parlor. The fire was crackling in the fireplace, and Roger's mother came over and greeted him with a kiss. "Hello, Mom."

"Son, we've got company. This is my good friend Thomas Craig—and this is his daughter Eileen. This is our son Roger."

"Glad to know you both." Roger shook hands with Mr. Craig, who was a tall, distinguished-looking man with some silver in his hair. The daughter, Eileen Craig, was of medium height had auburn hair and well-shaped features.

"Actually, Thomas is a relative of mine."

"A pretty distant relative. About sixth or seventh cousin," Craig said. He was studying Roger, and when they all sat down, he said, "I think your father has a confession to make, Roger."

Roger suddenly turned, his eyes flying wide. "A confession, Dad? What have you been doing?"

"Well, I've been bragging on you mostly. Professor Craig here is the head of the engineering department at MIT."

"The Massachusetts Institute of Technology?"

"That's the only MIT I know." Otis Langley grinned. "We kind of grew up together, and I've been writing Tom for some time telling about you."

"He even sent me your transcripts," Craig said, "and he tells me you want to be an engineer."

"Yes, sir, I would like to be."

Craig studied the young man and said suddenly, "Well, if you mean business, I think I can help you."

"Help me? How is that, Mr. Craig?"

"I can get you an assistantship in my department."

"An assistantship? How does that work?"

"You'll take some classes, and you'll work so many hours a week for me sharpening pencils or whatever I need having done." He reached over and put his arm around his daughter. "Eileen here takes care of me since we lost her mother, at home that is, but at work I need somebody else. I need somebody to keep me from going wrong."

"I doubt if I could do that, Mr. Craig."

"Do you think you might be interested? I know it comes as a shock, but the semester's just starting, and I've got to get back. I'd like for you to go with us."

"We've got this big old house," Eileen said, her eyes shining, "with lots of room. Daddy said you could room with us."

Roger was stunned. He stammered, "I—I never thought of such a thing, but I do want to study engineering."

Martha Langley said quickly, "Why don't you take Eileen and show her the town. She can tell you more of what it's like living in Massachusetts. Then you can come back, and we'll have dinner together."

"I'd like to see the town, Roger," Eileen said.

"Well, it's not much to see after Massachusetts, I'm sure, but I'll be glad to show it to you." The two left, and Otis Langley said, "That's a beautiful daughter you have there, Tom."

"She's her mother all over again. Smart, pretty, and sweet. That's about all a woman can be, I suppose."

"You're right," Otis Langley said and put his arm around his wife. "Martha here has always been those things."

"Do you think your son will be interested?"

"He'd be crazy to turn you down."

Martha said nervously, "But you have to let him make his own decisions, Otis."

"I know. I've been guilty of pushing my children at times. Hard to take your hands off, but I think he'd be interested. All he talks about is engineering, and MIT is probably the best school in the country."

"Well, he'd be kind of like a member of the family." Craig smiled. "I hope he decides to go with us."

Lanie came out of Pink's Drugstore and came face-to-face with Roger and a very attractive young woman.

Roger blushed as he said, "Why—why, hello, Lanie."

"Hi, Roger." She waited for him to introduce her, and when he simply stood there, she said, "You're supposed to introduce people, Roger."

"Oh—I'm sorry. Lanie, this is Eileen Craig. Miss Craig, this is Lanie Freeman, a very good friend of mine."

Lanie thought that was somewhat odd since he had asked her to marry him, and now she was a very good friend. "How do you do, Miss Craig?"

Roger began to speak rapidly. "Eileen came with her father to visit our family. Her father's Professor Craig. They're from Massachusetts."

"Are you on a vacation?"

"Well, we did go to some Civil War battlefields," Eileen said, smiling. "Daddy's fascinated by the Civil War, and we don't have any battlefields in Massachusetts."

"Well, I hope you enjoy your visit here," Lanie said. "It's good to meet you."

"And it's good to meet you."

Lanie turned and walked away, and Eileen asked, "She seemed like a very nice young woman. Have you known her long?"

"I guess everybody in Fairhope knows everybody else. Yes, I've known her quite a while. Come along, and I'll show you the town."

As soon as Lanie returned home after running several more errands, she found that the gossip about Roger and the young woman had already reached there.

"Henrietta Green saw Roger and some pretty young woman walking around town," Maeva said. Henrietta Green was the telephone operator and used her position to spread the news. "Henrietta was dying to know who she was."

"I know who she was. She and her father are here visiting the Langleys. They're distant relatives, I think."

"Were you jealous?"

"Oh, not really. She is a fine-looking woman though. She talks like a Yankee."

"Well, that's what she is, being from Massachusetts."

Corliss came bursting into the room. "Maeva—Lanie, Dakota's here."

Forrest suddenly appeared at the door. He went over and looked out window. "Oh, no," he groaned, "it's Dakota. She's found me!"

"Brace up, Dad. She can't eat you." Maeva laughed.

They all went out on the front porch, and Corliss ran at once to Dakota, who jumped out of the wagon. She was wearing a pair of clean overalls and had on a broad-brimmed straw hat. "Well, honey child, I brought you a pony."

Corliss stared at Dakota and then ran to the pony that was tethered to the back of the wagon. It was a beautiful small horse, speckled and spotted. Dakota went quickly to say, "I think he's just about your size. Let's see if you'll fit." She reached down, picked up Corliss, and sat her on the pony's back. "There, how does that feel, honey?"

"Is it really for me?"

"Why, you're the only one that asked for a pony."

Forrest had watched this with apprehension. He came down and said, "You can't be giving horses away, Dakota."

"That ain't no horse, Forrest. That's just a pony. I ain't got a use in the world for that little mare, but Corliss will have, I'll bet." She turned and said, "Cody, you get that plunder out of the wagon."

"What is it, Miss Dakota?"

"It's the fixings for the most bodacious supper you ever et."

Cody and Maeva carried the baskets and a bucket inside, and as soon as they were in the house, Dakota looked around. "My, ain't this a fine place. It's your old homeplace, is it, Forrest?"

"Yes, my grandfather built it."

"Well, it sure is fine. Now, let me see that leg of yours."

"My leg's all right."

"Don't argufy with me, Forrest. You just set there." She put her hand on Forrest's chest and practically shoved him into a chair. Kneeling down, she pulled his pant leg up and studied the leg. "Well, them bruises is about gone. I reckon you're feeling all right."

"I'm feeling fine, but Dakota, we can't afford that pony. We can't afford to feed one."

"That ain't no problem. I brought enough feed with me. I grow my own oats, and I brought enough to feed that little lady for a month."

"It's too big a gift," Forrest protested. "We just can't take it."

"Daddy, you got to let me have her."

Dakota put her arm around the girl. "You need to pamper this pretty little thing, Forrest."

"You'll spoil her, Dakota."

"Well, she needs to be spoiled a little bit. Now, you show me around your place, and then I'll come back and fix your supper."

Dakota disappeared into the kitchen to be sure the food she brought was being taken care of, and Maeva came to stand beside Forrest. "That woman will drive me crazy."

Maeva laughed and her put arm around her father. "Don't talk that way about her, Daddy. After all, she's going to be our new mama."

"You need a spanking, Maeva Freeman, and you may get one yet!"

"Come on. She saved your life, Corliss gets a pony, and we get a free meal. We'll see what kind of a cook our new mama's going to be."

❦

The supper was on the table. Dakota had cooked all afternoon. She had brought a bucket full of turtle meat and made turtle soup, which none of them had ever tasted before. She had made deviled crab eggs and brought five guinea hens all dressed. "They ain't big," she said, "but there ain't nothing more tasty than young guinea hens."

Finally, they got to the dessert, which was honey pumpkin pie.

"I got the honey myself, and I raised the pumpkins myself."

"This is the best pie I ever had!" Cody exclaimed. "I bet they have honey pumpkin pie in heaven."

Dakota laughed. "I wouldn't be a bit surprised about that."

"It's a wonderful meal, Dakota," Lanie said. "How did you learn to cook?"

"Seems like I could always cook. Now tell me about this place of yours, Forrest."

"Well, it used to be a big plantation with over a thousand acres at one time. Land was cheap back in those days. But hard times came—" he shrugged—"and it got sold off piece by piece. This five acres with the homeplace is all that's left." A sad look crossed Forrest's face. "No way to get it back."

"Why, shore there is," Dakota said, and Forrest looked up in surprise. "I've got over seven hundred acres. A lot of it is in timber, which ain't worth much these days, as you know, but there's plenty of cleared land to raise feed and pasture horses. There's money in horses. People are buying horses more than tractors these days."

"That's a big place for a woman to keep by herself," Forrest murmured.

"Well, it is hard, and I can't keep it going. I just have to let things go, but when you and me get married, with you there, Forrest, we could make that farm a jewel of a place."

Forrest threw up his hands. "Dakota, I've got no idea of marrying anybody."

Dakota went on as if he had not spoken. "You probably don't know much about horses, but I can teach you." She plunged into a description then of how her place could be made into something like the Freemans' place before it had been broken up. Forrest sat there, a gloomy look on his face, but all the rest of the family was fascinated by Dakota. Her eyes were beautiful, and her features were good, but her hair was simply tied back with a thong, and the overalls concealed her figure thoroughly.

Finally, she looked around the table and said, "I never saw such fine looking young ones." She looked then at Forrest and nodded firmly. "Our young ones will be every bit as good looking as these."

She started to get up. "Well, I've got to get started home."

Kezia shook her head firmly. "You'll have to stay the night."

"Why, I can't do that."

Kezia insisted. "You can't be going home in the dark like this."

"That's right," Lanie said quickly. "You've got to stay."

"You can put a cot in my room," Kezia said.

Dakota looked at Forrest who said nothing at all, and it was Davis who said, "Come along, Ma. I'll help you put the horses up."

Dakota Jones looked at the young man. The fact that he had called her *Ma* touched her, and she said, "Well, I reckon I could stay just one night."

Thirty minutes later the horses were up, and Dakota was up in Kezia's room. Lanie and Maeva had brought in a cot and fixed it up with sheets and a blanket.

"You mean what you said about God telling you He was going to send you a husband?"

"I sure did, Miss Kezia."

"No *Miss* about it, not at my age. I'm Kezia and you're Dakota. You really believe God told you that?"

"Yes, I do. Do you believe God tells people things?"

"I do."

She hesitated, and then Dakota said, "Forrest don't seem to like me much."

Kezia said, "From what I hear he loved his wife to distraction, but he needs a companion."

"I don't know. He just don't take to me."

"Well, if God's going to make a match out of you two, He'll do it. Forrest may kick and scream. Some men do, but these children already take to you—especially Corliss. That child is hungry for a mama."

"I don't know, Kezia. I talk big, but I get kind of scared sometimes."

"What are you scared of?"

"Growing old by myself."

"I know what that's like. I was in a sorry, no-account nursing home when Lanie and Merritt came. They took me out of that place and brought me here and made me a part of the family." She looked at the big woman and said, "I think they'll do the same thing for you. Just don't give up, Dakota!"

CHAPTER 20

When Lanie opened the door, she was surprised to see Roger standing there—and somewhat amused to see how awkward and ill-at-ease he seemed. "Why, good morning, Roger," she said brightly. "Come in."

"I can't stay long," Roger said as he stepped inside, "but I have to talk to you about something."

"Well, come on into the kitchen. You're late for breakfast, but there's still some coffee."

"No coffee for me," Roger said. He hesitated and then asked, "Where is everybody?"

"Daddy took the boys squirrel hunting, and Corliss is upstairs. Aunt Kezia is reading *The Wizard of Oz* to her—again. She does love that book." She walked into the kitchen, poured herself a cup of coffee, then turned to say, "What is it you wanted to talk about, Roger?"

"Well ..." he began, then cleared his throat as if to give himself a stronger voice. "I guess you probably heard the gossip about me and Eileen Craig."

"Yes, I have. Dorsey Pender keeps us well posted. I think he keeps his job as a mailman simply to have an opportunity to talk about people."

"Well, I came by to tell you something, and it may sound odd to you."

Lanie studied Roger and saw that for some reason he was having trouble meeting her gaze. She was genuinely fond of Roger. They had been friends ever since she had beaten him out for a prize when he was a senior in high school. She had always admired him because he was able to take that loss with a good spirit. She also admired him because when his family had been totally opposed to the Freemans, especially his father, Roger had insisted on remaining her friend. He'd even left his father's house for a time. She had read her diary recently, tracing her feelings about Roger, and had come to the conclusion that most of what she felt for him was the remnants of a crush that a freshman would have for a fine-looking, accomplished senior.

"Why don't you just tell me what's on your mind, Roger? I can see you're troubled."

"Well, I am. You know I told you about Professor Craig's offer?"

"To go to Massachusetts as one of his students?"

"Yes. Well, I've been thinking about it."

Suddenly Lanie knew why Roger was there. "You've decided to go to Massachusetts, haven't you, Roger?"

Words came rapidly to Roger's lips, and he shifted his feet nervously. "It's just too good an opportunity to pass up, Lanie. I'll get free room and board with the professor. He'll give me an assistantship, and MIT is one of the finest engineering schools in the country."

"It's a wonderful opportunity for you."

"Well, it is. I've decided to go, but I hate to go off and leave you."

"An opportunity like this doesn't come along every day, Roger," Lanie said. "I think you have to take it."

Roger looked down at his feet for a long moment, and the silence filled the kitchen. Lanie could hear the sound of the chickens out in the yard clucking, and from far off, a dog was barking at something, but she waited until Roger broke the silence.

"I've asked you to marry me, and if you will, I'll stay here and get some kind of job."

A warm feeling of affection came to Lanie Freeman at that moment. She knew how badly Roger wanted to be an engineer and what he would be sacrificing, but she did not hesitate for an instant. "No, that's no answer for us, Roger. If we married, we might have a baby, and then you'd have a family to struggle with as well as getting your education. I can understand, and I'm so happy for you."

"Don't you care at all for me, Lanie?"

Lanie felt a wave of sadness. She put the coffee down, came forward, took Roger's hand, and held it in both of hers. "I have a great affection for you, Roger. I always have. You're such a good man, but the road you are taking is going to be long and difficult, and you're going to need all the strength you have to make your way."

"All that is saying you don't love me."

There was an honesty in Lanie Freeman, and she looked into Roger's eyes and said quietly, "I don't think we care for each other in the way that a man and a woman ought to who are thinking of marriage."

Roger gnawed on his lower lip and then forced a laugh of sorts. "Well, I guess that's it then."

"When will you be leaving?"

"They're leaving tomorrow, and they want me to go back with them. It's late in the semester to start, but he says he can help get me registered in some classes and start my work if I go now."

"I hope you'll write me. I'll be praying for you, Roger, every day. I know you're going to be successful."

"Well, there's nothing to this talk about me and Eileen. I like her, but she's not the woman you are."

Lanie had the impulse to say, *You'll be living in the same house with her. I think you might change your mind.* But she wisely refrained. "I'm sure she's a fine person, and you must write and tell me all that goes on."

"Will you answer me?"

"Of course I will." Lanie squeezed Roger's hand and then removed her own. He suddenly leaned forward, kissed her on the cheek, and then muttered, "Good-bye, Lanie."

Lanie watched Roger as he left the kitchen, then followed him. He left the house, and she stood in the doorway watching as he went to his car. He got in, started the engine, and then he took one look at her. Roger waved, and then Lanie waved back. As the car moved away, she felt that a door had closed that would never be open again. She knew she would write about all this in her journal, but somehow she felt no sorrow nor grief. As she went about her work that morning, she thought about what had happened. Finally, she went upstairs and sat down beside Aunt Kezia.

"Look at that child. She's gone plum to sleep while I was reading to her."

Lanie looked over at Corliss who was lying flat on her back on Aunt Kezia's bed. Her eyes were closed, and she was breathing deeply. There was a pleased smile on her face as she lay there sleeping. "I was reading to her, and I got interested in this silly story. Then when I finally looked up there she lay."

"She loves that book."

"It's kind of a foolish book, but I've read it so much to her I like it myself." Kezia looked up and studied Lanie's face. "What's the matter, child? You look troubled."

"It's not that, Aunt Kezia, but Roger just left here. He told me that he's leaving Fairhope. He's going to Massachusetts to study engineering."

"With the professor that's a friend of his daddy's?"

"Yes."

Kezia studied Lanie's face. She had grown to love this young woman dearly and had followed Roger's courtship with a close intensity. She put the book down, folded her hands, and said, "How do you feel about that? His leaving, I mean."

"It's something he had to do. It's a wonderful opportunity for him."

"Did he ask you to go with him?"

"He said if I'd marry him, he'd stay here and get a job."

"That was a good offer for that young man to make. It must have been hard for him."

"Roger's one of the best young men I know. He always has been."

Kezia did not move her eyes from the face of the young woman who had come to mean so much to her. "Are you going to grieve over him?"

"I'll miss him, but it's something he had to do."

"Well, I can see it didn't hurt you too much." She suddenly laughed and said, "I remember I fell in love with a young fellow once. I guess that's what you young people call a crush. He drove a stage from the Butterfield Line. Oh, was I ever gone on him!"

Lanie loved to hear Kezia's stories. "What did he look like?"

"You know that movie actor, the cowboy, John Wayne. He looked like him."

"Did he like you?"

"I'm afraid that was the trouble. He liked all young girls. Of course, I was too young and inexperienced to know then, but I found out he was going to marry Ellen Raines, and it just about broke my heart — for about a week. But I got a little wisdom out of it."

"Not to fall in love with stagecoach drivers?"

"Not to fall in love with anybody unless there was something more real than I had for him. Well, that simplifies your life, don't it now?"

"Yes, it does. Well, I'm going down and do some canning."

"I wish I could help you, but my arthritis is pretty bad today."

"You help a lot just taking care of Corliss."

"I wish everything was as easy as taking care of this baby. She's better than going to a picture show."

⚭

Two days after Roger left town with the professor, Owen had come by to check on Kezia. He liked the old woman tremendously and often came by even when there was nothing wrong with her.

He sat and talked with her for over an hour, and then when he came down, Lanie said, "I just made fresh cherry cobbler. I don't suppose you'd want any."

"I can refuse anything except temptation and fresh cherry cobbler." He sat down at the table and waited until Lanie had put down a deep dish full of cherry cobbler and a thick mug. Owen dug in and said, "Ow, that's hot!"

"Now, don't burn your tongue."

Owen blew on the cobbler and ate it, and between bites, he talked of the patients he had seen. Finally, he looked at her directly and said, "How do you feel about Roger going to Massachusetts?"

"It was too good an opportunity to pass up."

"That young fellow had a heart for you."

"It was one of those things, Owen. I admire Roger tremendously, and I hope I'll always be good friends with him, but we didn't love each other enough to get married."

"How much is that? How do you measure it, Lanie?"

Lanie sat down, folded her hands, and looked across the table at Owen. He had become such an integral part of her life that she could not imagine not having him there. Ever since she had been fourteen, he had been there for her and for the family when they needed help. She knew that she had a special feeling for him, but it was harder to understand his feelings for her. At times, she wanted to ask him point blank, "Do you love me, Owen Merritt?" but the time had never come for such a thing as that. Finally, she said, "I don't know how you measure love. It's not like a pound of sugar or two feet of some kind of material, is it?"

"No, it isn't, but I've always thought that you and Roger might make a match of it."

"It's easy to make a mistake." She started to tell him that Roger had offered to stay but then changed her mind. She sat there silently, and finally Owen saw the talk was making her uncomfortable.

He sipped his coffee. "What's going on with Forrest and this woman Dakota Jones? It seems a twisted tale to me."

"Oh, it's a strange thing. Dakota pretty much saved Daddy's life, but she thinks God's sent him into her life to be her husband."

"That's the talk I heard, but I didn't know whether to believe it." He laughed. "I'm wondering how many women have felt that way when a man came into their lives?"

"Don't laugh at her, Owen," Lanie said. "She's a fine woman. A little rough around the edges, but I like her."

"From all I understand she's had kind of a hard life. How does your dad feel about her?"

"Oh, he claims she's driving him crazy, but I don't think it would be a bad thing if Daddy did marry again. You know, sooner or later all of us will be leaving to go to school or to get married. Davis may go off and play professional ball. This would be an empty house, and Daddy needs somebody to share it with."

"A man does get lonely."

Quickly Lanie looked up. "Surely not you? You're so busy with your doctoring."

"Doctoring takes part of a man, but you know most men, I think, have some kind of a picture of the kind of woman they want to marry in their heads. Usually it's a picture made up of the best he's seen in different women, one of them's beauty, another one's goodness, another's fiery desires."

Lanie stared at Owen. "That's not very fair. It sounds like he's got to have the ideal."

"Well ..." Owen smiled and it made him look much younger. "I think when a man finally gets a woman, he sees those things in her he wants to see."

It was the first time Lanie had ever heard Owen talk like this — how he felt about love and marriage and the woman he would spend his life with. "Are you saying love is blind?"

"No, I think it's just the opposite. When a man really loves a woman it makes him see things he would have missed otherwise."

"What sort of things?"

"I think he sees a sweetness that others miss, and he can see honesty and humor. Oh, all the things that a man wants."

"Do you think you'll ever find such a woman?"

A long silence followed Lanie's question, and finally Owen Merritt said, "I hope so, Lanie. You say your dad would get lonely, and I'll get lonely too."

Owen got up then, and she walked to the door with him. Cap'n Brown followed him, his loud raspy voice attracting Owen. He reached over and stroked the big cat's head, and then he straightened up. "Well, I guess the gossipers can talk about you and Brent then."

Lanie suddenly knew she had to be honest with Owen, who had been so kind to her. "Brent asked me to marry him. He says that we could live in the big city where there are lots of publishers and writers."

Owen's eyes narrowed, and he studied her intently. "Well, how do you feel about that?"

"Oh, I don't know, Owen. I guess I'm all mixed up."

"Well, you've had two men who want to marry you. If I wasn't so much older than you—" He didn't finish what he was going to say, but he shook his shoulders, turned and said, "I've got some calls to make. Thanks for the coffee."

Lanie watched him go, and when his car turned the corner and was out of sight, she leaned against the door and thought long and hard about Owen Merritt. *He still thinks of me as a fourteen-year-old, skinny and scared. I don't know if he'll ever learn to see me as a woman.*

❦

"Well, I sure hope Maeva and Logan do good with that record they've gone to Fort Smith to make." Forrest was salting down a ham that John Stevens, a neighbor, had brought by. He took great pride in preserving food, and he had made up a concoction composed of molasses, hot peppers, and some secret ingredients he refused to discuss and was rubbing it into the ham.

Lanie loved to watch her dad work, and for a while, the two stood there talking. Once Forrest looked up when he heard a horse and wagon approaching. There was relief in his eyes when he turned back and began working on the ham. "I sure hope Dakota doesn't come today. She's been here almost every day. I feel like running off and hiding."

It was the opportunity Lanie had been waiting for. "How do you really feel about her, Daddy?"

"Why, I think she's got too much imagination. She's talked herself into this thing. She wants a husband, and she came up with all this talk about God sending me by."

Lanie was not satisfied with this. "I don't think she's that kind of a woman. She's really convinced that God's got a man for her to share her life with. What if she's right? What if God does want you to marry her?"

Forrest looked up with astonishment. "Why, Muff, that couldn't ever happen!"

"Daddy, how do you feel about her as a woman?"

"Well ..." Forrest wiped his hands off on a cloth. He turned to her, and there was a furtive expression in his face as if he were afraid that something was close to him that he did not want. "She doesn't seem like a woman. She dresses in overalls most of the time. She works like a man."

"You know she had to do that to hold her place together."

"I know, and I admire her for that. Everybody knows about her horses. They're the finest in the county."

"Don't you ever want to marry again?"

"Why, I never think about it. Your mother and I were so close."

"She'd want you to be happy, Daddy."

Forrest suddenly turned to face Lanie and studied her. He was intensely proud of this young woman, and she had a strength and a pride and a dignity that she had gotten partly from him, he knew, but mostly from her mother. And now as he looked at her, he admired the womanliness that could not be mistaken. Forrest had been scarred by his failure to be with his family—although it had not been his choice. He knew it had been Lanie's determination that had held the family together, and he wanted the very best for her as he did for all of his children. Suffering had left a broad and painful track in him, but he knew it was God who had gotten him out of prison, and now his chief interest was seeing that his family did well. He said as much to her then asked, "Why are you talking like this, Muff, about my getting married again?"

"Mostly because of you, I guess. I want you to have someone, Daddy. You're not a man who needs to be alone, and you will be someday."

"That may be a long time off. Corliss is just a child."

"I was thinking as much about Corliss as about you. We all like Dakota, but Corliss adores her."

Forrest Freeman stood absolutely still and thought about the future. True enough, the children would all be leaving, one at a time, to take up their own lives. Corliss was so young he would have her for a long time, but he was aware that she was lacking something, a woman that a young girl would need as she grew up. He thought about Dakota, and something flitted through his mind, but he put it away. "I just can't think of Dakota in that way, in the way a man thinks of a woman he loves."

"It went real well," Maeva said. She was beaming, and her eyes were dancing. She and Logan had come back from Fort Smith, and she sat in the kitchen telling Lanie about making the record. "We had to do the record five times before the man that runs the studio was satisfied."

"Do you think anything will come of it?"

"All the people that were there making the record loved it, at least they said so. It was fun. The owner of the station said if the record does well, he can get us some bookings just for singing gospel." She looked around and quietly said, "What about Daddy and Dakota? Did you talk to him like we said?"

"I tried to, but he's gun shy."

"Well, it's not all his fault. Dakota's a fine woman, but she's not a kind that a man would fall in love with."

"She's got a good heart, and she loves God."

"A man's looking for more than that. While I was gone, I got to thinking about it. I've got a plan. Now, you just listen to me ..."

⌐═◄►

Dakota sat and stared at the two young women. She had been repairing a fence when Maeva and Lanie had driven up.

"Hi, Dakota," Maeva said.

"Hello, Maeva. How did your record making go?"

"Real fine. I think it's going to open up a new world for me and Logan."

Lanie said quickly, "We came out to talk to you, Dakota."

Dakota looked from one young woman to another. "About what?"

"About you and Daddy," Lanie said.

"That's right," Maeva added, "we noticed you don't come around like you did."

"I—I didn't think your daddy liked it."

"He's a little bit backward. You know he only courted one woman," Lanie said, "and that was our mama, so he doesn't quite know how to go about thinking about getting married again."

"Well, I decided not to come anymore," Dakota said. She had always been so strong and full of life that it hurt both young women to see her so depressed.

"Listen," Maeva said, "men are pretty slow and sometimes down-right dumb."

"That's right, and Daddy's no exception. Dakota, you got a vision from God, and you got to stay with it."

"But Forrest doesn't even like for me to be around."

249

Maeva suddenly laughed. She went over and put her arm around the big woman. "We're going to change that. We all need a mama, especially Corliss, and Daddy needs a companion."

"That's right, and we're going to see that you're the one who fills that bill," Lanie said. "We've got a plan, Maeva and me. If you'll just do what we tell you, I think you'll see a change in Daddy."

Hope touched the eyes of Dakota Jones. She had been upset thinking that perhaps she had been wrong about God telling her anything about Forrest. Now she stared at the two young women so pretty and full of life. "I don't know what to do."

"Well, *we* do," Maeva said. "We're going to make you over, Dakota Jones. We're going to make you the best-looking woman Daddy ever saw, and we'll show that Daddy of ours!"

"Yes, indeed!" Lanie nodded. "We'll show that man what he's missing!"

CHAPTER 21

Corliss adores that pony!" Lanie exclaimed, shaking her head with wonder. "I believe she could become an idolater with very little encouragement." Corliss had christened the pony Ruth, and ever since Dakota had left her, it had been a constant battle to keep Corliss from riding her every hour of the day.

Maeva came over to stand beside Lanie, and they watched as Forrest walked in front of the pony and Corliss bounced up and down, screeching like a wild Indian.

"I don't think she's had a thought but that pony since Dakota brought her here."

The mention of Dakota caused a wrinkle to appear in Lanie's smooth forehead. She bit her lip and said, "Do you think we did the right thing?"

"About what?"

"About doing a makeover for Dakota."

"Of course we did."

"I'm not sure. Daddy told me one time my spiritual gift was meddling, and that seems to be what we've done."

Maeva shook her head and said firmly, "That's a different thing altogether. This is for Daddy's own good. Besides, it was fun, wasn't it?"

The two young women had spent much time with Dakota Jones during the past few days. They had taken her to Fort Smith to a beauty parlor and got her hair completely redone, and they had visited every shop that sold ladies' wear in town. Dakota had protested that she didn't need such fancy dresses, but Lanie and Maeva had simply ignored her. They had outfitted her from the skin out including three pair of shoes and three different hats. Dakota had fallen into a daze and finally just given herself over to the two young women who had delighted themselves in making a change in Dakota Jones.

On the way home, she had mentioned that Carl Ritter who owned the farm next to her had been trying to court her for a long time.

"Do you like him, Dakota?"

"Well," she said with a shrug, "not all that much, but he's come around for a long time wanting to marry me."

"But you don't want to."

"No, he's got lots of money and a big farm that adjoins mine. He keeps saying that if we put our two places together, we'd have the finest farm in the county. But I never felt that it was the thing to do."

At once Maeva had said, "Get him to take you to church Sunday."

"Take me to church? He don't go to church."

"If he's trying to court you and marry you, he'll do anything you say. You're going to put on makeup and pretty clothes, and you're going to march into that church with this man Ritter."

"Why would I want to do all that?"

"To make Daddy see that you're a desirable woman," Maeva had said firmly. "Now, you promised to do everything we said, so that's the next order of business."

⚬—‹-

Maeva could now see that Lanie was troubled, and she put her hand on her sister's shoulder. "It'll be all right. You'll see."

"I hope so. You'd better go tell them to get ready for church."

Maeva giggled. "I can't wait to see Daddy's face when he sees Dakota come in looking like a movie star." She turned, went to the back door, and opened it. "Daddy, you bring Corliss in; it's time to get ready for church."

Immediately Corliss began protesting. "I don't want to go to church. I want to ride Ruth."

"Well, you've ridden her for an hour. You can ride her when we come home from church. Now, get off so I can unsaddle her and put her to pasture," said Forrest.

Under protest, Corliss jumped off the horse. She led her to the barn. She waited while Forrest stripped the saddle and the blanket from the small pony and put them inside. When he removed the bridle, Corliss took it from him and said, "I'll lead her to the pasture. Come on, Ruthie."

Forrest followed along, thinking how the pony had made such a difference in his child's life. He had been opposed to taking the gift from Dakota, but Dakota had not listened. She had, more or less, simply dumped the pony and run. He could not be completely sorry, for Corliss, who was always a happy child, was ecstatic over the pony.

He watched as she petted the pony on the nose. "Now you go rest for a while. As soon as we get back from church, I'll ride you again." She came outside, shut the gate, and then as they started toward the house, she looked up and said, "Daddy, why hasn't Dakota been back to see us?"

Forrest felt a twinge of guilt. He knew he had been cold toward Dakota, and it bothered him. The woman had saved his life, been kind to his children, and put a new dimension in his little girl's life. "I guess she's just been busy, honey."

"She never was too busy before."

Forrest had no answer for that, and when they had reached the porch, Corliss turned and looked up at him. "When are you going to marry her, Daddy?"

Caught off guard, Forrest cleared his throat while he tried to think of an answer. "Oh, that was just something Dakota thought of. It wasn't a good idea."

"I think it was a good idea. I'd like to have a mama, and Dakota would take care of me. When she stayed all night, she put me in bed, she read *The Wizard of Oz* to me, and she pulled the covers up, and kissed me just like a real mama does. I'd like to have a mama."

Forrest Freeman was speechless. He saw the woebegone expression on her face, reached down, and ran his hand over her silky hair. "We'd better get ready for church, honey."

After they entered the house and Corliss went upstairs to change clothes—and before he could sit down to drink the coffee Maeva had poured for him—Cody said, "Dakota hasn't been here for a week. Corliss misses her."

"So do I," Maeva said. "I think she got her feelings hurt, Daddy."

"How did that happen?"

"Daddy, you'll have to admit you weren't very nice to her. As a matter of fact, you treated her so coldly that I don't blame her for not coming back."

"Yes, you ran away and hid every time she came to the house," Cody said. "That wasn't right. You'd get all over me if I treated company like that."

"I didn't do that!"

"Yes, you did," Maeva said firmly. She came over and stood firmly in front of Forrest. "She looks rough, Daddy, but she's a very sensitive woman, and I think you treated her very badly indeed."

"Why, I didn't mean to do that. She did save my life."

"Yes, she did, and she's been good to us," Lanie said.

Forrest hesitated and then tried to think of an answer. "I didn't mean to hurt her feelings. I'll try to be more sociable, but she scares me with this talk about God sending me to her for a husband."

Davis had been sitting at the table eating the last of the scrambled eggs and bacon. "If you'd marry her, Daddy, why we'd have a real plantation. She's got over seven hundred acres. It would be just like the place your grandpa had."

Forrest stared at Davis and snapped, "I'm not marrying a woman for her money or her farm!"

"Of course you're not," Lanie said. "Come on. Let's go to church. Everybody get ready."

⚬━◆━

Forrest was glum all the way to church, but Lanie and Maeva, who were in the backseat, had to stifle their giggles. They whispered about the makeover and couldn't wait to see their father's face when he saw the new Dakota Jones.

"What are you two laughing about?" Forrest demanded, glancing back over his shoulder.

"Oh, nothing," Maeva said.

"Yes, you two have been up to something. You've been acting funny all week long."

"I'm just happy, that's all," Maeva said.

"So am I," Lanie chimed in at once.

"I am too," Corliss said. "I'd rather be home riding Ruth, and I don't want us to stay around and talk after church. Let's go right home."

They pulled up in front of the church and went inside and took their usual seats. They had not been there more than ten minutes when suddenly Forrest turned around and studied the couple that had entered the auditorium. "That's Carl Ritter," he said. "I never saw him in church before."

"No, I never did either," Maeva said. "He's not a churchgoer."

"Who's that woman with him?"

"Hush, Daddy. The service is starting."

Maeva sat beside her father with Corliss on her right. Several times during the service, she caught Lanie's eye in the choir loft and winked at her.

As soon as the service was over, Lanie ran to the choir room, doffed her robe, and was out in a flash. She met the rest of the family as they were going outside. "That was a good sermon, wasn't it, Daddy?"

"It's always good when that young man preaches." They shook hands with Colin Ryan, and Lanie said, "That was a good sermon, Brother Colin."

Colin grinned broadly. "One woman one Sunday tried to pay me a compliment. She said, 'Preacher, every sermon you preach is better than the next one.' If you get that all figured out, it means my sermons are getting worse all the time."

They moved on outside, and the bright sunlight filtered down through the tall walnut trees that surrounded the church. "Maybe we ought to go and welcome Mr. Ritter. He's a first-time visitor," Maeva said.

"Yes, Daddy, I think that would be nice."

Forrest had never cared for Carl Ritter. The man seemed, to him, to have a blunt arrogance that Forrest didn't care for, but he shrugged and said, "All right." They went over and he gave the woman a quick glance. She was tall, very well proportioned, and wore a light blue dress that caught the color of her eyes. Her lips were broad, and her eyes deep-set and almost a magnetic blue. Forrest turned to say, "Good morning, Carl. It's good to see you in church."

"Why, thanks, Forrest. I haven't seen you since you got out of jail. I'm glad to hear the good news."

"That was a right fine sermon, wasn't it, Forrest?"

Forrest turned, for the woman had spoken. Something went off then in his head, and he stared at the woman. He was confused for the voice reminded him of something. It was then that Maeva said, "I love the way you've done your hair, Dakota."

"Dakota?" Forrest said loudly and blinked. He stared at the woman. She was watching him carefully with a smile playing around her lips. "Dakota?" he said and could think of nothing else.

"Why do you keep saying *Dakota*, Daddy?" Corliss said. She pulled her hand loose from Maeva's grip, went over, and put her arms up, and when she was picked up and held closely she said, "Dakota, you haven't been over to see us."

"No, but I bet you're taking good care of that Ruth, ain't you?"

"Yes, I am. You look so pretty, and you smell so good. I've never seen you in a dress. You always wear overalls."

"Well, I jist decided to dress up a mite."

"Dakota—is it you?" Forrest said almost hoarsely. He could not believe his eyes. The woman did not faintly resemble the one he had known as Dakota Jones. Her skin was smooth and creamy, and there was an attractiveness about her that he would never have dreamed.

"Why do you keep saying her name, Daddy?" Lanie said. "You look so nice. Dakota."

Forrest cleared his throat and said, "You haven't been over to see us lately."

"Well, I've missed all of you. Are you ready, Carl?"

"I sure am, Dakota. Good to see you folks."

Forrest watched the pair go and seemed to be rooted to the spot. "Come on, Daddy, let's go home. I want to ride Ruth."

Numbly, Forrest turned as Corliss pulled at his hand. He got into the car, and when everyone else had loaded up, he said, "I didn't recognize Dakota."

"She's a fine-looking woman," Maeva said. "She just needed to dress up a little bit."

"She told me," Lanie said loudly, "she was going to do less of the real work."

"That's right." Maeva nodded. "Carl Ritter's helping her. She told me that much."

Forrest frowned and shook his head. "I never liked Ritter. He was a hard man with his family. His children left as soon as they were old enough, and he wore his poor wife out with too much work. He's a miser."

"He's a pretty good-looking fellow though," Maeva said. "I hear he's been trying to court Dakota for a long time."

Forrest turned to stare at Maeva, started to speak, and then clamped his jaws. He didn't say anything all the way home, and when he got out of the car, he said, "Davis, you saddle Ruth. I'm going for a walk."

The family watched as Forrest turned and headed toward the woods.

"What's wrong with him?" Cody complained. "He acts like he's mad."

Maeva winked at Lanie. "Daddy's just a little bit confused. He'll be all right though."

⌒━◦━

For two days Forrest had very little to say. He stayed out in the woods a great deal, hunting squirrels, and finally on Thursday he came in and found Maeva and Lanie in the kitchen canning apples. "I'm going over to see Dakota," he said. There was a challenge in his voice as if he expected to be rebuked.

He turned and walked upstairs, and as soon as he was out of sight, Maeva's eyes danced. "It's working. He hasn't said ten words since he saw Dakota."

The two young women talked about how different their father had been, and when he came down, he was wearing some new clothes that Lanie had helped him pick out—a pair of dark blue slacks and a pale blue shirt that matched.

"Why, you're all dressed up."

"Get tired of wearing old work clothes," Forrest said evasively.

"Why are you going to Dakota's?" Maeva asked.

"Well," Forrest said, "somebody's got to warn her about Carl Ritter. What kind of a man he is."

"I wouldn't do that if I were you, Daddy," Lanie said. "It's her business."

Forrest shook his head stubbornly. "I owe it to her for saving my life."

"Tell her we said hello and to come and see us," Maeva said as he left the house.

As soon as he was outside, Maeva nodded her head firmly. "Good, he's jealous. I hope Dakota remembers what we told her about throwing Carl Ritter up to him."

"She doesn't really care for him, Maeva."

"I told her to act like she did. Nothing like green-eyed jealousy to make a man come running."

As Forrest stepped out of the truck and walked up to the front door of Dakota's house, he was reminded of how helpless he had been when she had brought him here after finding him in the woods. The memories stirred him, and he had thought about that time almost constantly the last two days. He glanced over toward the horse lot and saw six beautiful horses grazing—but no Dakota. Usually she was out with the horses or doing some work in the barn, but there was no sign of her. He saw smoke rising from the chimney, but when he stepped up on the porch and knocked on the door, there was no answer. He was puzzled and wondered if, perhaps, she had gone to town. After a few minutes, the door opened.

"Why, hello, Forrest. I didn't expect you."

"Hello, Dakota." For some reason Forrest had expected Dakota to be wearing her working clothes: shapeless overalls and oversized brogans and a floppy straw hat, but instead she was wearing a dress he had never seen before, a print dress that clung to her figure and a pair of black patent shoes. "Were you going somewhere, Dakota?"

"I'll be going to town in an hour or two. Come in, Forrest. Would you like some coffee?"

"That would be nice."

They went into the kitchen, which was as neatly kept as the farm itself. Dakota picked the coffeepot off the stove, filled two large mugs, and set them on the table. "It's nice and fresh. They got that there new machine at the Kroger store. You buy the beans and grind them up yourself. That way you know it's fresh."

Forrest took the cup and sipped it cautiously. "Well, this is mighty fine."

"How are all the younguns?"

"They're well."

"Corliss still foolish over her pony?"

Forrest smiled. "You couldn't have given her anything that would have made her any happier. It's the biggest thing in her life right now."

The lamp on the table threw its lush beam against her smooth skin, and her lips lay softly together. Light points danced in her eyes as she met his glance, and she smiled at him in a way that was both warm and yet still enigmatic. Forrest watched her over the width of the table. The fragrance of her clothes came to Forrest, and it slid through the armor of his self-sufficiency. For one instant he admired her, then the admiration was overcome by the strange feeling that hits a man when he looks on beauty and knows that it would never be for him.

"Did you come for something, Forrest?"

"Well, as a matter of fact, I did, but to tell the truth you've got me a little confused."

"Why is that?"

"Well, you look so different, and you act different."

"Do you think so?"

"Well, of course I do! You always wore those shapeless overalls, and you never took any care with your personal appearance. What happened to you?"

"Oh, I just got weary of workin' like a farmhand." Dakota shrugged. She was a tall, contoured woman, and there was a vitality in her that somehow affected Forrest strongly. To his shock it fanned up the close-held hungers that had been in him for many years and that he had learned to ignore.

"Well, I think that's fine. You work too hard."

"Well, Carl is helping me, and I hired a feller to come and do the heavy work."

"I was surprised to see you in church with Ritter."

"Well, I guess maybe you was. He don't go to church, but I asked him to take me."

"Why didn't you ask me?"

"Because you was plumb scared of me."

Forrest dropped his eyes for he knew she had spoken the exact truth. "I don't know what you mean by that."

"Oh, course you do! It was all my talk about God sending you by to be my husband." She laughed, and it made a rich, full sound. "It would have scared any man."

"Then you don't think it was real, all that you said about God sending you a husband?"

"It's right hard to know the will of God, Forrest. I know God wants me to have a husband, but I reckon I jumped too quick to believe it was you that God was sending. It all seemed so *right*. There you were helpless, and I'd been praying for God to do something—" She hesitated and ran her hand over her hair. "But I can imagine how it must have sounded to you."

Forrest had not the foggiest idea of what to say, but finally he cleared his throat and said, "Well, I must admit, it caught me a little bit off guard." He asked with caution, "Do you really want to get married, Dakota?"

The smile left her lips, and for that one moment, a look of sadness came to her. "I get downright lonely, Forrest. My first marriage wasn't very good, but at least there was someone to talk to. I think a woman needs somebody to share her life with."

Forrest tried desperately to think of some way to put what he came to say so that it didn't sound too harsh, but he knew he had to say something. "I won't talk about a man behind his back, but I don't think Carl Ritter's a man that could make you happy."

"Why would you say that?"

"Why, it's plain enough to see he's after your farm."

"That's what you think?"

"That's how he got such a big place by buying land next to his. I expect he's always wanted this place."

Dakota sat very still, and her words were as cold as polar ice. "So no man would want me as a woman? They'd just want my farm?"

At that instant Forrest knew he had stepped over the line. "I—I didn't mean to put it like that, Dakota."

"I wish you'd go, Forrest."

At once, Forrest stood up feeling as empty as he had ever felt in his life. He looked at Dakota who had risen and was now facing him, her arms folded across her breast. A great sense of wrongdoing came to him, and he knew he had not treated this woman fairly. "I'm sorry, Dakota." She did not answer, and as Forrest Freeman left the house and got into his car, he muttered under his breath, "Well, I made a big mess out of that!"

"Don't you snap at me, Doctor Owen Merritt!" Bertha Pickens said.

Owen had come into the reception room and thrown a piece of paper down in front of Bertha, the nurse. "You've got this wrong, Bertha. Can't you do anything right?"

He stared at her and saw that her dark eyes were snapping. She was always a strong-willed woman, but she had been a godsend to him since he had come, a green young physician to his first charge. Now he hesitated then said, "I'm sorry. I'm just snippy today."

"You work too hard. That's what your trouble is."

"That's not what you said when I first came here." Owen grinned at the thought. "You'd bawl me out constantly for not working hard enough."

At that moment, Doctor Givens entered the office. He looked around and said, "Well, did all the patients die?"

"No, I worked through them," Owen said.

"Come into the office. I want to talk to you."

"Well, tell him to behave more decently, Doctor Givens," Nurse Pickens said. "He's as techous as a cat with a sore tail."

The two men went into the office, and Givens said, "What's the matter between you and Bertha?"

"Oh, I was short with her. I'm sorry. I'll have to make it right."

"Bring her some flowers, something like that." He sat down in his chair and waved at another chair. When Owen was seated, he said, "I'm retiring."

Owen Merritt stared at the old man. Doctor Givens had often threatened to retire, but it had always been something vague and dim and way in the future. "I don't believe it," he said.

"Oh, I know I've made talk before, but this time I mean it."

"What are you going to do with yourself, Oscar?"

"I bought a place on the beach in Florida. It's got a back porch right out over the water. I'm going to sit out there and fish right off my porch."

"Why, I always thought if you did retire, you'd stay around here."

"I thought so too, but there's something about the beach I like. I like the sound of the water. I like to watch the pelicans fly over in formation like a bunch of airplanes." He went on talking for a long time, and finally he said, "The practice is yours, Owen. We'll work out something, whatever you like, about the money."

"I don't know what to say, Oscar."

"You know I never thought you'd make it here in Fairhope. When you first came I wouldn't have bet five cents that you would be able to survive but you have." He studied Owen and said, "What's the matter with you? You're depressed."

"I don't know. I'm just out of sorts."

"I think it's more than that, Owen."

Owen looked up, startled. Oscar Givens had perception that most men lacked. He had thought at times that it was almost as if the old man could look right into his mind.

Without preamble, Oscar Givens began telling a story. "When I was a young man I fell in love with a young girl named Olivia. I was just getting started, and I thought I had to have more to offer her so I didn't ask her to marry me. I put it off."

Doctor Givens fell silent, and Owen said, "Well, what happened?"

"I waited too long, son. She gave up on me and married another man. I never got over it. Never found another woman I loved, so here I am a crusty old bachelor." He got to his feet and gave a look at the younger man. "Don't let that happen to you, Owen."

Owen spent the rest of the day calling on patients, but that night sleep eluded him. He could not get away from Oscar Givens's words. He slept fitfully and had an awful dream. All he could remember was that he was in a big, ugly room and could never get out of it.

Chapter 22

Lanie had gotten up early and now she sat down at her desk and wrote carefully at the top of the page. *December 3, 1932.* She looked back through her journal and studied some of the records she had made of her feelings. At times, she had to smile, but then she shook her head, went back to the blank page, and began to write:

> *I've just gotten my second letter from Roger. He's so happy there in Massachusetts, and I'm glad for him. I must admit it does hurt my feelings a little bit. I didn't love Roger like a woman should love a man she's going to marry, and I don't think he ever loved me in that way, but he mentioned Eileen in both letters several times. I guess my pride's hurt a little bit that he could move on from asking me to marry him to being interested in another woman. But I'm actually happy for him. He's found his place, and it's going to turn out well.*
>
> *Maeva and Logan are in Fort Smith singing with Ernest Tubb and some other country western singers. Their record is doing so well! Logan's sure they'll be able to get a contract with a California agent.*

There was a scratching at her door, and she went over and found Cap'n Brown with a tiny morsel of a mouse in his jaws.

"Give me that mouse!"

Reluctantly Cap'n Brown dropped the tiny creature, and Lanie shook her finger at him. "Shame on you." Then she laughed. "But then I guess that's what cats do. Now you leave."

Moving across the room, she put the tiny mouse into a cigar box and closed the lid. "I'll let you loose later. Some place where Cap'n Brown won't be able to get to you. Cap'n Brown has no conscience." She went back and began to write again, this time more rapidly.

I'm worried about Daddy. He hasn't been able to find a job yet, a steady job at least, and I know he feels bad about Dakota. He watches her at church. She's always with Carl Ritter, and I can tell that he's upset about it. He's just not himself. He isn't happy and he goes out with a gun and claims he's hunting, but he comes back without anything so I know he just goes out to think.

I'm worried about Owen too. He's behaved so strangely lately. He told me he had a bad dream, but he wouldn't tell me what it was. He's come by the house every day it seems claiming to see Aunt Kezia, but he always manages to get me off in the kitchen and talk to me, and he always brings Brent into the conversation. I just tell him that Brent's been helpful to my writing and me.

But really, it's more than that. I'm worried about what to say to Brent. He hasn't said anything else about wanting to get married, but I know he will. I don't want to live in New York or Chicago, and he doesn't really fit in here in the mountains, so it would never work out. I think I'll —

The door suddenly flew open, and Maeva came in. "You never knocked on a door in your life, Maeva. Why don't you —"

"Lanie, Corliss is very sick."

At once Lanie got to her feet, closed the journal, and slipped it in the drawer. "Why, she hasn't been feeling well for a couple of days, but I thought it was just an upset stomach."

"It's more than that. We need to get Owen here to look at her."

"I'll go get him."

"Well, hurry up. I'm afraid for her."

Owen stepped back from the bed and looked down at Corliss, who was flushed and weak. She hadn't been able to keep anything down, and Owen turned and walked out of the room. Lanie followed him, and as soon as they were outside, she asked, "What is it, Owen?"

"I think it's pretty serious."

"How serious?"

"Well, it may be diphtheria."

The word brought a chill of fear to Lanie. Diphtheria was a deadly disease, and there seemed to be almost nothing doctors could do for it. She felt her hands begin to shake. "She keeps calling for Dakota. I think she'd come and help."

"Then I think you should send for her. It's going to take a lot of around the clock nursing."

Lanie was pale and her lips were trembling. "I'm afraid, Owen."

At once Owen came over and put his arm around her shoulder. "I know it's foolish to say 'don't worry.' We all do that. We just have to pray. God's able to heal her. We've seen Him do miracles." He saw the tears well up into Lanie's eyes and said gently, "It's all right to cry. I do it myself sometimes."

Suddenly, Lanie turned and put her arms around Owen. She held onto him tightly, and he could feel her body convulsing with a paroxysm of weeping. It was so unlike her. She was such a strong young woman, always had been. "Hold me, Owen!"

He put his arms around her and stroked her hair. They stood like that until finally the tremors ceased. Lanie stepped back, gave him a strange look, and then wiped her eyes with a handkerchief drawn from her pocket.

"I'll send Daddy to get Dakota," she whispered.

As Lanie turned and left the room, Owen had the impulse to speak, to go after her and tell her how he felt, but he had missed his moment, and he knew it.

◦═◦

As Forrest stepped up on the porch, the door opened, and Dakota stood there. "Hello, Forrest."

She seemed somewhat stiff, not like herself at all, and Forrest knew that there was still some resentment in her. He had regretted a thousand times telling her that Carl Ritter was only after her farm. He knew it was a stupid, foolish, untactful thing to do, but he could not unsay the words. "Corliss is sick, and she's calling for you."

"What is it, Forrest?"

"Owen thinks it might be diphtheria."

Instantly, Dakota said, "Let me get my coat." She disappeared but was out almost at once, pulling her coat on and fastening it. They walked to the car, and she got in.

Forrest got behind the wheel and moved away from the house. She said nothing, and he struggled to find some way to change the past, which he knew was impossible. Finally, he gave up. "Dakota, I'm sorry about what I said about Carl Ritter. It was a fool thing to say."

Dakota turned and studied Forrest. His jaw was set, and she knew that he was utterly serious. "It's all right. You may be right. He's always wanted to buy my farm."

"I shouldn't have said it. I'm sorry."

"Don't worry none about it."

They reached the house, and Forrest stopped the car. "Go on up at once, Dakota."

Stepping out of the car, Dakota ran up the steps. Lanie met her on the porch. "I'm so glad you're here, Dakota. Corliss has been crying for you."

"How is she?"

"Very bad. She's going to take around the clock nursing."

The two women climbed the stairs, and as soon as Dakota entered the room, her heart seemed to contract. Corliss was always such a lively, healthy child, and now she looked terrible. At once Dakota slipped out of her coat and dropped it on the floor. She went over, pulled Corliss up, and held her to her breast.

"Is that you, Dakota?"

"Yes, it's me, honey."

"Don't leave me!"

"I won't leave you. You're going to get well. It's going to be all right"

❖

For the next four days Maeva, Lanie, and Dakota took turns sitting with Corliss. Owen came by every day, and many times the family noticed that as soon as Dakota went into the kitchen to get coffee or something to eat, Forrest was always there.

The change had almost been miraculous. On the third day of Dakota's stay, Corliss seemed as sick as ever, but when she awakened on the fourth day, her eyes were clear and her fever was gone.

Now as Lanie walked into Corliss's room, she saw with a smile that Corliss was sitting in Dakota's lap, and Dakota had a copy of *The Wizard of Oz*.

"I believe she could read that book to you, Mama," she said. She had started calling her that, and she saw that it pleased the older woman.

"I'm all well, Doctor Owen says," Corliss said. "I can ride Ruth now."

"Pretty soon. As soon as Owen says it's all right."

Dakota got up and gave Corliss a kiss on the cheek. "I've got to go home now, honey."

"No, I don't want you to go."

"Well, I'm sorry, but I have to."

She left the room, and Corliss stared after her, heartbroken. "Don't let her go." Forrest entered the room to say good-bye before he took Dakota home, and Corliss cried out, "Daddy, don't let her go!"

"I wish she wouldn't go, but I can't make her stay."

Corliss looked up at him, her eyes big. "You can marry her. That's what God said to do."

The words seemed to enter Forrest with the force of a blow. He kissed her and said, "I'll be back soon."

Going downstairs, Forrest found that Dakota had already left. He went out and saw her sliding into the car. Getting in, he started the engine and pulled out. Lately he had had great trouble talking to Dakota, and now he said, "I guess I'm all mixed up, Dakota."

"About what?"

"Well, about you and me."

Dakota turned and faced him. "That's my fault, Forrest. I never should have told you about wanting a husband and then telling you God had sent you."

Forrest smiled. "It scared me, I got to admit. I don't have the words to tell you how I feel."

"You don't have to say anything, Forrest." She got out of the car when they arrived at her house and said, "I need to be alone, Forrest. Come and get me if you need more help with Corliss."

The family had gathered in the parlor as if for a meeting—all except Forrest. He was outside on the porch staring off into the distance.

"What's he doing?" Cody said curiously.

Davis was peering out the window. "Nothing. He's just standing there looking."

"Go tell him to come in," Aunt Kezia spoke firmly.

Lanie looked at her with surprise. "Why should I do that?"

"Because I've got something to tell him. Now you do what I say."

Lanie, along with the others, had learned that it did not usually pay to disobey Aunt Kezia. She went to the door. "Daddy, come in. Aunt Kezia wants to tell you something."

"All right." Forrest entered and followed her into the parlor. He looked around and said, "Why are you all here?"

"We're here to mind your business," Kezia said.

"What are you talking about?"

"You'd be a fool to let that woman get away."

"That's right, Daddy," Davis said. "You two were made for each other. You need to marry her."

"Why, she won't hardly talk to me," Forrest protested.

Cody spoke up. "I know about women. I'll give you some hints."

"You hush up!" Maeva said abruptly. "Daddy, you need to let her know how you feel."

"How can I do that? I've acted like a fool with her."

"Why, court her, you!" Kezia snapped. "If you don't, she's going to marry Carl Ritter."

"You can't let her do that, Daddy," Lanie said quickly. "You've got to marry her. We need a mama around here."

"I wouldn't know how to court anybody."

"Well, if you can't beat Carl Ritter's time, I'd be ashamed of you!"

Forrest glared around the room. "It's funny how everybody knows how to mind my business."

"It's because we love you, Daddy," Maeva said. She went over and put her arms around him, and Lanie came on the other side. "Yes, you're lonely and you're miserable and you know it."

"That's right," Cody said. "Now, what I'd do if I were you—"

Kezia broke into Cody's instruction. "She's a woman, and she needs to be courted."

"It's been years since I courted a woman. I've forgotten how."

"It won't be hard," Maeva said. "She wants to be told that she's attractive. She wants to be told that she's admired. She wants somebody to pay her some very special attention."

"Go over there, take her some flowers or some perfume or something. Forget about being a fool. We're all fools at one time or another."

For some time the entire Freeman family kept encouraging Forrest Freeman, and finally he said, "I'll have to think about it." He turned and walked out of the room abruptly.

"I'll go tell him some more," Cody said with determination.

"You stay away from him," Davis said. "You don't know anything about this. All you do is run away from Lolean Oz."

"Well, that's different."

"Davis is right," Aunt Kezia said. "We've told him the truth, and now he's got to act on it. So, we'll just pray that God will give him a little bit of common sense."

CHAPTER 23

The family had taken their places around the table for breakfast, but the head of the family was conspicuously absent.

"Where's Daddy?" Cody demanded. "He's always here for breakfast."

Lanie glanced toward the back of the house. Forrest's bedroom was on the first floor, and she was wondering as much as the rest where Forrest was. "I don't know," she said. "Maybe he's just sleeping late."

"Why, shoot, Daddy never sleeps late!" Davis exclaimed. "He's always up by daylight."

"Maybe I'd better go knock on his door. He might be sick," Maeva said.

Lanie shook her head and was about to reply, but at that moment they heard a door slam, and every head turned toward the door that led into the kitchen and dining room area. Forrest stepped inside and then hesitated. He was wearing new clothes that no one had ever seen. He wore a pair of light brown slacks with a razor-sharp crease, a light blue long-sleeved shirt open at the neck, and a pair of shiny shoes that looked nothing at all like the heavy work shoes that he usually wore.

"Well, what are you all staring at?" Forrest said belligerently.

"Why are you all dressed up, Daddy?" Corliss asked. "Is it Sunday? Are we going to church?"

Forrest could not be strict with the child. He had been frightened out of his wits during her sickness, and now he shook his head and smiled. "No, Corliss, it's not Sunday."

"Then why are you all dressed up? You look so pretty."

"You do look good, Daddy," Lanie said. "I don't believe I've seen those clothes before."

"No, they're new. I bought them yesterday. Do you think I look all right?"

"All right for what?" Cody said. "You're not going to go out and cut wood in those clothes."

"Of course not."

"Sit down, Daddy. You need some breakfast."

Forrest nodded then sat down. He waited until Lanie filled his plate with three eggs and four slices of bacon and two freshly made biscuits. The rest of them continued to eat, but conversation was sparse. Finally, Maeva said, "You've got to tell us why you're all dressed up, Daddy."

"Well," Forrest said, chewing on a biscuit, "I've been doing a lot of thinking lately, and I've made a decision."

"What have you decided?" Davis asked curiously.

"I've decided that I've been acting like a fool." He took a swig of coffee and then added, "I don't know what you'll think about this, but I've decided that I'm in love with Dakota."

There was an instant of utter silence, and then a cheer went up from the table. Forrest looked around with shock. Every face was beaming with smiles, and Corliss was clapping, her eyes dancing with delight. "Does that mean you're going to marry her, Daddy, and bring her here?"

"I don't know if I can do it, but I'm going to court her and try my best to get her to marry me."

"Good for you, Daddy," Maeva said. She jumped up from her chair, ran around, and threw her arms around her father. She kissed him soundly on the cheek, and her eyes were mischievous. "You'll have to beat old Carl Ritter's time though. I know you can do it."

"Sure you can," Cody said. "I wish you'd do it in a hurry."

"Why are you in such a hurry?" Lanie smiled.

"Well, I need someone else to talk to. I don't get any sympathy from anybody here. Dakota always listens to me talk."

"You go have at it, Daddy," Davis nodded firmly. "You can beat that old Carl Ritter's time, I'll bet."

"Of course you can, but you've got to have a little tact," Lanie warned. "You can't go barging in like a bull in a china shop."

"I don't know any way to do it but just to go over and camp on her doorstep."

"You got to take her flowers or perfume or little gifts, and you got to be gentle with her. She's a very sensitive woman," Maeva said.

For a time advice poured in until finally, Forrest gave up on breakfast. "I'm nervous as a long-tailed cat in a room full of rocking chairs," he said. "I'm going now."

"You haven't finished your breakfast," Cody pointed out.

"You can have it, Cody." Forrest got up and went to the door. He turned around and smiled. "You kids better pray for me. I'm not sure how to go about this courtship business, but I'm aiming to give it my best shot."

He turned and left, and Maeva took a deep breath. "He'll do all right. Daddy's a fine-looking man."

"And Dakota really thinks God picked him out for a husband so he's got a head start over Ritter there," Lanie said with satisfaction.

❦

When Forrest got to Dakota's house, he had his speeches all prepared. He didn't have any flowers, but he had brought a quarter from a deer that Davis had shot three days earlier. *Not a very romantic gift, but it was all I could grab on the spur of the moment.*

As he pulled up to the house, he saw Ritter's Chevrolet parked out in front and muttered, "What's he doing here this time of the day?" He got out of the car, grabbed the quarter of meat, and hurried up to knock on the door.

It opened almost at once, and Dakota stood there before him. "Why, Forrest, what are you doing here this early?"

"I came to see you. Here, I brought you some fresh venison."

"That's right thoughty of you. Bring it on into the kitchen. I'll slice it up later." She hesitated but then stepped aside.

Forrest walked in and on the way to the kitchen he glanced into the parlor and saw Carl Ritter, who was standing there, staring at him. "Hello, Ritter," Forrest said coolly.

"What are you doing here this early?"

"The same thing you are. I brought Dakota a gift."

Dakota stared at the two men who were glaring at each other angrily. "Come on, Forrest. You kin put the venison over here on the table." She led him into the kitchen and said, "Just put it down right over there." He put the meat down, and she covered it with a clean cloth to keep the flies off, and then said, "I need to talk to you alone."

Dakota was wearing a dress that became her quite well. She had been enjoying her new life, looking more attractive as she learned how to dress and do her hair. She had even taken to wearing some makeup.

Ritter suddenly appeared in the door. "I guess you'll be on your way now, won't you?"

"No, I won't."

"Well, I'm not going either."

"What's the matter with you two?" Dakota said. Actually, she was enjoying the attention she was getting. She knew both men had come over to see her, and it was obvious that each was determined to get ahead of the other. "Why don't I fix some coffee, and we'll all set down and talk."

"That's fine with me," Forrest said. "I don't have anything to do."

Ritter stared at him. "Well, some of us have to work. You may be a gentleman of leisure, Freeman, but I've got a farm to run." He turned to Dakota and said, "I'll pick you up tonight."

"All right, Carl."

Forrest waited until the door slammed, and then he turned and said, "I apologize for barging in, but I just had to see you, Dakota."

Dakota had not missed the fact that Forrest was dressed in new clothes. She did not comment on it but said instead, "Do you want to set a spell?"

"No, I've got something to say." Forrest had been practicing his speech trying to make it as eloquent as possible, but now as she stood before him, he knew that there was no way that he could spout a memorized oration. He stood for one moment trying to collect his thoughts and was aware that she was staring at him in an odd fashion. He still could not accustom himself to the fact that this was the same woman who had pulled him through his accident. The physical transformation was miraculous, but he realized as he stood there that he himself had gone through a similar change. He had not realized how lonely he had been since the death of his wife. He had had a good marriage and had known what it was to have a harmonious life with a good woman. Lately all that had come back to him, and he yearned for something like that again.

"I want to tell you how much I've come to care for you, Dakota."

Dakota stared at him, unable to speak. It was the sort of thing, she knew, that men said to women — but no man had ever said it to her. Her first husband had not been a man who expressed his emotion. He had shown little affection toward her, hardly ever complimented her for her looks or any other quality. Her heart was so full, she could not answer.

"I know that I've made some bad mistakes with you, but I want to make them right." He came closer to her and saw that a faint color stained her cheeks and that her lips were parted with some sort of expression that he could not read. He saw the quick rise and fall of her bosom, and his vision of her at that moment was like the lens of a camera narrowing down until he saw only the full swell of her lips and the strength and grace of her face. He had no other words to speak to her, but a boldness came to him, and he stepped forward and took her in his arms. He pulled her closer, bowed his head, and kissed her.

As he put his lips on hers, there was, for that one moment, a wild sweetness and an immense shock that she responded to his kiss like a woman of passion and strength. "I reckon I love you, Dakota. I don't know how to say it better than that."

She did not answer, but her cheeks were filled with color, and she was staring at him in a way that she never had before. "I'm not real sure of anything, Forrest."

He nodded and saw that she was uncertain. "I don't want to rush you," he said, "but I intend to make you love me. I'm going to be here every day telling you that in one way or another."

"You can't come tonight. Carl's comin' for supper."

Forrest suddenly laughed. He felt like a young man again. "Better set the table for three," he said, "because I'm coming." He reached forward, kissed her again, and said, "I'll leave now, but I'll be back for supper tonight."

Dakota stood there until he left, and then she went to the window and watched him drive away. She found that her hands were trembling, and she was still in shock over the response she had made to his caress. For a long time she stood there until the car disappeared, and then she said, "I have to know your will, God. I thought I knew it, but I got to know it for sure now."

⌑⋇⌐

"Why isn't Daddy here?" Corliss asked.

Lanie looked over at her. "He's gone to Dakota's."

"He's been going over there all the time. Why doesn't he ever take me with him?"

"He doesn't need you around, punkin," Davis grinned. "He's doing some serious courting."

"So is Carl Ritter," Cody said. "He just glared at Daddy in church. He's used to getting his own way."

Maeva laughed out loud. "I'd sure like to be a fly on the wall. Those two sitting around glaring at each other must make Dakota nervous."

"I bet it don't." Kezia grinned. "I bet she likes it. Here all these years she ain't had no male attention, and now she's got two men ready to fight over her."

"Are they really going to fight?" Corliss said. "I'd like to see it."

"So would I," Cody said. "That old Ritter is mean as a snake."

❦

The meal had been a painful thing. The two men had stared at each other across the table. At first Dakota had been nervous, but finally it amused her. It was true enough that she did appreciate some attention after getting none for all these years, but tonight her nervousness returned. Ritter had made several cutting remarks to Forrest, and Forrest's eyes had glittered more than once. She knew Carl Ritter had a hot temper and had the reputation of being a brawler in his youth. He was older now, of course, but the anger was in him.

Forrest had been determined to behave as well as he could while at Dakota's house. He told himself, *You've got to keep calm, Forrest. Don't let him get your goat.*

The meal had been well cooked, as it always was, but as soon as it was over, she said, "Why don't you two go in the parlor while I clean up."

"I'll help you with the dishes," Forrest said at once.

"I reckon I can do that," Ritter interrupted, his eyes narrowing.

"I didn't hear Dakota asking you to help." Forrest got up and began cleaning the table.

"Didn't you hear what I said?" Ritter demanded. "I said I'd help with the dishes." His patience was at an end. He reached over and snatched the dish from Forrest's hand, and Forrest glared at him then reached out and snatched it back.

"Watch what you're doing, Ritter," he said. His voice was soft, but there was a threat in his eyes.

"Why don't you get out of here. Nobody invited you."

"Yes, they did. I invited both of you," Dakota said. There was tension in the air and somehow danger. She watched Ritter carefully.

"I've had enough of you, jailbird!" said Ritter. "Now you get out of here. You come and see Dakota when I'm not here."

"I'll have to hear her say so," Forrest said coolly.

"You're hearing me say so! I've had enough of you. You're nothing but a bum." Ritter reached out and grabbed Forrest's arm. "I told you to leave. I'll help you to the door."

"Take your hands off me, Ritter."

For an answer, Ritter suddenly gave way to an explosive burst of temper. He swung a hamlike fist at Forrest catching him high on the chest. Forrest went reeling backwards, the back of his legs striking against the table. The dishes crashed, and Dakota cried out, "Don't do that, Carl!"

But Carl Ritter was beyond reason. He threw himself forward and struck again. This time Forrest parried the blow and caught Ritter with his fist exactly on the nose. The blood spurted. His eyes grew wild as he saw the blood, and he came roaring in. "I'll kill you!"

Forrest was a smaller man but quicker. Grabbing Ritter, he whirled him around and threw him up against the wall. The dishes on the shelf came crashing down, and Dakota cried out again. But neither man heard her. Ritter pushed himself away from the wall and began raining blows on Forrest. Forrest caught most of them on his forearm, but some came through to strike him in the face. He threw a mighty punch right into the stomach. He felt Ritter's stomach cave in, and a *whoosh* came from his lips. Forrest lowered his head and made a wild run, catching Ritter around the middle and driving him back. They struck the wall and fell to the floor kicking and striking at each other.

Forrest was the first to get to his feet, and as Ritter came up, blood covered the front of his shirt. He was breathing hard and still full of fight.

"Stop it, both of you!" Dakota cried out.

But there was no stopping now. The two fought across the kitchen, upsetting the table. Forrest knocked Ritter back on his heels, and Ritter snapped up a chair. Seeing that Ritter intended to hit him with it, Forrest grabbed another chair and caught the blow. He shoved forward pushing at the chair, and caught off balance, Ritter fell backwards.

The room was full of the sounds of the two men grunting and straining with Ritter cursing. Dakota could do nothing but keep out of the way. The fight continued until finally Ritter's face was a bloody mass. Forrest was marked too, with a cut on his eyebrow draining blood, and a blow to the mouth that brought blood streaming on his chin. His ribs were sore from the blows he had taken, but he pinned Ritter in a corner and poured blows at him until Ritter sagged, his eyes glazing.

"That's enough, Forrest."

Dakota pulled at him. He was breathing so hard he could not answer. "Are you through, Ritter?"

Pain showed in Ritter's eyes. Without a word, he turned, and weaving unsteadily, made his way out of the kitchen. Forrest stood there trying to breathe, and finally they heard a car start.

Dakota came over to face Forrest. "He's cut you all to pieces. Here." She pulled the chair up. "Set down, Forrest. I've gotta clean you up." Dakota poured water from the kettle into a deep bowl, dipped a soft cloth in it, then began cleaning his face. "I'll have to put something on these."

She left the room, and Forrest fell into a chair, his breath coming in deep gasps. She came back with a bottle of something Forrest did not recognize, poured its contents onto the cloth, and began to rub it on his face. When he flinched, she said, "I know that stings, but you don't want to get infection."

As she bent over to treat him, Forrest laughed. It hurt, for his ribs had been bruised, and he had a cut on the inside of his lips.

"What are you laughing about?"

"I'm laughing at us. Two grown men fighting like a couple of high school kids!"

Suddenly Dakota smiled. "It's a wonder. I never saw such a thing. Nobody ever fought over me before."

"Come here." Forrest rose, and the fact that he was bloody didn't bother her when he pulled her close. "Well, it's been a pretty active courting, and I'm willing to keep it up until you give in, Dakota, but I want to tell you how much I care for you, and I want you to marry me, and I want us to live together for the rest of our lives. I want you to be a mother to my children." And then he smiled, though it gave him some pain. "And I want us to have some children."

At that moment, with Forrest standing in front of her bloodied and marked from the fight, Dakota knew what to do. She reached forward, put her arms around him, and put her head on his shoulder. She hugged him gently and then whispered, "I'll bet we're going to have beautiful younguns, Forrest."

"I'll bet we do, sweetheart."

The two stood there, and Dakota Jones knew that what God had spoken to her was indeed true.

"Come on," he said.

"Come on where?"

"I'm wanting you to be there with me when I tell our kids what's going to happen."

⟊

As soon as the car drove up, Corliss screeched, "There's Daddy, and Dakota's with him!"

The whole family started toward the door, but Lanie said, "You stay right where you are. Let them get in the house."

But when they stepped inside, they all gasped.

"Daddy, what happened? Were you in a car wreck?" Maeva said.

"No, this is not all my blood. Some of it belongs to Carl Ritter."

A silence ensued, and Dakota laughed. "You ought to see your faces."

"Did you pound him good, Forrest?" Aunt Kezia demanded.

"Sure did!"

"What happened, Dakota?"

"They fought over me! Ain't that wonderful!"

Kezia said, "Two men fought over me once. Neither one of them was worth dried spit, so I didn't care who won. Sure was a good fight though."

Forrest looked at his family. "You're all going to have a new mama, kids, and here she is."

Kezia said, "Well, I hope you marry him soon, Dakota. I'm too old to keep him in line."

Dakota found herself swarmed by the Freeman children. All of them hugged her, and she picked up Corliss and held her, whispering, "We're going to have a real fine time, you and me."

Cody kissed Dakota. "Well, now that you're going to be our new mama I got some things I need to tell you about this family. They've all got some weak spots. I've been working on them, but it ain't done yet."

Dakota was amused. "What about *your* weak spots, Cody?"

"Me? Why, I don't have no weak spots!"

A howl went up, and Dakota hugged him. "I don't think you do, Cody. You and I will straighten this family out." Dakota winked at the others as she said this, and Forrest watched as his children swarmed around Dakota.

He stood back, pleased. *At last I've done one right thing!*

⇢ CHAPTER 24 ⇠

Brent Hayden stood before Lanie, and something in his glance made her nervous. It was the day before Christmas, and she had been busy decorating the house along with the others. When Brent arrived she had pulled him off into the kitchen, and he had stood there watching her in a peculiar way. She did not know exactly how to react to this man. He had not mentioned his proposal of marriage again.

"I sent the first chapters of your novel to Random House," Brent said. "They want to see the rest of it."

"Oh, Brent, that's good, isn't it?"

"It sure is."

"I don't know if I can ever finish it though."

"You can finish it," Brent said. The sound of laughter came from the parlor, and Brent shook his head. "Another Christmas." He waited for her to speak, and when she did not he said, "I'm moving back to the city, Lanie."

Lanie expected him to ask her to marry him and go with him, and she searched desperately trying to find an answer that would not hurt him.

Brent saw the disturbance in Lanie's face and spoke first. "Don't worry. I know I asked you to marry me, but it would never work. I'd never fit in Fairhope, and you'd never fit in the big city."

"Oh, Brent, you've been so good to me and you've been such a help!"

"I hope so. We're going to get this book of yours published and then another one after that. Maybe I'll be your agent."

"Would you do that for me, Brent?"

"Sure, I would." Brent suddenly laughed. "You know, you're losing your suitors pretty quickly, Lanie. First Roger goes off and leaves you flat, and now on the day before Christmas you lose me." He reached out and touched her cheek. "I'm just teasing."

"I admire you so much, Brent."

"I'll always be your friend, Lanie, and you can name your first boy after me."

❦

The sun was down, and the family had eaten an early supper so that it was quiet in the house when Owen came by. He brought in a box, and Lanie said, "What's that, Owen?"

"Why, it's Christmas gifts. Tomorrow's Christmas. Haven't you heard?" His cheeks were red from the cold, and he put the box down. "I had a lot of fun shopping for these."

"You shouldn't have done it."

"Something I wanted to do. I didn't have much Christmas growing up. My folks didn't believe in it too much."

"What have you got everybody? Let's put them under the tree, and you can tell me what they are."

"All right."

The two spent the next few minutes arranging the presents under the tree. With each one, Owen told her what the package contained.

When they were all under the tree, she said, "Come on into the kitchen. It's cold out. I made some hot chocolate."

"Sounds good."

The two went into the kitchen, and he sat down at the table. "You know, it seems like I've sat at this table a thousand times. The first time you were just fourteen."

"I remember. I pestered you to death, didn't I, Owen?"

"Oh, you were a real pain in the neck." He grinned at her and sipped the chocolate. "What have you been doing?"

"Decorating." Lanie knew she had to tell Owen about Brent. She took a deep breath and said nervously, "Well, Brent's leaving Fairhope."

Owen had been lifting the cup to his lips, but he stopped. He put the cup down on the table and placed his hands flat. "Are you leaving with him?" he asked, and his voice was tight with some sort of apprehension.

"Oh no, Owen! There was never anything like that."

"He asked you to marry him."

"I know he did, but I think we both knew from the beginning that we didn't suit each other."

"Well, you lost two men. Roger and now Brent."

"That's what Brent said." Lanie felt better now that the news was out. She studied Owen and thought again how she had always considered him handsome. He was a limber man with a looseness about him, and she saw at that moment that something was pleasing to him. Humor slid into the angles of his tanned face, and time ran slow as she watched him. He smiled and suddenly seemed younger than his thirty years. "What are you smiling about?" she demanded.

"I've got some news for you."

"What, Owen?"

"Doctor Givens is retiring. I'll be taking over his practice."

"Oh, I'll miss him. He's been so good to us."

"I'll miss him too," Owen said, "but it's been coming for some time." He sipped the hot chocolate and then said, "You notice there was no gift for you in that box I brought in?"

"You don't have to give me anything, Owen."

"Oh, I've got you something."

Lanie saw that he was smiling, and some humor was dancing in his eyes. "Well, where is it?"

"I'll give it to you tomorrow on Christmas day."

"You like to tease me, don't you?"

"Yes, I do." He put the cup down, reached across the table, and captured her hands. He held them, the pressure warm and intimate, and the two of them did not speak for a long time. Finally, they heard footsteps coming, and Lanie drew her hands back.

Cody burst in through the door. "What are you two doing back here in the kitchen? I thought we were going to make candy tonight."

"We are," Lanie said quickly, her face flushed.

"Come on with me, Doctor Merritt. I want to show you the tree. I decorated it all myself."

☞

Christmas morning had come, the presents had been opened, and everyone was happy. Owen was there, and for some reason Lolean Oz had come.

Davis asked Cody, "What's she doing here?"

Cody had scratched his head and said, "Well, somehow I asked her to come. I don't know how it happened, but I did."

"You ought not to let that girl put words in your mouth," Davis said.

Cody gave Davis an injured look but ignored him. "Hey, everybody," he yelled. "it's time for you to see my latest invention."

A groan went up, and Dakota said, "You've invented something, son?"

"Sure I have, Mama. You're going to love it."

"Watch out for him, Dakota." Forrest grinned. "The last invention he had he nearly killed himself and the preacher."

"And he did kill my favorite hen," Lanie chided.

"Oh, it was that hen's turn to die, sister. I've told you that. Everybody come on."

"We've got to get started cooking," Maeva said.

"Well, this is part of it. Come on."

Kezia was staring at Cody and shook her head. "What is that boy up to?"

"Who knows?" Davis said. "But it'll be interesting, I'll bet."

"Come on, everybody. You've got to go out to the barn with me."

They all trooped out of the house, and when they got to the barn, he walked inside and said, "Here's my newest invention."

He patted something covered with a canvas, and Lolean said, "What is it, Cody?"

Cody pulled the canvas back and tossed it on the ground. "There it is. Ain't she a lalapaloozy?"

They all crowded around, and Davis said, "What *is* that thing? I never saw anything like it."

"Of course you never saw anything like it. It's the first one that ever was," Cody said.

"Well, it sure is interesting. What does it do, son?" Forrest said. He had moved closer to Dakota and put his arm around her, and when she looked at him, he winked and said, "You better stand back. Somebody always gets plastered with his inventions."

"Ah, it ain't so, Daddy."

"What is it?" Maeva demanded.

"This," Cody said in a loud voice, "is going to be called the Cody Freeman No-Work Chicken Plucker."

A laugh went up, and Kezia said, "You mean that thing plucks the feathers off chickens?"

"It sure does, Aunt Kezia. I'll bet you plucked lots of chickens and turkeys and ducks in your lifetime."

"A whole mess of them, boy, but I don't see how that thing will work."

"Well, I'll show you. I brought the turkey out here. Killed it myself."

"I didn't think I heard that turkey I brought," Dakota said. She had brought two fine turkeys and put them in a pen.

Now Cody marched over and lifted them off the hook where they were hanging. He grunted for it was a big turkey. "Let me show you how this works." He put the turkey down on a table and pointed out how the chicken plucker worked. "You see these rubber things fastened to the drum?" He picked up one of the many strips of rubber that were fastened to a wooden drum with screws. "See how they flop around? Well, when the drum turns, these things just kind of stand out."

"What makes the drum turn?" Lolean demanded.

"This motor down here. You see?"

"Where'd you get a motor?" Davis demanded.

"I took it off an old washing machine. The motor works fine. Had to get a pulley for it, you see. So, when you turn it on the engine starts, the pulley turns, and the chicken plucker spins."

"But how does it get the feathers off the chickens?" Dakota asked in a puzzled voice.

"You see these rubber things? I made them myself out of an old tire. When the tips of them hit the turkey, it knocks the feathers off. All you have to do is hold the turkey and let the chicken plucker do the work."

"Well, if that don't beat hens a-pacing!" Aunt Kezia said, her eyes wide. "Does the thing really work?"

"Well, I haven't actually tried it yet. Didn't have no turkey," Cody said. "Besides, I wanted all of you to be here to see it. You'll be telling your kids and grandkids how you was there on the day that the Cody Freeman No-Work Chicken Plucker was first used."

Forrest said, "Well, let's have a demonstration, son."

"Sure, Daddy. You all watch close now. History is about to be made."

They all watched as Cody picked up the turkey and then nodded. "Here's the switch right here." He reached over and flipped the switch. Instantly the drum started turning a little bit slower at first and then picking up speed.

Cody picked up the larger of the two turkeys and slowly advanced it toward the whirling rubber strips. "Watch now," he shouted. "Here we go!"

To the amazement of everyone except Cody, the turkey feathers began to fly, plucked off by the rubber strips.

"It works!" Cody yelled. "Look at 'er go!"

Cody's audience cheered as the bare flesh of the turkey appeared. "Well, I'll be dipped in gravy!" Davis yelled. "The thing really works!"

The air was filled with flying turkey feathers, and everyone cheered until Cody shut the turkey plucker off and turned to display the nude carcass of the big bird. "Ain't she a doozer!" he cried.

"You're wonderful, Cody!" Lolean ran forward and hugged Cody, giving him a noisy kiss right on his mouth.

"Now, Lolean, that's unseemly," he muttered, but he didn't protest when she did it again.

"Let me do the other turkey, son," Forrest said, grinning from ear to ear. He took the smaller bird and turned the machine on. In no time, the job was done, and he turned off the turkey plucker. He handed the bird to Lanie and went to hug Cody. "I knew someday one of your inventions would work."

"Well, Daddy, you might have mentioned that to me." Cody laughed.

"I always wanted to marry a rich younger man." Lolean winked at Lanie, who was as happy for Cody as she could be.

"Well, you better get a lawyer to see that this contraption is patented," Davis said.

"Gimme that bird," Dakota said. "Until you invent a cooker, Cody, somebody's got to do it."

As they all followed Dakota inside, Lolean clung to Cody and whispered, "You're so smart, Cody! I'm so proud of you I could just kiss you again."

"Well, it might be unseemly with all these folks around," Cody said. "Maybe you better wait until we're alone."

"It won't be unseemly then?"

"Why, shucks, no! It will be one of them holy kisses you told me about. I'm looking forward to it!"

"Christmas was wonderful," Lanie said.

"What was your favorite part?"

Lanie's eyes danced. "I think the chicken plucker was the most exciting."

Owen laughed aloud. The two were sitting on the couch in front of the fireplace. Owen had built it up so now it was burning brightly, popping, and sending a myriad of sparks up the chimney. "That boy! He may turn out to be an Edison, after all."

They sat there talking about what a good meal it was and how everyone had enjoyed their presents.

Finally, a silence fell across the two, and Owen moved closer and put his arm around her. "I've been wanting to tell you something for a long time, Lanie."

Lanie was very conscious of Owen's arm pulling her closer. She felt the warmth of his body, and somehow there was a peace and a security in the moment that she knew she would never forget. "What's that, Owen?"

"I've never really told you how much I admire you. Back when you lost your mother and we first met, you were just a kid, but you had to grow up in a hurry. I watched you do things that no fourteen-year-old ought to have to do, but you did it, and you never complained. Then when your dad went to prison, you had to quit school and go to work to take care of the family. Your family survived because you're strong, Lanie, and I admire strength."

Lanie could not answer. The words were a balm to her spirit, and she leaned over against him, putting her head on his shoulder. "It's so nice to hear you say that, Owen, but you know I couldn't have done it if you and others hadn't helped me."

"Well, it's all going to be all right. Davis is going to be fine. You know, he's talking about becoming a veterinarian. He's going to take over Dakota's horse breeding."

"He'll do well at whatever he wants."

"And Cody—well, he hasn't actually killed anybody except your chicken, and he'll make a fine preacher. And Maeva, she's one of God's miracles. I think she and Logan will make a match out of it, and they're going to be a success. And Corliss? Well, that's the smartest young one I've ever seen. Sweet along with it. She can be anything. Your dad's happy, and I predict that he and Dakota will have a beautiful crop of babies. And you, you're going to be a famous writer. So, sweetheart, I'm in awe of what you've done."

When Owen called her *sweetheart* something seemed to turn over inside of Lanie Freeman. She had loved this man since she was fourteen. At first, it had been simply gratitude and later, as she had grown up, her affection had changed to something else until she knew she loved him as a woman should love a man, full and free and without reservation.

Owen said, "I didn't put your present under the tree, but I've got it in my pocket." He shifted himself, reaching into his pocket. He pulled out a small box and gave it to her.

Lanie grew still, her eyes fixed on the box.

"Go ahead and open it," Owen urged her.

Lanie took the box with fingers not quite steady, and she opened it. The reflection of the fire caught the diamond in the ring. "Oh, it's beautiful, Owen!"

He turned and took the ring and whispered, "It's an engagement ring, Lanie. I want you to marry me, and you'll be stuck with an old man in this one-horse town forever. But I love you, and I can't think of living without you."

Lanie's eyes filled. She took the engagement ring, put it on her finger, and then she turned to face him and threw her arms around him. "I've loved you since I was fourteen years old."

The two clung together. He kissed her tenderly and then as she rested in his arms, he said, "I've got something to confess."

"You don't have another wife somewhere, do you?"

"No, but I knew you were going to say yes when I asked you to marry me."

"You did not!"

"Yes, you told me so."

"What are you talking about? I never said anything about marrying you."

"Oh yes, you did. I copied your words down." He pulled a fragment of paper from his shirt pocket and said, "It says, 'I love Owen so much! I want to marry him and have a family with him and grow old with him beside me.'"

Lanie grew very still, and her eyes were wide. "Why, that's from my diary."

"Yes, it is. You left your diary out one day when I was over taking care of Corliss. This was written on, let's see, November 13, 1932. I copied it down because I wanted to have it when I asked you to marry me."

"Owen, you're so awful!"

"Oh no, I'm not awful. Let me show you."

Cap'n Brown had been sitting beside the fire watching the two. Now he watched a moment longer, and deciding there wouldn't be any more food to be had from either of them, he curled up and went to sleep at once.

They were quiet for a time, and then Owen said, "You'll be my child bride."

"Lolean says she's going to marry Cody because he's younger than she is. She says she can take the bad habits out of him. So, I guess you can do the same for me."

Owen Merritt smiled. "I can't believe that we're going to be together for the rest of our lives."

Lanie Freeman pulled his head down, kissed him, and laid her head on his shoulder. "It's what God intended from the first."

The Homeplace

Gilbert Morris, Bestselling
Christy Award–Winning Author

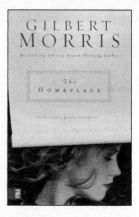

Lanie took out her journal and dated it
April 12, 1928. She started the habit of writing down everything that happened to her
when she was no more than eight years
old, and now she had six journals completely full. She thought about the prize at
school, almost prayed to win, but somehow she could not. "God,"
she finally said, "I'll do my best, and if you'll help me, that's all I
ask."

Fourteen-year-old Lanie Belle Freeman of Fairhope, Arkansas,
has high hopes for her future. Happy on the five-acre family homeplace, she dreams of going to college and becoming a writer. And
with her father launching a new business and her mother expecting the fifth baby, the bright days of an early Southern spring seem
to herald expansive new beginnings for the Freeman family.

But her mother isn't as strong as she should be, and it's going
to take time for the business to pay back the mortgage. When
unexpected tragedy strikes, it is left to Lanie to keep the family together and hold on to their home. In a world shaken by the
Great Depression, it is faith in God and love in a tightly knit family
that will help Lanie and her siblings overcome the odds and create
a future that promises the fulfillment of love.

The Homeplace offers a warmhearted and inspiring saga of a
courageous young woman who holds her family together through
the Depression era.

Softcover: 0-310-25232-6

Pick up a copy today at your favorite bookstore!

The Dream

*Gilbert Morris, Bestselling
Christy Award-Winning Author*

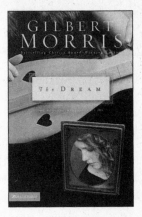

Lanie Freeman had to grow up fast. Her
mother died when she was just fourteen
and now her father is in prison. The oldest
of five children, seventeen-year-old Lanie
has transformed into a surrogate mother
… and a beautiful young woman. Not only
must she keep her family together, but lately she has drawn the attention of Roger Langley, son of the richest man in town. Tensions
run deep between the Freemans and the Langleys. And on top of
it all, Louise Langley accuses Lanie of trying to snatch away her
handsome fiancé, Dr. Owen Merrit. Dr. Merrit has long helped out
the Freeman children, but Lanie isn't sure he even notices that
she's no longer a child. Then Fairhope is thrown into chaos when
the new preacher arrives — wearing blue jeans and riding a mo-
torcycle. In only a month, dashing Brother Colin Ryan shakes the
entire town to the core of their beliefs. With the town embattled
over the preacher, her family struggling to survive, and her own
heart in turmoil, Lanie seeks solace in her writing. She pours out
her heart to God, trusting his promises. But when things fall apart
at every turn, will Lanie continue to trust? *The Dream* continues
the inspiring saga of one woman's struggle to hold together her
family and follow her dreams in the midst of America's darkest
hour.

Softcover: 0-310-25233-4

Pick up a copy today at your favorite bookstore!

The Miracle

*Gilbert Morris, Bestselling
Christy Award–Winning Author*

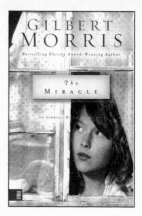

Raising four strong-willed younger siblings
after her mother's death and her father's
imprisonment, seventeen-year-old Lanie
Freeman never knows what new adventure will roll into view — such as her brother's wild idea to turn the family's old truck
into a traveling store.

The Freeman Rolling Emporium could provide the financial security Lanie and her family so desperately need, or it could tear
them apart. Yet it's only a prelude to other changes. Author Brent
Hayden's arrival in Fairhope breathes fresh life into Lanie's dream
of becoming a writer. And then the hammer descends ...

Lanie's father is diagnosed with cancer, and the faith and unity
of her family are stretched to the limit. And on top of this shatter-
ing news, a crisis is about to strike that will rock the whole town of
Fairhope — and shatter Lanie's dreams of love.

The Miracle continues the story of a young woman's valiant
struggle to uphold her faith, her family, and her dreams during
the height of the Great Depression.

Softcover: 0-310-25234-2

Pick up a copy today at your favorite bookstore!

ZONDERVAN®
.com

God's Handmaiden

Gilbert Morris, Bestselling
Author of The Spider Catcher

A historical and romantic adventure woven
around the story of Florence Nightingale.

Gervase Howard is in her mid-teens
when her working-class mother dies and
she must go to live with relatives in service to a wealthy, noble family, outside of
London. While learning various jobs, she is drawn to the eldest
son, Davis. Her fascination with him grows deeper, but more hopeless, since the two are separated not just by class, but also by
Davis's love for Roberta.

When Davis announces his engagement, he asks Gervase to
join them as Roberta's maid. But instead Gervase becomes a companion to Florence Nightingale and accompanies her when the
Crimean War breaks out and she is asked to create a corps of
nurses. On the field, Gervase crosses paths with Davis, who has
become disillusioned in his marriage and is drawn to her warmth
and care. Both know, however, there is nothing more for them
than friendship.

Upon her return to England, Gervase receives word that Davis
has been seriously injured in a fall and is asked to nurse him back
to health. As he regains consciousness, he reveals shocking news
that plunges them both into danger.

Softcover: 0-310-24699-7

Pick up a copy today at your favorite bookstore!

Edge of Honor

Gilbert Morris

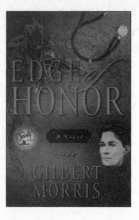

A powerful novel of honor, forgiveness, and unquenchable faith — set at the end of the Civil War.

Quentin Larribee is a surgeon, but in the confusion of war, his healing hands brought death to an enemy soldier. To ease his troubled conscience, he visits the man's impoverished widow, only to find himself falling in love. Now he is torn between two choices: a bright medical future with his wealthy fiancée in New York City, or an impossible love with a woman who knows nothing of his terrible secret.

In this unforgettable novel, good is found in the unlikeliest places, and God's unseen hand weaves a masterful tapestry of human hearts and lives.

Softcover: 0-310-24302-5

Pick up a copy today at your favorite bookstore!

Jordan's Star

Gilbert Morris

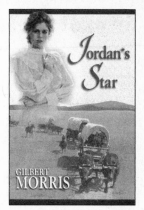

It is Jordan's special star — a celestial token of hope for the life and love she dreams of. How brightly will it shine in the night's darkest hour?

A host of stars crowds the desert sky, arching from the east, with its thriving towns, to the western mountains and an unknown future. Bound for the Oregon frontier, Jordan Bryce and her new husband, Colin, a dashing ex-mariner, face danger from both man and nature: a deadly buffalo stampede ... tragedy at a river crossing ... hostile Indians ... and hatred within their wagon train, escalating from bitter words to the point of bloodshed. All that separates the Bryce's party from disaster is seasoned leadership, the skillful guidance of Ty Sublette, and the hand of God.

For Jordan, the journey west is more than a trip into an untamed land. It is a passage from a teenage girl's romantic fantasies to the wisdom and character of womanhood. But nothing can prepare Jordan for the testing that awaits her beyond the journey's end. There, in the face of staggering circumstances, she will face an impossible decision ... as two good men — one wounded by past grief, the other branded by his own impetuousness — struggle with the demands of faith and honor on behalf of the woman they love.

Softcover: 0-310-22754-2

Pick up a copy today at your favorite bookstore!

The Spider Catcher

*Gilbert Morris, Bestselling
Author of Jordan's Star*

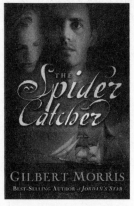

He is a young Welshman who forsook
the family shipbuilding business to study
medicine ... until, poised at the brink of
a brilliant career, tragedy broke his heart
and shattered his dreams.

She is a daughter of London's inner city,
a woman-child weaned on life's harsh realities who has learned
much about fending for her living and her virtue but little of what
it means to be loved.

Thrown together by circumstance, Rees Kenyon and Callie
Summers head across the ocean toward a new life during the
stormy beginnings of the American Revolution. As a new nation
struggles for independence, Rees employs his medical knowledge
to save lives, and his shipbuilder's skills to build the potent fighting
vessel known as the "Spider Catcher."

But it is Callie, whom Rees scooped from the mud of the
London streets, on whom his own life will soon depend ... and
who can help him find for himself the faith, hope, and love he has
taught her.

Softcover: 0-310-24698-9

Pick up a copy today at your favorite bookstore!

Three ways to keep up on your favorite Zondervan books and authors

Sign up for our *Fiction E-Newsletter*. Every month you'll receive sample excerpts from our books, sneak peeks at upcoming books, and chances to win free books autographed by the author.

You can also sign up for our *Breakfast Club*. Every morning in your email, you'll receive a five-minute snippet from a fiction or nonfiction book. A new book will be featured each week, and by the end of the week you will have sampled two to three chapters of the book.

Zondervan *Author Tracker* is the best way to be notified whenever your favorite Zondervan authors write new books, go on tour, or want to tell you about what's happening in their lives.

Visit *www.zondervan.com* and sign up today!

ZONDERVAN.com/
AUTHOR**TRACKER**
follow your favorite authors